The Barbecue at No. 9

Also by Jennie Godfrey

The List of Suspicious Things

Jennie Godfrey

The Barbecue at No. 9

HUTCHINSON
HEINEMANN

HUTCHINSON HEINEMANN

UK | USA | Canada | Ireland | Australia
India | New Zealand | South Africa

Hutchinson Heinemann is part of the Penguin Random House group of companies whose addresses can be found at global.penguinrandomhouse.com

Penguin Random House UK,
One Embassy Gardens, 8 Viaduct Gardens, London SW11 7BW

penguin.co.uk

First published by Hutchinson Heinemann in 2026
002

Copyright © Jennie Godfrey, 2026

The moral right of the author has been asserted

Map © Darren Bennett at DKB Creative Ltd (www.dkbcreative.com)

Line on p. 85 from 'Rat Trap' by The Boomtown Rats (written by Bob Geldof)
Line on p. 88 from 'My Generation' by The Who (written by Pete Townshend)

No part of this book may be used or reproduced in any manner for the purpose of training artificial intelligence technologies or systems. In accordance with Article 4(3) of the DSM Directive 2019/790, Penguin Random House expressly reserves this work from the text and data mining exception.

Set in 13.3/16.2pt Garamond Premier Pro
Typeset by Six Red Marbles UK, Thetford, Norfolk

Printed and bound in Great Britain by Clays Ltd, Elcograf S.p.A.

The authorised representative in the EEA is Penguin Random House Ireland, Morrison Chambers, 32 Nassau Street, Dublin D02 YH68

A CIP catalogue record for this book is available from the British Library

ISBN: 978-1-529-15501-3 (hardback)
ISBN: 978-1-529-15502-0 (trade paperback)

Penguin Random House is committed to a sustainable future for our business, our readers and our planet. This book is made from Forest Stewardship Council® certified paper.

For Rachel, Guy, Eva and Hugo.
My family.

'It's twelve noon in London, seven a.m. in Philadelphia, and around the world it's time for Live Aid.'

Richard Skinner, Wembley, 13 July 1985

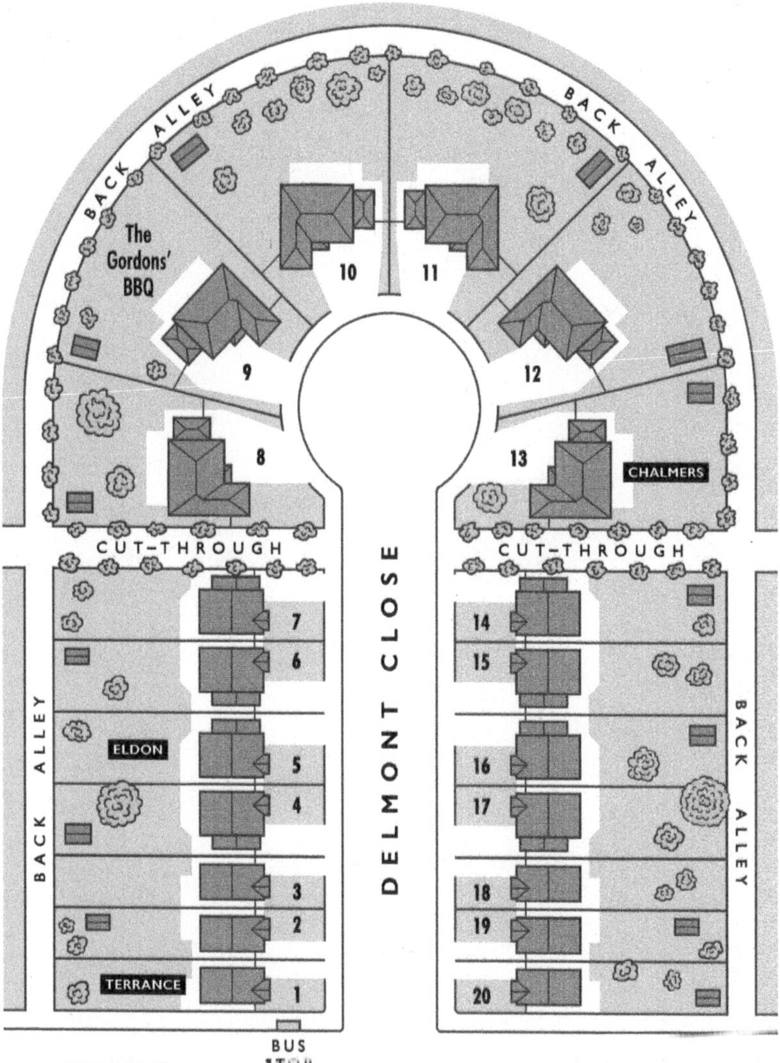

1 The Pauls (including Rosie)
2 The Howletts
3 Ryan & his mum
4 The Greenwoods
5 The Watsons
6 The Andrews
7 The Parkers
8 The Lloyds
9 The Gordons
10 The Chamberlains
11 The Barkers
12 Mr & Mrs O'Leary
13 The Wilsons
14 The Smiths
15 Rita
16 Davina & her daughters
17 The Sharps
18 The Prentices
19 The Thomases
20 Tina & Steve

PART ONE
The Invitations

Thursday, 11 July 1985

Two days before Live Aid

Hanna – No. 9

Hanna Gordon was as yet unaware of the person who was closely watching the residents of Delmont Close. She was too busy being mortified. Given that Hanna suspected her mum, Lydia, had no idea where Ethiopia was, she was already cringing at her plan to host a barbecue on the day of the Live Aid concert 'in aid of the children', but when her mum insisted they invite all their new neighbours in the close, Hanna thought she might die of embarrassment.

She was upstairs in her bedroom – which also happened to be the smallest one, a fact she noted with frequent resentment – carefully folding clothes and putting them into the school bag she normally used for PE. Her room was decorated in the lilac, densely floral Laura Ashley wallpaper her mum had chosen when they moved in, which Hanna had covered up immediately with moody posters of The Damned and Dead or Alive, sellotaping them neatly to the walls. Since Hanna only wore black these days, the wallpaper served as even more of a reminder that she no longer belonged in this house. Or in this family.

The cry of 'Come and deliver these invitations round the close!' from downstairs was a reminder of a different variety: of how annoying her mum was. In fact, of how annoying her whole family was. They never gave her any peace. This wasn't how she had planned to spend her summer. She slumped down the stairs, determined to show her reluctance in every possible way.

'Muuuuuum,' she wailed as she headed to the living room, 'do I have to?'

She walked in to her parents arguing over her mum's request.

'I thought this was meant to be friends and family,' Hanna's dad, Peter, said. 'It'll cost a fortune to feed the whole bloody street as well. And do we really want them tramping through our house all day? We barely know half of them.'

Hanna's dad was heading to work in his usual grey suit. He looked faded and pale next to her mum, who, obsessed with aerobics, was wearing a Day-Glo outfit involving cycling shorts so bright and tight they made Hanna want to keep blinking. Their Jack Russell, Prince, was weaving his way in and out of Lydia's legs as a show of support. The little dog adored her, despite her apparent and frequently announced loathing of him. Lydia waved Peter's concerns away, then swatted Prince from under her legs using the wad of invitations clasped in her hands.

'Nonsense,' she said. 'It's outside for a start, and I'm

sure hardly any of them will come.' She paused before delivering her masterstroke: 'Anyway, it's for the poor starving children in Africa. It's about charity, and where do they say charity starts, my love?' Tapping Hanna's dad lightly on the nose with the invitations, which only riled him further, she handed them to Hanna and turned on her heels, disappearing into the kitchen with Prince trotting behind her. 'You can take the dog with you!' she called as a parting shot to Hanna, shooing Prince back towards her. 'Get him out of my bloody way.'

Hanna's dad sighed, his forehead creasing. He looked exhausted, Hanna thought, noticing this for the first time. He took a deep breath in and looked at Hanna with a more mischievous expression while he called out, 'Keith and Beverley have confirmed they're coming!'

Hanna's mum's face reappeared around the kitchen door, a mask of horror on it. 'What?' she said. 'But your brother's snooty wife never comes to anything we put on. And why didn't Beverley let me know?'

'Well, they're coming to this,' Hanna's dad said. 'Keith told me when I rang to see how he was.'

Her mum's expression changed from horror to confusion: Hanna's dad had an almost allergic aversion to the phone. 'Why spend money on a phone call when you can have a conversation face to face for free,' he was fond of telling them all with some frequency, usually when he heard a number being dialled. He seemed to have bionic ears when it came to the sound of the receiver being lifted, detecting it from miles away. He had threatened to install a lock on the phone numerous times, but thankfully hadn't followed up on the threat yet.

'Well, that changes everything!' her mum exclaimed. 'We're going to need to get the good china out.' Her head disappeared back into the kitchen and Hanna and her dad grinned at each other.

'Thought it was about charity,' he muttered in a voice so quiet it was impossible for his wife to hear before he left the house, intercepting the postman on his way down the path.

Hanna suspected that there was nothing charitable going on here at all. That this was instead her mum's way of establishing dominance over the rest of the residents of the close. *Look at us*, she was saying, *we have a fancy new barbecue, and we can afford to feed all of you. Oh, and look at our state-of-the-art television and stereo system while you're at it*. But Hanna decided not to make too much of a fuss. What was the point? She went upstairs, grabbed her Walkman and was just about to leave the house when a tinny voice came out of the small transistor radio on the hall console: 'In just two days the greatest show on earth will begin, with performances from some of the most famous musicians of a generation.'

'I can't WAIT!' shouted her eleven-year-old brother David from his bedroom – much bigger than Hanna's, despite him being younger and a boy. 'It'll be like watching *Top of the Pops* ALL DAY,' he said, that idea

THE BARBECUE AT NO. 9

being heaven for them both. She couldn't begin to count the number of times they had fought over which one of them got to be in charge of the pause button on the tape player when they recorded the Top 40 on a Sunday afternoon. David usually won, as his reaction time was faster. Hanna always ended up with the DJ's voice on the end of the tracks.

She didn't reply to her brother's excited words: she was a teenager now, which meant she was no longer allowed to express enthusiasm; it was against the rules. But the truth was, she felt it too, the stirrings of a giddiness she'd not felt for some months. Maybe this *was* something to be excited about? In spite of what else was happening in her life: her plans for the future, the mess she had made. She had heard there was a girl in the year above whose cousin's friend's next-door neighbour actually had a ticket for the concert. Though she had also heard that the same person was going to Disneyland in Florida for the summer, so who knew if it was true. Either way, what wouldn't she give to be going to Wembley on Saturday, rather than being here. Anywhere but here.

'You coming for a walk, Prince?' she called, and the little dog came hurtling out of the kitchen, his stubby tail wagging, happy to accompany anyone who said the word *walk*, willing to abandon his beloved Lydia if it meant going outside.

'Turn the radio up on your way out, would you,

love?' her mum shouted as Hanna left. Her eyes rolled, almost automatically. 'You don't even like pop music,' she muttered as she yanked the dial on the radio to full, let Prince out and slammed the door, a move that blew her almost white-blonde hair across her face.

She had long despaired over the colour of her hair. It was one of the things she was planning to change after leaving here, even though, or maybe because, her mum said it was her best feature. She would dye it black as soon as she could. She put her sunglasses on, placed her headphones over her ears, pressed play on her bright yellow Walkman and set off, before any thoughts about the future took hold.

Hanna surveyed Delmont Close. Modern, neat and safe, with nothing out of place, it was part of a new Wimpey estate and consisted of a large horseshoe shape of around twenty homes, with the Gordons' house located on the curve at the bottom where the bigger, detached houses with the largest gardens were. Hanna's mum insisted on continuing to use the Wimpey catalogue names to differentiate the houses on the close, always referring to their own five-bedroomed house as 'The Chalmers', as opposed to 'The Eldon', which had four bedrooms, or 'The Terrance', which had three.

Her mum and dad had selected the house from a glossy brochure as though it was the Argos catalogue at Christmas. Hanna sometimes wondered whether her mum wished she could have chosen her daughter from a

THE BARBECUE AT NO. 9

catalogue too. If she could, she definitely wouldn't have chosen Hanna – at least, not as she was now. Maybe as she was a few years ago, when her dad still called her 'princess' and she wore the same kinds of clothes as Antoinette Chamberlain from next door and looked pretty and demure. But not now.

Hanna made her way to the top of the close, starting at no. 1, her best friend Rosie's house. Rosie had already been invited to the barbecue by Hanna – both for the company and to act as a human shield against her mum and friends – but now her parents would be invited too. As she carried on down the street, dropping invitations into each house as she went, Hanna thought about how she would have known just from the front gardens which houses contained people her mum disapproved of versus those that passed muster. Even if she wasn't already fully aware of her mum's judgements on their neighbours, which she mostly was.

As she walked past her own house again and went up to the Chamberlains', it was clear to Hanna that they belonged in the latter category. Manicured to within an inch of its life, their front lawn was the picture of symmetry, the neat green lines looking as though they had been painted on with a roller.

The Chamberlains' house was a Chalmers, just like theirs, which already marked them out as worthy of her mum's time and attention. As well as living in the kind of house she approved of, the Chamberlains were also the kind of *people* she approved of. They were, to use her mum's expression, 'a proper family'. Proper families were referred to by their collective surnames, an honour which bestowed almost the same respectability as a royal title in her mum's eyes.

Hanna posted the piece of paper through the Chamberlains' door and turned back towards the rest of the close. As she did so, she caught sight of the back of a person disappearing down the cut-through between the houses to the next cul-de-sac on the estate. They must have passed right by her. She felt an uneasy prickling at the back of her neck. The thought that she hadn't heard anyone behind her flashed through her mind, which she immediately dismissed on realising that she was still wearing headphones that were blasting 'She Sells Sanctuary' by The Cult at full volume. Of course she hadn't heard anyone. She looked around for Prince, who seemed wholly unbothered and was at that moment weeing on Mrs Chamberlain's geraniums.

Something about the sight of the person unsettled her though. Maybe it was how close they must have been to her, without her being aware. She felt unnervingly as though someone had tapped her on the shoulder and run away. She took her headphones off for a moment and looked down the alleyway and around the close. It was both unnaturally hot and unnaturally unpopulated. She half-expected to see tumbleweed cross the street in front of her, like in the Westerns her dad loved to watch.

THE BARBECUE AT NO. 9

The day felt so dusty and parched, the only signs of life the distant drones of lawnmowers, and the sounds of radios playing through open windows, net curtains fluttering whenever there was a breeze.

She moved on to the next few houses, Prince on her heels, until she got to no. 13, where she felt the beginnings of a familiar flutter in her chest. The door to the house opened, and she took a sharp breath in.

'Hello, Hanna,' he said, his deep voice soft and low.

'Hello, Mr Wilson,' she almost squeaked in reply, feeling her face glow.

He laughed, not taking his eyes from hers.

'I think we're beyond "Mr Wilson" now, don't you? It's Mike, and what do we have here?' he said, taking the invitation out of her shaking hand. She watched as he read it. 'Tell your mum and dad thank you and that we'll both be there,' he said, and bent down to pat Prince. As Hanna turned away to go to the next house, she thought she heard him quietly say, 'See you on Saturday,' just as she was putting her headphones back on, but she couldn't be sure.

The first time she had met Mike Wilson she had been with Rosie, sitting on the kerb outside no. 9. He had driven up in his red sports car – a car her mum disparagingly called 'a midlife crisis on wheels' – music blaring from the open window. Hanna had been surprised that it was one of Depeche Mode's songs; she associated adults with easy listening like Dire Straits and The Carpenters, or Queen, her dad's favourite band. Before going into the house, Mike had stopped, smiled and said, 'Hello, you two,' and Hanna hadn't been able to stop herself from saying, 'I love that song.'

'So do I,' he'd replied and winked at her.

They'd watched him go into the house before they had both burst into giggles. Hanna hadn't been sure what exactly they were laughing at, but once Rosie had caught her breath she said, 'He's a huuuuunk,' using the language of the *Jackie* magazine photostories they used to read but were now too cool for, or at least Hanna was. He was indeed a hunk, Hanna had realised. He looked like Face from *The A-Team*. But that wasn't what she had come to like about him. She liked the fact that he talked to her as an equal. That was why her crush had started.

Hanna waited until she had posted the invitation into the next house before she looked behind her to see whether Mike had gone back into his house or if he was watching her still, as she sometimes sensed he was. There was no sign of him, however, so she turned the volume on her Walkman up as loud as it would go and sank into the music. She always felt as though she disappeared when she did this, like it made her invisible to other people. She found that she was less self-conscious with her headphones on, more able to observe the world. Music made her forget herself. It was the only thing that did. Maybe that was why she loved it so much.

THE BARBECUE AT NO. 9

She almost felt like skipping or whirling around in a circle like she and Rosie used to do when they were younger, but she was still aware enough to know she wasn't really invisible and should be too old for that kind of thing now. Instead, she sauntered, singing the words in her head instead of out loud, wishing she were able to fully let go.

She thought she saw a shadow pass the window at no. 15, as she popped the invitation into the letterbox. This house was inhabited by the latest arrival on Delmont Close. Their new neighbour was 'single, divorced no doubt', according to her mum. 'Do we really need another divorced person on the close?' she had said when the woman moved in. 'Don't we already have one?' Divorce sat alongside renting or living in a council house on Lydia's list of mortal sins.

Hanna was confused by her mum's preoccupation with mortgages, which was second only to her obsession with house prices. She seemed to think that having a mortgage somehow made you morally superior to other people, but as far as Hanna was aware – informed mainly by her dad's grumbles about paying theirs – mortgages meant worrying about money all the time.

Next, she posted an invitation through the door of the other divorced person on the close: Davina, or 'Three Dads Davina' as she was called in reference to the paternity of her three daughters. Maybe Davina and the woman at no. 15 might make friends, given there was little chance of them becoming part of Lydia's social circle. Hanna smiled to herself at the idea of them joining forces against the might of her mum's friends and their moral judgements.

She unconsciously stood taller as she walked down the Thomases' drive at no. 19, as though Ned, their very handsome, somewhat wayward son was watching her from inside the house. Not that she wanted him to come out and talk to her or anything; in fact, the opposite. Ned Thomas was dangerous territory. He was regarded as the most fanciable boy on the estate, mainly because he was in a band and went to private school (even though they lived in one of the 'Terrance' houses, as her mum was quick to point out), making him more exotic and unattainable than the boys they saw every day. She'd noticed that other girls behaved differently around him, almost instinctively, herself included at first. Like Prince when begging for treats, all the girls sat up straighter, eyes pinned on him, mouths open in his presence. There seemed to be no one at home, however, and she remembered her mum saying something about them going on holiday.

Finally, she focused on the somewhat crowded garden of no. 20, the next and last house on the close. It stood out from the rest, its cluttered front marking it as different. The hordes of gnomes and ornaments outside the house, and the thick net curtains inside, made the mother and son who lived there the subject of much discussion by

THE BARBECUE AT NO. 9

the Neighbourhood Watch (as Hanna had labelled her mum's group of friends), but it was the fact that the son was so rarely seen in person that made him the equivalent of the close bogeyman. This was not helped by him being tall and physically awkward, his dark hair impeccably neat, and that he always wore strangely formal clothes – suits in black, brown and navy – earning him the nickname Lurch from Ned Thomas and his friends.

Hanna felt slightly ashamed to realise that she didn't know Lurch's real name, had only ever heard him referred to as Lurch, even by adults. His mum, Tina, was the opposite of her son in every way: tiny, bleached blonde and chaotic, with a cigarette permanently dangling from the side of her mouth and a voice so grating it could sometimes be heard from the Gordons' back garden, earning sighs and eye-rolling from her mum. She was surprised that Lydia hadn't told her to skip this house. Maybe she assumed they wouldn't come, but that only made Hanna more determined to make sure they were invited.

Despite herself, the thought of Lurch still made her uneasy. Even though she tried not to judge people by how they looked, there was no denying he was weird. She kept her wits about her as she walked down the drive, noting that the summer sun seemed to dim as she reached the front door, though it was just the shadow from the house.

Prince didn't follow her, preferring to sniff each

of the gnomes in turn, and there were no signs of life within as she posted the piece of paper through the door and forced herself to walk at her usual speed back to the pavement. She was very practised at feigning nonchalance; she had been doing it for months now, and everyone was fooled.

PART TWO

The Barbecue

13 July 1985
Hour One: 10–11 a.m.

Two hours before Live Aid

Hanna – No. 9

When Hanna eventually emerged that morning, no. 9 was quiet, apart from the radio on the console table, which was full of the lead-up to the Live Aid concert. According to her mum, her dad had gone to the shops to get the last remaining bits for the barbecue and to buy enough video tapes to record the whole thing. David was upstairs getting ready by listening to their dad's old Queen cassette tapes on his Walkman, and her mum was busy cleaning their wall-to-wall pine kitchen to within an inch of its life.

'We don't want the neighbours thinking that we live in a pigsty. We're not going to be known as *that family*,' she said, as Hanna walked into the kitchen and Prince flung himself at her, as though they had been parted for weeks. Lydia slapped Hanna's hand out of the way of the freshly baked sausage rolls that were cooling on the side before she could grab one of them.

'I'm hungry,' Hanna said, and as she said the words, she realised just how true they were. 'What can I have?'

She felt her cheeks flush as her mum's eyes looked her up and down, appraising her, then turned to look pointedly at the fruit bowl. 'There's apples there, and cereal in the cupboard. Now you can either give me a hand or get out of the way,' she said. Hanna picked up an apple and headed back upstairs again.

She wondered what it would be like to have a mum like Rosie's. Their house at no. 1 Delmont Close was nowhere near as big (as Hanna's mum was fond of pointing out), or as floral, but Mrs Paul, who insisted Hanna call her Julie, dispensed frequent hugs and laughed a lot. Hanna couldn't imagine her eyeing her daughter's body with the expressions that Hanna's mum pulled. Hanna might even have thought it possible to tell Julie the truth of what had happened, but then, if she'd had a mum like Julie, maybe it never would.

Hanna often thought about who she might be if she was part of a different family. Even before everything had changed, she had sometimes wondered if she'd been adopted and had daydreamed about how one day her 'real' family would come and get her. She had imagined what they would be like, trying on different families for size in her mind, wondering like Goldilocks which one might be 'just right' for her. But nowadays, she couldn't avoid feeling that mostly she was the one who was all wrong.

She imagined what it would be like to be the child of 'Three Dads Davina' too. Her three daughters all seemed effortlessly cool. They didn't go to the same school as Hanna, Davina preferring a more progressive education for her children. Davina wore paint-splattered dungarees, had dyed red hair, smoked roll-up cigarettes and occasionally protested about nuclear weapons at the Greenham Common airbase, much to the horror of the Neighbourhood Watch. 'Common is right,' they muttered among themselves. Davina was the sort of person who talked about her children as though they were her friends, a fact which Hanna's mum found perplexing, preferring the parent-and-child relationship to be clearly delineated. 'No wonder those girls look so feral,' Hanna had heard her say to her dad one evening.

If she was one of Davina's children, she would be called something exotic. Her life might feel exotic too, in a family like that. It wouldn't matter what trouble she got into, they would 'handle it together', like hippy musketeers. Hanna felt a longing so visceral it almost winded her, but then her little brother appeared on the landing, making her jump. He pointed at her, singing 'Don't Stop Me Now' at full volume, shaking his hips in time. He stopped when he looked at her properly, presumably taking in her pale face and pained expression.

'What's the matter with you?' he asked.

'Nothing,' she replied, and carried on up the stairs towards him.

'Well, you look awful,' he said, a smile on his impish face.

'Fuck off, David,' she said, also smiling.

David swooned dramatically, as though her words

had physically wounded him, then shouted, 'MUU-UUUM, Hanna just swore at me!' before leaping out of sight, the door to his room slamming before Hanna even had the chance to go after him. Hanna paused for a moment, waiting to hear her mum's steely-voiced response, but there was nothing. Lydia was either setting the garden up or ignoring them. Hanna trudged slowly up the remaining stairs to her room and lay on the bed. She should be nicer to her brother.

She wondered for a second whether she should write him a proper letter, explaining everything, but he was too young to understand, and she couldn't burden him with the mistakes she'd made, or the ways people hurt each other. She would make an effort for the rest of the day, so that at least he would know she loved him and didn't really want him to fuck off.

A scream from downstairs jolted her out of thoughts of David and she instinctively sat up. She was used to her mum's dramatics, so didn't immediately move, imagining she had seen a mouse or a spider. Her assumption was confirmed on hearing her mum shout, 'Get out, get out!', presumably to whatever creature she had stumbled over. She was about to lie back down again when David burst into the room. 'There's someone in the garden,' he said, wide-eyed and breathless, then turned on his heels and jumped down the stairs two at a time. Hanna reluctantly followed him, sure this would turn out to be nothing but intrigued nonetheless.

She was met by her mum, quivering in the kitchen, spatula in hand, Prince practically welded to her, his rotund little body shaking too. David was already rustling about in the bushes at the end of their long rectangular garden, the high fences and strategically placed trees shielding them from their neighbours.

'What happened?' Hanna said, then waited for her mum's panting breaths to return to normal so that she could speak.

'There was... There was someone in the garden,' her mum finally said, 'in the bushes.'

'Are you sure?' Hanna said, though as soon as the words left her mouth, she knew they were the wrong ones. The depth of the red her mum's face turned, and the volume of her reply, left her in no doubt whatsoever.

'*Of course I am sure.*'

'Okay, okay, sorry, what did they look like? What were they doing?' Hanna asked, hoping to divert her from her anger with details.

'I couldn't see them clearly,' her mum said, her voice staccato. 'The sun was too bright. But they were definitely there. A person. Dressed in dark colours. They were just stood there. Watching. As soon as I called out, they ran.' She was starting to hyperventilate again now, and Hanna could see that she was genuinely frightened, her expression taut and drawn. She somehow looked younger, vulnerable even. It was an expression Hanna saw only rarely, when her mum thought no one was looking, and she briefly let herself show the person behind the wall of big hair and lip gloss. Something tugged inside Hanna.

'I've asked your father a hundred times to fix the lock on that back gate and now look what's happened. And the bloody dog was useless as well. Didn't even bark,' she said, though Hanna couldn't help noticing she was stroking Prince's head, who stayed glued to her side. It reminded her of the many times that, despite her mum's insistence that she disliked having a dog around the house, Hanna had seen her move Prince in closer to her and absent-mindedly stroke him whenever they watched telly in the evenings.

'Well, I mean, at least we're all safe,' Hanna said, her intention being to reassure. She still couldn't quite bring herself to believe there had been an actual person in the garden, and if there had, that they would have been scared off by her mum's spatula-wielding defence of the house, or Prince's wholly non-threatening presence. But then she remembered the person she'd seen when she was posting the invitations the other day – disappearing into the cut-through – and the sense she'd had that they'd passed right by without her realising. Maybe her mum wasn't going *completely* mad.

'That's not the point,' Lydia said, and Hanna was relieved to see David running back up the garden.

'They were in the alleyway,' he said, giddy with excitement, 'but they saw me, and ran off.'

THE BARBECUE AT NO. 9

So, there had been someone there after all. Hanna instinctively reached out her hand. She was surprised when her mum took it and squeezed hard in return. Eventually she released it, and Hanna left her mum and brother breathlessly rehashing the drama, realising that this was her moment to finish packing before the barbecue started, without any interruption. She mustn't let this distract her. She needed to be ready to go when the moment was right.

Back in her bedroom, Hanna pulled her sports bag out from under the bed. On opening the zip, her eyes immediately alighted on the wad of tissue she had wrapped the pregnancy test in and laid carefully at the top. The sight of it made her slump down. Little did her mum know that the intruder in the garden was only the beginning of her family's dramas today. Hanna wasn't even sure why she had packed the test that had confirmed the end of her life as she knew it.

This wasn't one of those scenarios where she might happily share the good news, showing her friends the stick and basking in the joy of their 'oohs' and 'ahhs' and 'what are you hoping fors'. No one would see this as anything other than the worst thing that could ever have happened to her.

Rita – No. 15

The problem with cleaning an almost empty house, Rita realised, was that it didn't take long enough. What was she supposed to do with the hours sprawling ahead of her, as sparsely filled as the rooms she was dusting? Although maybe she should be thinking of this as one of the benefits of starting again, a clean slate, or more accurately a clean mantelpiece, or an empty wardrobe. All that possibility. What was that hymn Des loved, the one he sang around the house at full volume?

Count your blessings, name them one by one,
Count your blessings, see what God hath done . . .

She carried on dusting, humming the hymn while she went, and tried to think about what her blessings were, not getting much further than the weather being sunny – she had been missing the searing heat of the dusty Australian country town she had come from – and the fact that it was the Live Aid concert today. She would never normally indulge in television during daylight hours, but this seemed like it would be an occasion where it might be *allowed*, like the Royal Wedding or the Olympics.

She was in the living room dusting the mantelpiece

THE BARBECUE AT NO. 9

when she was reminded of the invitation to the barbecue at no. 9, which had been sitting there since Thursday, when she had heard the letterbox rattle, making her jump. It hadn't been the right time for the postman. When she had peered around the curtain, she had seen it was the young girl from no. 9 walking down the road, her scrappy little dog behind her. The girl was all in black, despite the heat, her blonde hair bobbing as she nodded along to whatever music was playing out of her headphones; Rita had smiled at the sight. Partly from relief, and partly fond memory. Oh, to be that young again. That carefree.

She picked the piece of paper off the shelf and read it again. She almost giggled, as though she was a teenager being invited to her first party with boys in attendance, instead of an exhausted woman in her forties, living alone for the first time in her life, feeling as faded as the cut-off jeans she was wearing. But it was such a lovely surprise to be invited. She'd not lived on Delmont Close more than a few weeks and she had been very busy, in her head at least, and had not really had time to get to know anybody in the close yet, so this overture of friendship was very welcome. Yet another sign she had done the right thing in moving here. She needed signs like this.

She tried to remember the last time she had been to a barbecue, or even a party, outside of her own home. Des had preferred it if they were the ones to entertain, and with his role in the community that meant frequently.

She had a vague recollection of a party in a garden where she had danced for so long, she'd had to stop, breathless and laughing. She had also been shoeless, which made her smile. It must've been the early days.

The memory became clearer, like a Polaroid photograph slowly developing. It was seventeen years ago, judging by the shoes she was carrying by their straps. They were strappy blue platform sandals that she couldn't possibly imagine walking in now but were just becoming fashionable in the late sixties. Her dress had been the same baby-blue colour, long and floaty, with a psychedelic pattern on it. She had been so proud of her handiwork, having made up a pattern from her own design. She avoided looking down and taking in the blue vest and old jeans cut down at the knees into shorts that she was wearing today. She rarely gave a second thought about what she put on each morning nowadays.

Where was Des? she wondered, looking for his curly brown hair among the people standing around in the photograph she could almost see in front of her. He didn't seem to be there, but he must've been, surely: they went everywhere together in those days. Then she remembered that the party they had gone to was round at Matthew and Miriam's – the church treasurer and his wife – and Matthew had a full shed of various woodworking tools, where he would spend hours, much to Miriam's delight given how much she disliked him being 'under her feet', as she put it. No doubt that would have been where Des was.

She tried to wind the picture forward – to see if Des appeared in it, to get a glimpse of his handsome face – but all she could see was that momentary snapshot of joy, her carefree expression. It would have to be enough for now. Tears began to mingle with the smile on Rita's face, so she turned her attention back to the invitation, wondering what she should do. On the one hand, the barbecue would be a way to meet people on the close, and maybe even make friends. On the other . . .

As she pondered, Rita began to feel a now familiar wave of heat start to progress through her body and she waved the invitation frantically across the front of her face, a face which – even though she couldn't see it – she knew was turning puce. Though the day was blisteringly hot, this wasn't caused by anything external. It wasn't that kind of heat. Despite knowing this, Rita found herself moving through the house at speed in her eagerness to get outside. It would make no difference temperature-wise, but she had to get into the fresh air: she could already feel her breaths shortening and catching as her anxious mind whirred into action.

She stood in the shade of her back garden, arms outstretched so that they didn't touch her now scorching body. If the garden hadn't been overlooked, she would have removed every item of clothing too, but she hadn't quite lost all her senses; decorum just about remained intact. Thankfully, the stillness of the garden began to calm her, along with the straight lines and soothing symmetry of the houses on the close. The only noise was the faint rhythm of someone playing the drums, a sound she found somehow comforting.

Slowly but surely her body and mind began to settle, and she was just about to go back inside when she sensed rather than saw that someone was in the back alley behind the house. She froze, her body on high alert. This was unusual. The alley was there to provide another route into the back gardens for the short row of houses, but no one ever really used it, preferring to access their gardens from their homes. This wasn't the sort of place where people were in and out of each other's back gardens without being invited. It was one of the reasons she had moved here.

'Hello,' Rita called out, her voice unsteady. She could now almost make out the shadowy figure. They were wearing a baseball cap which obscured their face and were standing behind next door's gate. But whoever it was ignored her, turning their back and walking away. Rita felt her heart rate increase once more, but they had gone. She felt unsettled, and the thought crossed her mind that maybe it might be someone looking for her, but she tried to dismiss it. How would anyone find her here? She had made sure it wasn't possible. It was probably nothing, she told herself, in an attempt to convince herself that was true. With one last deep breath in and out, Rita went back into the house, but the thought that someone had been lurking there wouldn't leave her.

Maybe if she did go to the barbecue, she could tell her neighbours that she'd seen someone prowling around. Be a helpful citizen. Show them she was a person to be trusted. She hadn't felt helpful in a while. That was certainly a point in favour of her attending the party. Yes, maybe that's what she should do. Although perhaps prowling was too strong a word for it. She might be overthinking things. Des used to rib her about that. At least her hot flush was over now.

Rita had discovered she was going through the menopause from her hairdresser, Angela, whose salon, Tangles, Rita had gone to for years before she moved to Delmont Close. At first, she'd wondered whether Angela knew that perhaps Tangles wasn't the best name for a hair salon, but given that it was the only one in their small country town, apart from the barber's, more appropriately named Shorn, that Des went to, she soon realised it didn't matter in the slightest what Angela called it, nor did the fact that Angela's own hair was less than coiffured.

Before she'd told Angela what was going on, she'd gone to the doctor and described her symptoms to him – the heat, the fear, the fury, oh the fury – and he had looked over his half-moon glasses and down his aquiline nose at her and said, 'Well, Mrs Hargreaves, that sounds like life to me.' Despite having no medical training, Angela had given her a more definitive diagnosis as Rita had sat in her chair, getting her regular trim, watching her face turn the colour of rhubarb in the harshly lit mirror as her body overheated.

'Don't worry about it, darl. It's The Change,' she had pronounced with the certainty of a woman who *knew* these things. All Rita had felt was an overwhelming sense of relief that she wasn't deathly ill or – even worse in her opinion – going mad. It had a name, and it was natural.

'Forty-one is on the early side to start, but I was that age too. You should ask your mum when she went through it,' Angela had added, before realising what she'd said and putting her hand over her mouth, her eyes meeting Rita's in the mirror. Rita's mother had died recently, and it wasn't something Rita talked about but somehow everyone knew. She wondered if Des had told people, in order to excuse her strange behaviour. She shook her head, indicating to Angela not to worry, and the conversation moved on, Angela gaily informing her of the horrors she had to look forward to for the next 'five or ten years, my love. You might as well get used to it.'

Rita remembered thinking that it was funny Angela called it 'The Change', since she couldn't imagine a life with *less* change in it than hers. But then everything happened, and now there was nothing left of how it was before, so maybe Angela had been right.

THE BARBECUE AT NO. 9

She knew not to let this kind of reminiscence take hold, lest it lead her to spiral, so, ever practical, Rita decided to plan what she might wear to the barbecue if she *were* to attend. She made her way upstairs, studiously ignoring both the wallpaper and the 'artwork' on the stairs, both of which were beige to the point of boredom.

Due to the haste of the move, she had purchased this place sight unseen. It had been the only house left on the estate and was far too big for one person. It was also so newly finished she could still detect the smell of paint, which only added to the feeling she had of being a guest in her own home. It was a former show home, used previously to let people see what their empty plots would look like with decoration and furniture. Nothing was to her taste. Although what was her taste? She wasn't actually sure that she knew. Or had ever known.

In her pink-as-the-stairs-were-beige bedroom, she quickly confirmed that, as she had suspected, her scant wardrobe would not be up to the task of her first social outing in months. She was surprised to feel a flicker of excitement at the thought that she might have an excuse to buy an outfit, to select something suited to this new life, to make a choice rather than have everything happen to her. Even if she decided not to go to the barbecue in the end, it would still be a worthwhile investment to have more clothes than the paltry selection in front of her. Everything in her wardrobe was what she had fitted into the suitcase as she left, more suited to her life in small-town Australia than suburban England. She walked downstairs again, took her handbag off the back of the chair it was hanging from, and left the house before she could talk herself out of it.

Steve – No. 20

Steve sat at his makeshift surveillance station, smoking a cigarette. It was situated in the small alcove in his bedroom at the front of the house by the large bay window, giving him the best view of the entire close. He had surrounded himself with everything he needed: comfortable chair, table with binoculars on, along with pens, paper, cigarettes, ashtray, and a half-filled mug so tea-stained the inside was the colour of the tobacco in his Benson & Hedges.

He'd checked one night that none of this was visible to people passing by, and, thanks to the thick net curtains his mother had installed throughout the house, it wasn't. 'We don't want the whole street knowing our business,' she had said at the time. The rest of the house, apart from his sparsely furnished room, was filled to the rafters with what he and his brother, Andy, affectionately called 'Tina's trinkets'. Ornaments galore and souvenirs from various seaside locations spanning decades, now old and faded, even though the house was brand new.

You could hardly move around the place without bumping into something Tina had bought in

Cleethorpes in 1973 'to remember it by', or a mug from the Silver Jubilee. Both boys had gently suggested that the move to Delmont Close might present an opportunity to sort out some of her things, to no avail. 'It's a new house, Mum,' Andy had said. 'You could have some new things in it? I mean, there's been about five royal weddings since this.' He'd been holding up a commemorative coronation plate, mouth twitching, making Steve want to laugh, one of the rare occasions they had exchanged a joke in recent years. But she hadn't taken the hint.

He finished his cigarette and went downstairs to make a cup of tea. The house was quiet, meaning his mum must be out. He was likely asleep when she left; he'd been sleeping a lot lately. Opening the fridge, he smiled wanly at the cling-film-covered plate piled with sliced white bread inside. She'd left him some sandwiches, knowing from his mood the day before that even pouring a bowl of cereal or making toast for breakfast might be too much for him today. It was ham and cheese, by the look of it; his mum had a deep distrust of any green food.

He wasn't hungry but he would eat them anyway, he thought, feeling the usual flash of shame that his mother was still looking after him when he was supposed to be an adult now, a 24-year-old man. He'd been to war, for goodness' sake, yet there were times when the simplest of tasks were beyond him. He let himself wonder what

Cameron would have made of the situation, then put the thought firmly to one side. No good would come of adding Cameron into the mix.

He took the plate to his alcove and settled back in, lighting another cigarette. The close was as peaceful and quiet as the house, he realised, until the silence was broken by a loud rat-tat-tat.

Steve dropped immediately to the floor.

His body in a state of emergency, eyes and ears sharpened to a point. He crawled slowly to the side window, where the sound seemed to be coming from, his head moving from left to right to ascertain the source of the noise.

The recognition that this was a rhythmic repetition of the same beats broke through his terror, and he realised it was simply the son of his next-door neighbours, drumming in the shed. There had been a welcome silence for the past few weeks while the family were away (in Tenerife, according to Madge from the corner shop, who had imparted this information with a raised eyebrow and a throwaway 'lucky for some'). They must be home from their holidays.

The drums had been a present the Christmas before from Ned's overindulgent parents. Mrs Thomas always looked at her son with such doe-eyed adoration it made Tina snort. She wasn't a fan of other mothers fawning over their children, though the irony of just how much she looked after him was not lost on Steve.

Since then, the drums had haunted him. The first few times he'd heard Ned practising he'd become so distressed it had led to a full-blown 'episode', as his mum called them, but eventually the sound had become so commonplace he had become somewhat inured to it. He was disappointed to realise that the peace and quiet created by the family being away had put him right back at the beginning, and he would need to get used to the noise all over again.

He sighed then got back up, returning to his chair and cigarette. There was little else to report, but he picked up his pad of paper anyway and headed it with the date, time and weather conditions, adding that the Thomases had returned and wincing as he realised just how late it was. He at least found the action of writing comforting, his body beginning to settle down again from the state of emergency of a few minutes before.

He'd missed observing any early morning activity. It had not been a good day, or in fact a good week. However, he knew from experience that it was important to be thorough regardless. That the smallest detail might end up mattering. He scanned the close, making a note of which houses had their windows open and which closed, which cars were parked and which were missing. There were none he didn't recognise.

Steve's attention was drawn by a sudden movement, and he watched as the woman from no. 15 left the house at speed. She was striding with purpose, almost

THE BARBECUE AT NO. 9

marching. She was a definite person of interest, Steve realised, and he made a note on his pad. She had moved in recently, and since then she'd had no visitors. He hadn't seen any removal vans either, or deliveries. It was as if she had appeared from the sky. Her clothes were so bland as to fade into the background, which might well be deliberate. He could see that she was beautiful, her facial structure one of almost perfect symmetry and her feline eyes a striking green, but it was almost as though she wanted no one to notice her. He had, however. He must remember to find out if Madge at the corner shop knew her name.

Madge was the only 'friend' he'd made since moving here. He'd never intended for this to happen, but Madge was the sort of woman who, once she had decided something, made it happen, and for some reason she had decided she liked Steve. This was curious to him, given that, unlike his mum, Madge could not be described as chipper. In fact, considering how rarely she smiled, it was ironic that she worked in a Happy Shopper. But she loved a gossip and was therefore a vital source of intelligence for Steve, and he took comfort in her stable presence at the till every time he went into the shop. Madge was how he knew many of the people's names who lived on the close, and most of their personal histories.

The woman from no. 15 had disappeared off into the distance, and Steve had just put his binoculars back on the table and stood up to stretch when he heard the scream. There were enough children in and around the close for him not to overreact to the sound, though something about the tone made him freeze, heart pounding.

He raised the binoculars up to his eyes again and looked towards the bottom of the close, in the direction of the sound. He could see there was someone in the alleyway, but thanks to the shading of overhanging trees and their dark clothes and baseball cap – on a scorching hot day in July, he noted – there wasn't much more Steve could make out, as their face was turned in the opposite direction. But there was something about the stillness of the figure that put every one of Steve's senses on high alert. So much so, he could feel his whole body begin to vibrate. The person wasn't moving at all; they seemed to be just watching. Steve tried to work out what they were looking at, given the angle at which they were facing. It could have been any one of the houses at the bottom of the close. Steve's body stilled, as though he was a mirror of the figure in the shadows.

This was the kind of thing the military had trained him for. He slowed his breathing down to keep himself calm, focusing everything on the person in the alleyway. He was aware that at moments such as these, time seemed to slow down too, so although he felt that the person had been there for many minutes, it could just have easily been seconds. He kept one hand on the binoculars while bending slowly to find his pen and paper on the table with the other. He knew he needed to record everything – you never knew what might end up being important, and he could write it out more neatly later – but as he pressed down on the pad it slipped from the table and he instinctively reached down for it.

That momentary lapse was all it took. By the time he had picked the pad up and focused on the alleyway again, the figure was gone. 'Fuck,' Steve said, under his breath, as though his mum was there to hear and admonish him for his language, despite her own being ever-colourful.

Who was this person watching the close? What did they want?

Hour Two: 11 a.m.–12 p.m.

One hour before Live Aid

Rita – No. 15

In her haste to leave the house to buy a new outfit, Rita had failed to look up any bus times or pick up the timetable. It was too far to walk to the 'brand-new, state-of-the-art' shopping centre – which according to the Wimpey salesman was a 'USP' for the residents of the close. So far, she had only been to it once or twice, to get essentials for the house. She preferred the closeness and relative safety of the local shop to buy her food from, it reminded her of home – as she still thought of it – whereas the sprawling shopping centre felt like something out of an American TV show. Luckily, a bus to take her there arrived not long after she had got to the stop at the end of the close, otherwise she might well have turned around and gone back to the house again, dismissing the idea of new clothes or neighbourhood barbecues.

As the almost empty bus pulled away from the stop, Rita turned back to look at her new house, hoping to imprint the scene on her brain, so that she might eventually replace her home with this one. She liked the symmetry of the boxy houses, and their newness. She was wiping the slate clean, and the close was the perfect location to do so. It had no history, no story to tell, so she could pretend that she didn't either.

She found herself humming '*The wheels on the bus go round and round*', only realising how loud she had got when another passenger turned around and gave her a long look. Rita couldn't remember if Angela had mentioned anything about talking or singing to yourself as being part of The Change, but she supposed it could just as easily be due to her being alone far too much in the last few months. All the more reason she should go to this barbecue, before she lost all her social graces and ended up even more like the kind of madwoman people avoided on public transport – though she was starting to wonder if she had always been more like that kind of woman than she'd appreciated.

It was only when she got to the shopping centre that she realised she had no idea where to start. She could almost hear Des's amused voice saying, *You haven't thought this through, have you, love?* The rows of brightly lit, garish shop names meant nothing to her. She'd left London as a miniskirt-wearing Mary Quant fan – after marrying Des in 1968 – though even then she had sewn most of her clothes using her mother's old Singer sewing machine. All manner of fashions and trends had passed her by since then, none of them suitable for a pastor's wife in an Australian country town. She had continued to make her own outfits, still stylish at first, but more modest than those earlier designs. All of which meant she couldn't actually remember the last time she had been clothes shopping, and she had no real idea what she should be wearing.

The one shop name that jumped out at her was Chelsea Girl – a reminder of 1960s London – so she decided to start there. Even though she was conscious it would most likely be too young for her, they might at least steer her in the right direction. Her concern was confirmed by the teenage sales assistants' facial expressions as she walked in. A combination of boredom and disdain settled on the identically made-up faces, all frosted lips and black eyeliner, of the two girls who had been chatting over racks of luminously coloured batwing tops and leggings, their heads bobbing to the synthesisers blaring over the shop speakers.

They looked Rita up and down as though she was another species, which she supposed to them she was. She felt an inexplicable urge to laugh. The folly of youth, not understanding that life, circumstances, the passing of time meant that they would end up just like her one day. Well, maybe not exactly like her. Not if they were lucky.

'Hi,' she said, her voice croaky with underuse, 'can you direct me to a shop that might be more suitable for me?' She indicated her shorts and vest-top-clad body with a self-effacing smile, hoping she might win them over with her awareness that this wasn't the shop for her.

She failed. They instead looked at each other as if to say, *Who's going to take this one?* and one of them pointed at a large shop further down the concourse.

'You'll be wanting C&A,' she said, her expression unchanging. As this was a store that Rita had actually heard of, she nodded her thanks and left the bright colours and now giggling shop assistants and headed straight for where the girl had indicated.

The clothes inside this shop were considerably less colourful and seemed to consist mainly of coats. Rita stared at rack after rack of navy and brown, but as she wandered around in an almost hypnotised state, she realised that in among the coats were some other clothes, and she began to haphazardly pick hangers from the rails whenever she saw something in her size. She had little idea what was in the pile of clothes in her arms as she drifted towards the changing rooms, just hoping that something might suit her or at least make her feel like the kind of person who goes to a barbecue in a new neighbourhood on her own.

It wasn't until she faced herself in the mirror of the changing room that she realised her mistake. The pale pastels, flowing dresses and skirts she had unconsciously selected were for the woman she had left behind in Australia. It was almost a shock to see her short, dark brown hair and pale skin reflected back at her. She still expected to see the long, blonde curls that Des loved so much, and the always tanned face of a woman who spent most of her time outdoors in the Australian sun. Her hand strayed to her head, and she ruffled the hurriedly shorn, now slowly growing locks for what felt like the first time. Who was she now? What clothes did a woman like the one in the mirror wear?

A quiet voice came from behind her: 'I think this would look great on you?'

The shop assistant who was manning the door of the changing room pointed to a navy-blue boiler suit hanging on the rack next to her. 'You could roll the legs up to three-quarter length,' she said, 'and the fabric is really lightweight.' Rita stared at the outfit and the girl, trying to imagine it. 'Then if you tied a scarf in your hair – I can go get you one if you want – you'd look like the dark-haired one off Bananarama, or a bit Dexys.' Rita almost laughed: how young did this person think she was? She couldn't even picture the dark-haired one from Bananarama.

Secular music, and in fact television, had not been a thing at home, certainly not in the last few years, but as she looked back at herself in the mirror and tried to see herself objectively, she realised that her shorter hair had taken some of the last few years off her. She could perhaps pass as being in her thirties. At a push. Maybe she should try something different? So, she took the boiler suit into the changing room while the shop assistant went and got a scarf for her hair, and when she looked at herself in the mirror again, she found herself smiling the most genuine smile she could remember.

After being talked into some hoop earrings 'to finish the outfit off', Rita made her way to the bus stop in something of a daze, but as she sat on the bench and waited, all the courage and bravado she had experienced in the shop began to seep away. She felt as though she was slowly deflating. What on earth did she think she was doing? Who on earth did she think she was?

She was staring into space, trying to imagine herself going to the barbecue in her new outfit, when her attention was drawn to a familiar figure leaving the shop in front of her, huffing and puffing, his arms filled with carrier bags. Rita blinked hard a couple of times, as she realised it was the girl from no. 9's dad. Had she conjured him up from her imagination by thinking about the barbecue? No, he was real, and he was heading her way. Rita looked down, as though going to rummage in her bag, and he was just about to walk past her when he stopped.

'Rita?' he said. She was so unused to people saying her name out loud that she didn't look up for a moment, until it registered that he was in fact speaking to her. How did he know who she was? 'Yes?' she said, her brow furrowed.

'Sorry.' His face softened. 'It's Peter. Gordon. I live on Delmont Close, down the road from you.' Rita was momentarily wrong-footed, unsure what to say. How did he know this? He seemed to sense the question as he carried on, 'We met . . . the day you moved in.'

The memory was a mere glimmer. She had been on autopilot that day, not allowing herself to feel or experience anything other than what was immediately in front of her for fear of being overwhelmed. But just as she had let herself into her new house, her keys in the door, Peter and his wife had passed by, and his wife had called out 'Hello!' Rita had turned, smiled and said hello back – as was required of her – but on realising the woman was going to say more, she had swung back to the door and let herself in, not looking behind her.

'Of course,' Rita said, her pastor's wife's training kicking in, as she smiled warmly. 'Hello again.'

'Do you want a lift?' Peter carried on, swinging his carrier bags to signal towards the car park. His manner was stiff, and Rita wondered if he meant it or was asking out of politeness.

'Oh, no, don't worry,' Rita replied, though she knew it was silly to refuse. Here she was, waiting for a bus in the scorching sun without actually knowing when it might arrive.

'The buses here are terrible,' Peter said. 'Are you sure? I'm headed that way now. Got to get this lot set up.' He indicated the carrier bags again, holding one towards her. It seemed to be filled with video cassette tapes. 'The kids want me to video the whole bloody concert,' he said by way of explanation. 'And not just the Wembley bit!' Peter laughed, seeming to relax for a second before he remembered himself. 'We're having a party later actually, a barbecue. Hopefully you've had an invitation?'

Rita nodded, without giving any indication of whether she would be attending but thinking it might be a good idea to get a lift if she decided she was going. It might make her feel less awkward, having had more of a conversation with at least one person who would be there, and it would mean getting some practice in having the kind of casual, neighbour-style conversations where words are exchanged but nothing is really said. She thanked him and followed him to his car.

'How did you know my name?' she remembered to ask, as she put her seatbelt on. She had avoided introductions on the day they met, and had only seen them a few times since, in passing. He laughed in a way that was more of a bark. 'My wife. Lydia. She makes sure she knows everyone's name. Usually before they even move in. She'll have found it out somehow.' There was a pause. 'She likes to know everything about everyone who moves into the close. In fact, she'll be furious with me if I don't ask you a thousand questions about your life,' he said, and Rita froze.

'Oh, don't worry, I won't,' Peter said, seeming to sense her fear. In a softer, unexpectedly gentle tone he carried on, 'She doesn't mean any harm by it. It's just her way of keeping control. Fool's errand . . .' He trailed off then, lost in his own thoughts, before he seemed to remember she was still in the car. Rita was starting to wonder if he had been drinking – this all felt a little odd, and overfamiliar – but then he turned to her and said, 'Sorry. I'm talking rubbish. It's been a long week, well . . . a long year.'

'I hear you,' she responded with feeling, and they sat in a not uncomfortable silence listening to the Live Aid build-up on the radio as he drove them back to Delmont Close. Rita found herself intrigued by this person. She looked at him surreptitiously, taking in his profile. So far, each time she'd seen him he'd looked every bit the buttoned-up businessman. Even at the weekends he always looked ironed and slick, as though he was in a catalogue photoshoot, not a real person. He didn't look like that today. Beads of sweat were collecting on his forehead and his hair looked as if someone had been ruffling it. Unbidden, an image of him appeared in her mind. She had no idea where it came from, but she could almost see him sitting with his head down and his hands clasped in his hair, an expression of despair on his face.

Also, was there a faint smell of cigarettes behind the sickly-sweet air freshener that was hanging down from the mirror? He just seemed a little unmoored to her, though she supposed he could have said the same about her. Catching sight of her own carefully dyed, dark brown hair in the wing mirror, she wondered whether maybe he had secrets too. She started to feel the desire to ask him some questions of her own, but stopped herself just in time. She had no interest in prolonging the conversation after all. No interest at all.

Steve – No. 20

Steve's mum loudly announced her return home with her usual cry of 'Ding dong, Avon calling!' as she bustled in downstairs, a throwback to when he and Andy were kids. She had worked as an Avon lady in the evenings, leaving them in the company of their often angry father, a man Steve frequently felt he feared more than loved. They used to fling themselves off the sofa and into her arms as soon as they heard her come in the door.

Steve listened to the various sounds that always accompanied his mum's arrival – a series of clatters, bangs and thuds; though small in stature, Tina couldn't do anything quietly. Eventually he smoothed his hair, checked his clothes were straight in the mirror, and made his way to the kitchen. His mum, already absorbed in the ironing and tunelessly singing along with whatever was blaring from the radio, started at the sight of him in the doorway.

'Christ alive,' she said, placing a hand on her heart as though to steady it. 'You almost scared the life out of me.' She reached out to the glass ashtray she had perched on a shelf next to her, precariously balanced among the decorative plates and figurines crammed on it, and lifted the lit cigarette it contained up to her perfectly painted lips. 'You'll be the death of me, Steven, I swear to fucking God.'

Used to his mother's hyperbole and frequent blaspheming, Steve smiled.

'Morning, Mum,' he said and went to put the kettle on.

'I think you'll find it's nearly afternoon,' she said, and he winced, though her voice had no scold in it, just an observation of fact.

'Tea?' he asked, battling his way to the kettle via the SodaStream, sandwich maker, toaster and microwave crowding the kitchen top – his mum loved a new appliance – before turning around to look at her. She had picked up a piece of paper and was reading it in such a studied, self-conscious way Steve almost laughed. His mother could never have been an actress. It was only then that he remembered the young girl at no. 9's deliveries to each of the houses on the close that he'd recorded a couple of days ago. He hadn't left his room that day and had forgotten to follow up on what she had been posting.

He decided to indulge her.

'What's that you're reading?' he said, injecting a tone of nonchalance into his voice, almost as obvious as his mum's pretend reading.

'We've been invited to a party!' she said. 'Both of

us,' she added with meaning. 'At number nine, three o'clock this afternoon. It's for Live Aid – you know, *for the children in Africa*,' she added with a dramatic whisper. Steve was stunned into immediate silence. He was never invited anywhere. 'Typical of Lady Di at number nine though,' his mum carried on. 'It can't be a good old-fashioned street party, like we had for the jubilee, remember? She's got to go one better than that and have a fancy barbecue.' His mum held the piece of paper out to him, and carried on singing, smoking and ironing, an impressive juggle, while Steve made the tea.

His eyes kept returning to her as she sang. She was ironing an electric-blue garment. Tina could never be described as 'plain' – every outfit she wore made Steve think of tinsel; they were all shine and glitter – but this was one of her many party dresses, arguably her favourite. It had a ra-ra skirt, she had once explained to him. She was taking this invitation seriously if this was her chosen outfit.

She didn't return his gaze, and he was aware she was studiously resisting asking whether he would consider coming to the party with her. She knew him well enough not to have told him before, guessing correctly that giving him too much time to think about it would mean a certain no. His mum was definitely a trier. She wouldn't give up on the idea that he might one day become as outgoing and sociable as she was, even if all the evidence was to the contrary.

He took his cup of tea and the invitation upstairs before he read it for himself, and was surprised to see that it did indeed extend to both of them. He'd assumed his mum was just including him in the hope he might be persuaded to come. He couldn't think of a time he had exchanged even a neighbourly nod of acknowledgement with any of the family at no. 9, or indeed anyone else on the close. He always kept his head down while on one of his rare trips out, though he of course knew a lot about them.

Why would they include him in the invitation? Was there some ulterior motive? He couldn't even imagine how they knew his name, except of course through his mum, but she had never particularly liked Lydia and Peter Gordon, calling them Lady Di and Flash Gordon respectively. That didn't influence her attending though: Steve didn't think she had ever said no to a 'do' in her life.

There was only one person in the close Steve had said more than a brief hello to. Davina, who lived four doors down. He didn't think she worked, as he often saw her in the day, and she had once appeared in the corner shop at the same time as him, despite his best efforts to avoid bumping into anyone.

'Hello,' she'd said, blocking the shelves containing tinned tomatoes and beans that he was trying to get to. 'You live on Delmont Close, I think, same as me. I'm Davina.'

With this she'd held out the hand not holding her

basket of shopping. Steve hadn't taken it, but instead had looked down at his feet, nodded, and mumbled that his name was Steve. He'd watched her face turn slowly pink and her hand return to her side, and he'd felt guilty at the snub. But friendships weren't his thing. They were a distraction, and he had a job to do. Watching out for signs of danger, and keeping everyone on the close safe from harm, required his full attention.

He'd wondered afterwards why she had tried to speak to him. Maybe she was someone he should be keeping an eye on too, or maybe she had simply thought they would have more in common than the rest of the people living on the close, given they were both clearly misfits. She was dressed in shabby clothes, with the musty smell of charity shops about them, all holes and frays. He wondered how she could afford to live in Delmont Close and had made a note to that effect.

Madge had been keen to fill him in on the gossip about Davina.

'You know that one you were talking to, who smells of patchouli oil, with the three daughters – *Davina*,' she had said to him after seeing their interaction, her face scrunching up at the name, as though it spoke of an exoticness she disapproved of. 'Three. Different. Fathers,' she declared, a fact conveyed with much activity from her eyebrows, 'and not one of them around.'

She had told him in the same conversation that the Chamberlains, who lived next door to the Gordons, had marriage troubles, something he had gone on to confirm was true. He had no idea how Madge knew these things, but she was a mine of information and made her pronouncements with an air of rightness he couldn't imagine ever giving off.

He wondered what Madge – and indeed the rest of the close, the Gordons at no. 9 included – said about him. He knew the kids called him Lurch, had heard them chanting it from a safe distance, the lad next door particularly, sat astride his BMX, ready to speed away if Steve reacted, which he never did. He wasn't unaware of his apparent weirdness in the eyes of the outside world. He knew how he came across. He had once been one of them too. The kind of person who you said hello to in the street, and who regularly got invited to neighbourhood get-togethers. He knew only too well how different he was now.

The invitation was at least a good reminder about the Live Aid concert. It meant he needed to be even more vigilant than usual. While all eyes were on their televisions, someone needed to be watching for the enemy. He knew enough to know that any likely attacks would come when the country was distracted by something else. And a suburban neighbourhood like this would be the ideal target. Also, he realised, everyone would be watching it, which meant that the shops would be quiet, so he could use the time to go and get his weekly provisions.

The aforementioned bad week meant that he hadn't

gone at his usual time – Wednesday at 11 a.m. – and he was running low on cigarettes, the one thing his mum refused to buy for him, despite her own forty-a-day habit, and the large boxes of duty-free she would bring home from her frequent holidays to Spain with the girls. He suspected it was to make him leave the house.

He would go to the shop, stock up on a few things, then settle in upstairs and resume his surveillance for the rest of the day, though in truth he was no longer sure what exactly the danger was any more. In the army, the enemy had been delineated, obvious. Now, it seemed to move and morph at such a speed it made him dizzy. The only way to stay ahead of it was to keep his eyes open and his guard up at all times.

He thought briefly about doing his one hundred press-ups, he'd missed a few days, but they would have to wait. He cleaned his teeth, straightened his clothes again, ensuring no crumbs had made their way on to them, and brushed his hair once more. By the time he was ready to go to the shops, he found his mum in the kitchen, reading and smoking, the glasses she needed to wear all the time, but often didn't, perched on the end of her nose. She tended to alternate between Jackie Collins and, perhaps more surprisingly, Proust, who she said 'is very wise on the subject of life and loneliness', though judging by the red stilettos on the front of the book she was holding, this was more in the former ballpark than the latter.

'I'm off out, Mum,' he said. 'Do you need anything?'

'No, love,' she said, not taking her eyes from the page.

'Okay, see you later,' he replied, and was just about to leave when she lowered the book on to her lap.

'Maybe get me a bottle of Lambrusco? Or Blue Nun. Something fancy? It said on the invitation not to bring anything, but you know what Lady Di from number nine is like.'

'Okay.'

'And Steve . . .'

He knew what was coming.

'Would you think about joining me? It might be good for you. You know, to get out for a bit. We won't have to stay long.'

She raised the book back in front of her face and he left.

The walk was short and he kept his gaze low, using only his peripheral vision to observe and make a mental note of anything he needed to record once home, though there was little to report on the way there. No loud noises. No surprises. Nothing to set him off.

The door of the Happy Shopper was wedged open, and Madge was fanning herself with the laminated sign that read 'Don't ask for credit, refusal often offends', a picture of a cartoon dog on it for some reason. He quickly made his way down the two aisles, picking up various bits and pieces, along with the wine for his mum, before heading to the till.

THE BARBECUE AT NO. 9

'Morning!' Madge said. 'Missed you this week. Everything all right?'

Steve nodded – he wasn't about to share the truth of the last few days – and placed his basket on the side for her to begin putting the items through.

'Quiet one today?' he said, looking round the empty shop.

'Hardly anyone in the last hour or so,' she said, 'though it was busy before that. We've almost run out of crisps and beer – people planning to watch the concert, I reckon, or going to the Gordons' barbecue.' She studied him closely, as though to check whether he knew about either event.

'Oh yeah, I've been invited to that,' Steve said, not really knowing why he felt the need to tell her.

'You should go,' Madge said, her fingers moving at lightning speed as she typed the price of each item into the till. 'It would be good for you,' she added, echoing his mum's words. She paused for a moment, then said quietly, 'Ryan will be going.'

He had recently become aware of a young man who, like him, had come back to the close to live with his mum. According to Madge, his name was Ryan, and he'd been unable to get a job after graduating from university, so had moved home. 'I mean, he studied English, so I'm not sure what he expected,' Madge had said. Steve had learned over time that Madge wasn't a fan of education, particularly of the 'useless' variety. 'School of life, that's where I went,' she would say, 'and that's all you need if you ask me.'

'I suppose it could also be down to the current rate of unemployment,' Steve had said at the time, unable to stop himself from replying, pointing to the headline on the newspapers by the till which read *Three Million and Rising*, but Madge carried on as though she hadn't heard him, lamenting the choices of 'young people today' as if Steve himself wasn't a young man, also currently jobless.

Steve had kept an eye on Ryan since. He was shorter than Steve, with messy hair and a mad-professor look about him, his round steel glasses only adding to that impression. Steve had found himself drawn to him, and at first had told himself his interest was generated by their similarity of circumstance. Both had flown the nest, only to come back a few years later. Steve wondered if, like his, Ryan's view of the world had changed and become tainted. Though, of course, leaving to go to college, as Ryan had, was different from leaving to go to war.

Every time he saw Ryan, he felt the same physical responses that he had when an episode was imminent: the thudding heart, the dry mouth, the desire to run. He knew it wasn't that kind of fear though. No, this was something else. Something he hadn't felt for a very long time. Something equally scary for him.

'You okay, Steve?' he heard Madge say, and he realised he'd got lost in his thoughts.

'Sorry, yes, it's just hot,' he faltered, before pulling himself together and turning the attention away from the chatter in his brain. 'Has there been anyone new in?' he asked. 'Today even? Wearing dark clothes and a baseball cap?'

He was thinking about the person he'd seen in the close earlier, after the scream. If anyone had noticed someone hanging around, it would be Madge. Even if the person hadn't been into the shop, Madge had a full view of the street in front of her, and the close sat just off that street, almost opposite.

'No one I don't know,' Madge said, 'and I would've noticed in this heat! In fact, I've seen a bit too much of everyone who's been in. What is it about the sun coming out in this country that makes men think we'd like to see their white bits?' She mock shuddered. 'I'll keep an eye out though,' she added, 'and make a note. Anything I should be worried about?' Madge indulged Steve's vigilance and he was grateful for it.

'No,' he said, 'at least I don't think so. I'll let you know.' He paid for his shopping and left, moving slowly in the heat and breathing in the smell of mowed lawns as he headed back home, the candy-striped carrier bag knocking against his legs.

Steve, as always, kept his wits about him while he walked, alert for the sight of the figure in the baseball cap, and for Ned Thomas and his friends and the cry of 'Lurch', but the boy was rarely seen in daylight hours these days. He was probably in the shed, and the rest of the close was as still and silent as when he left it.

All that stretched in front of him, as far as he could see, were uniform-looking houses repeated over and over. Their newness and neatness like a fortress of symmetry; Thatcher's talisman against poor people. They were designed to protect the occupants, as though if everyone lived in similar houses, they'd live similar lives and there would be nothing to be afraid of any more. Though as Steve knew only too well, that wasn't true at all.

He was just turning into their drive when a Volvo passed him, one he recognised immediately as Peter Gordon's car. Peter was driving, but of interest to Steve was the fact that his passenger wasn't Lydia. Steve stopped for a moment, bending down as if tending to one of his mum's plants, forgetting temporarily that they were all plastic, so he could get a look at who it was once the car had stopped. When the woman from no. 15 got out and headed to her house, while Peter went into no. 9, he was intrigued. He knew from his notes that the new woman didn't have a car, so Peter was probably just giving her a lift, but she didn't strike him as someone that Flash Gordon would normally associate with. Not nearly showy enough. He realised he needed to know more about this new person on the close.

Hour Three: 12–1 p.m.

The Coldstream Guards, Status Quo,
The Style Council, The Boomtown Rats

Hanna – No. 9

Hanna listened to her mum and dad argue from her bedroom. She wondered how many times she had done so over the last year. This time it was about the gate, and the broken lock, and the number of times her mum had asked her dad to fix it. Except of course it wasn't. Lydia had practically pounced on Peter as soon as he had returned from the shops, and they were still standing in the hallway.

'It's like you don't even care that we could have been attacked in our own home.' Lydia's voice was taut. It had a quality that reminded Hanna of when she was first learning to play violin, the way it carried from her ears right into the centre of her.

'The point is that you weren't,' Peter replied, his voice much lower and ever logical, almost robotic, though something about his tone gave away that he too was concerned. It was a tremor most people would not have detected, but Hanna was so attuned to sound, and that of her dad's voice, she knew not only did he believe her mum, but he was worried too.

Hanna sighed. She knew that this wouldn't be

enough for her mum, that this kind of response was guaranteed to make her worse, and she was right. Lydia's voice became more staccato, every syllable like a prod of her glossily manicured finger. 'That is not the point at all. The point is that even when we've had as close a call as we did today – an intruder, for God's sake – you still don't seem to care about your family. The only thing that seems to matter to you is your bloody job.'

'And it's that bloody job that pays for this bloody family,' Peter said.

Hanna took a deep breath at this, hoping David had his headphones on and wasn't listening too. Downstairs, Peter sighed, saying, 'I'll fix the gate.'

He must have made to move, as Lydia screeched, 'Not now! We have the whole close coming round in a matter of hours, *plus* your brother and that wife of his, who'll no doubt be judging us as *that family* who can't even organise a neighbourhood barbecue, and there are a thousand things that need to be done.'

'Well, make your mind up.'

Hanna couldn't bear to listen to the circular argument go round again, and closed her bedroom door, turning the radio on, so she could listen to the concert instead, and let music perform its gentle hypnosis on her. She flopped down on to her bed. It didn't use to be like this, her family. Even though she had always felt like a misfit, her parents used to be normal: her dad funny, affectionate and embarrassing, singing 'Fat Bottomed

Girls' by Queen at full volume every opportunity he got; her mum a bit annoying, making her tidy her room and eat her vegetables, but ultimately loving, safe and comforting.

The screeching and the sighing were relatively new. Hanna remembered when everyone at school, including her, was obsessed with the Adrian Mole books. She hadn't read many other books all the way through, her preferred language being the lyrics of songs. In the first book, Adrian had been oblivious to his mum having an affair with Mr Lucas, and Hanna had been wondering if that might be what was happening with her dad and if that might explain her mum's anger. She'd been watching for signs, but her dad didn't seem to go anywhere except to work – or into his own head.

She'd even wondered if it was to do with her – the change in him – but how could it be? Her dad had no more idea of what was going on in her life than her mum or David did, or even Rosie. She might be able to blame herself for many things, but this wasn't one of them.

Both her thoughts upstairs and the argument downstairs were interrupted by the doorbell.

'Hanna,' called her mum in the sing-song voice she used for visitors, 'it's Rosie.' Hanna groaned and pulled herself off the bed. 'Coming!' she called back. As she headed down the stairs, she could see her dad had taken the opportunity to disappear, while her mum stood chatting to Rosie, all smiles and fake jollity, as though the raging argument of a few moments ago had not taken place.

'Don't be too long, Hanna,' her mum said when she reached the front door. 'There's plenty to be done to get ready for this afternoon.' She gave Hanna a hard look that belied the soft tinkle of her voice, and Hanna was reminded of the games you had to play to be part of her family. No wonder she was planning to leave. *Never raise your voice to each other in front of other people. We don't want to be known as 'that family'*, she could almost hear her mum saying. Worrying about being 'that family' took up an inordinate amount of her mum's energy.

'We won't be long, Mrs Gordon,' Rosie said. 'I've just got to go to the shop for my mum. Do you need anything else for the barbecue?'

Hanna almost laughed as Rosie smiled sweetly at her mum, knowing this would land her in Lydia's good books.

'No,' came her dad's voice from the living room, where he was noisily messing about with the video recorder and a pile of tapes, at the same time as her mum said, 'Yes.'

'Ignore my husband,' she said, the tinkle now so sharp it could cut glass. 'If you could just get a couple more bags of Twiglets, that would be lovely,' and she went to get her purse while the girls pulled faces at each other. 'No one likes Twiglets,' whispered Rosie, and Hanna shrugged, smiling in response. She knew from experience there was no point in arguing this with her mum.

THE BARBECUE AT NO. 9

'I thought I'd come and rescue you from party preparations,' Rosie said, once they were on their way to the shop. 'I bet Lydia has gone full Margo Leadbetter with the arrangements.'

Hanna snorted at this. They both thought of Rosie's relaxed, loving parents as Tom and Barbara Good from *The Good Life*, and Hanna's more uptight ones as Margo and Jerry. 'Mum has gone bananas, especially as Uncle Keith and Aunty Beverley are coming. I wouldn't be surprised if she hasn't got the red carpet out by the time we get home.'

'Sorry if you were about to watch the concert though,' Rosie carried on. She very rarely paused for breath, or listened to a word anyone else said, and Hanna was grateful for that, it was one of the many reasons the two of them were friends. Rosie never minded Hanna's quietness, and Hanna never minded Rosie's constant chatter.

'I did bring this so we can listen,' Rosie said. She opened the bag she had slung over her shoulder and showed Hanna a small portable radio with a wrist strap attached. 'But it's all old-people music at first anyway. As long as I get to see Wham! I don't care.'

Hanna took a surreptitious look at her long-legged, brunette friend as she talked. While Hanna's clothes had descended into darkness, Rosie still wore the candy pink, acid limes and yellows that graced every cover of their still-shared *Just Seventeen* magazines. The contrast between them now meant Hanna looked like the photographic negative of Rosie.

Rosie was so unselfconscious too. Even as they passed Mike Wilson's house, where he was outside mowing the front lawn, Rosie just waved and said, 'Hello, Mr Wilson,' and didn't freeze or blush like Hanna did when he grinned his handsome smile and replied, 'Hello, ladies.' Rosie was so comfortable in her own skin. Hanna wondered if it was because she was into sports and stuff. Her body had a job, a purpose, whereas Hanna had long felt that hers was just for other people to look at.

She glanced down at her curves, which felt alien to her, as though she was entirely separate from them. She longed for Rosie's easy grace. This was the kind of thing she would have once talked to Rosie about. They'd been friends since the beginning of primary school, their lives inextricably intertwined, and they used to share everything.

They had been thrown together – as all the best childhood friends are – by proximity, courtesy of their shared birthday, which meant they had been sat next to each other in class. When they turned thirteen, they had marked the transition from child to teen by changing the spellings of their names, from Rose to Rosie (after the TV cop show), and Hannah to Hanna (borrowed from the Hanna-Barbera that appeared at the end of their favourite cartoons), which bonded them even further. But at some point, Hanna felt she had left Rosie behind, though that sounded as though she thought she was better than her best friend, when actually the opposite was true.

THE BARBECUE AT NO. 9

They had gone from playing elastics and roller skating up and down their respective streets, to trying on blusher and loving Nick Rhodes (Hanna) and John Taylor (Rosie) from Duran Duran. But somehow that's where Rosie had stayed, while Hanna had raced on to the next thing, thinking she was ready to be a proper teenager when she really wasn't. She hadn't thought it was possible to grow up too fast, but it turned out it was. When both their families had moved to Delmont Close, Hanna had hoped it might be a chance to bridge the distance between them.

As they were nearing the shop, they spotted Antoinette Chamberlain and her three friends on their way out of it. To Hanna, they looked like three middle-aged women, wearing pearls and pastels, with their shirt collars turned up. Antoinette's expression was her usual superior, pouty one. 'Who does she think she is, Princess Diana?' Rosie whispered, as they approached them.

'If Princess Diana shopped in Etam maybe,' Hanna replied, the two of them dissolving into giggles. 'Why is she always soooooo miserable-looking?' And in an instant Hanna felt as though they were back together, the friends they had always been.

This was followed immediately by the thought of her leaving, and how Rosie would feel. Hanna shook aside the knowledge of what was to come. She was amazed by how easy she found it to compartmentalise, but then she'd had a lot of practice lately in lying to everyone she loved. She was now an expert at being two separate people. No matter how hard it was, that would be the great relief of leaving: no longer having to keep track of the stories she had told.

The girls all studiously ignored each other as they walked past, Hanna and Rosie still laughing while the others chewed gum and stared straight ahead, showing no emotion, like three mini Stepford wives. 'They haven't been invited to the barbecue, have they?' Rosie said, with an exaggerated groan.

'Only Antoinette, with her mum and dad,' Hanna replied. 'I don't reckon she'll come.'

The two girls got what they needed from the shop and headed back to no. 9, Rosie talking about the party, who she wanted to be there, and which bands she wanted to watch on the TV, while Hanna swung the bag full of Twiglets and a bottle of Lilt against her legs.

'Oh, I forgot to ask if Shane's coming,' Rosie said. 'I mean, I'm guessing he is, given you're officially boyfriend and girlfriend now,' she added, making a squelchy kissing sound with her lips. At the mention of Shane's name, Hanna couldn't help but smile. Then she remembered about the baby. How on earth was she going to tell him? Was she going to?

'Oh my God, will Ned Thomas be coming? Is he back from his holiday yet? Can you imagine how gorgeous

THE BARBECUE AT NO. 9

he's going to look with a tan?' Rosie's voice cut through her thoughts of Shane as they turned into Delmont Close. Hanna answered that she didn't know, but he'd been invited, and Rosie moved immediately on to what she would wear to the party and how she was hoping to attract his attention: she'd fancied him from afar forever, though up until now he hadn't even acknowledged her existence, and she was so excited that he was actually going to be there.

Hanna let her chatter on, wondering whether she should say anything more about Ned, maybe warn Rosie that he might not be good news, maybe tell her what she knew about him, what had happened; but she realised that she didn't know how to talk to her friend about him, she didn't have the words. That seemed to happen so often these days. Her words felt stuck inside her brain. She was starting to feel as if she didn't speak the same language as everyone else around her.

Her only consolation was that whenever she had a feeling that she couldn't put into words, she could find a song instead that would represent her happiness, her sadness, her yearning, her fear. As the two of them approached no. 9, she did what she always did and retreated into her mind, humming a tune she'd been thinking about earlier, barely listening to her friend and wondering if this was how her dad felt when he disappeared into himself.

The two girls arrived back at Hanna's house and were just about to go inside when for the first time Hanna felt a flutter in her tummy that somehow didn't feel as though it belonged to her. Was it the baby? Was it moving? It happened again and Hanna instantly wanted to cry; wanted to have Rosie put her hand on her tummy and feel it too.

As the girls stepped inside, it was clear they had interrupted Peter and Lydia arguing again. Hanna could almost hear the echo of it in the tense atmosphere of the house. Her parents were standing in the hallway, close enough to touch, but judging from the expressions on their faces, no touching had been taking place. Her mum's face was angry and pale, with flushed-red cheeks; her dad's shoulders were slumped, his expression dejected. On seeing Hanna and Rosie, her mum immediately bustled into action.

'You took your time. Are these for me?' she said, taking the carrier bags from both girls' hands and heading to the kitchen. 'I need you to start putting these in bowls,' she continued, over her shoulder.

'Right – I'm going to start organising the barbecue,' Peter said, his voice gruff, leaving the girls standing in the hallway.

Rosie looked at her watch. 'I think Nik Kershaw's on soon,' she said. 'I might go now so I can watch him while I get ready.' Her voice was low and her expression one of pity and she slipped back out of the door before

Hanna could beg her to stay. They wouldn't start arguing again with Rosie in the house, Lydia wouldn't want to be known as 'that family'. But she was gone.

Hanna stood in the hallway for a moment, then made her way upstairs. Before she went to help her mum, she wanted to check on David, make sure he hadn't heard what had been going on. The silence from his room told her he was wearing headphones, so she opened his door slowly, not wanting to startle him.

David's bedroom was all boy. Geometric patterns and lines in red and grey and the smell of socks. He was sitting on his bed, knees up, arms balancing on them, chin resting on his hands. He looked younger than his years. Prince was lying next to him, his nose touching David's feet.

'You listening to the concert?' she mouthed, indicating the headphones he had clamped to his ears. He nodded, taking them off, and Hanna noted his swollen cheeks and eyes. He shuffled up, making space, and Hanna sat down on the chequered bedspread. Prince jumped down from the bed, then back up again, settling himself in between the two of them. He was not remotely useful as a guard dog but had a nose for whoever in the family was in emotional distress. What that said about his adoration of Lydia, Hanna preferred not to consider, though she wondered how on earth he chose which one of them to comfort at the moment. It felt as if, at any given time, every single member of the Gordon family required his soothing presence.

'You okay?' Hanna said, making sure she looked straight ahead when she asked the question. She had learned that her and David's most honest conversations took place without eye contact, usually when they were playing on his Space Invaders game, or Frogger, and were focused on the screen rather than each other's expressions. David sighed, and she felt him shudder next to her. She was about to ask him again when she realised he was sobbing, silently. They weren't given to physical affection, their love more usually expressed in ruthless mockery, but her arm reached around him, and she felt her throat clench as he unexpectedly leaned into her.

The two of them sat that way for a while, Hanna almost holding her breath, not wanting to break the spell of their rare proximity. If she could have pressed pause on this moment, she would have. Eventually David spoke. 'Do you think they'll get divorced?' he said, his voice high-pitched. 'There's a boy in my class whose parents are divorced, and he only sees his dad once a month.' Hanna pondered for a moment. On the one hand, she wanted to be the reassuring big sister; on the other, she had never outright lied to him before, and given the betrayal he would surely feel when he found out she had gone, she didn't want to start now.

'I don't know,' she said. 'I know they're not happy. But think of all the times when you've been unhappy. Like, do you remember when we were little, and Gary died and both of us thought we'd never stop crying?'

She felt David's head nod against her arm at the memory of the goldfish they had won at the fair and brought home in a plastic bag filled with water. 'But we did, didn't we? Eventually. And maybe eventually Mum and Dad will stop being unhappy.'

She was just getting up, and about to ruffle his hair, a move that would make him furious, meaning they were back to themselves, when David said, 'But we'll always be stuck with each other, won't we.' The words were casual, as though a throwaway comment, so obvious it hardly needed saying, but Hanna could sense the weight behind them, the promise her brother was looking for her to make. She felt her breath catch. 'Come downstairs,' she said to him, hoping he wouldn't notice the wobble in her voice. 'We can watch the concert on the telly.'

They made their way downstairs with some hesitancy, hoping not to walk in on further arguing, but the only sound was that of Bob Geldof singing 'Rat Trap' and the roar of the crowd screaming, *'You've been caught'* back at him. More than anything, Hanna wanted to sit and watch the concert with David, and lose herself in it, but she couldn't let herself. Maybe it was some kind of penance for what she was going to do, but she needed to find her mum and dad, to help them get ready for the barbecue, or at least show willing.

'I'll be back in a minute,' Hanna said to David, now sitting on the sofa, Prince curled up by his side. David was so entranced by the sea of people crammed into Wembley Stadium, he barely noticed as Hanna wandered off into the garden.

It was just her dad out there, seeming to shimmer in the heat, looking at the brick barbecue they'd had built, as though mesmerised. They had decided to get one because a) they were the latest new thing, and b) Keith and Beverley had one already, which Lydia had been furious about. She was determined to be the first to have one on Delmont Close, if not the whole county.

Not wanting to interrupt whatever spell her dad seemed to be under, Hanna instead made her way to the end of the garden, shaded by trees, where there was a wrought-iron bench no one ever used. She sat down and looked back at her family, as though drinking them in for the final time: David in the living room, staring at the television; Prince by his side, staring up at him; Dad in the garden, staring at the barbecue; and Mum in the kitchen, staring at the recipe book in her hands. It was the perfect family tableau. Her presence would only spoil it. She was right to be leaving.

Her eyes drifted downward and caught sight of a cigarette butt, discarded to one side of the bench as if someone had sat there, smoking, taking in a similar scene to the one that she was observing now, perhaps with her in it too. Maybe her dad had started again; Mum would kill him if he had. But a thought kept hovering that she tried to swat away like a fly: maybe someone really was watching them.

Rita – No. 15

Rita wasn't sure about the concert so far. It seemed to be more like the Royal Variety Performances she was forced to sit through as a girl, with the Coldstream Guards playing the national anthem, and the camera panning to Prince Charles and Princess Diana, somewhat incongruously sitting next to Bob Geldof. She left it on anyway, picking up her copy of the *Radio Times* to check when The Who would be on. She hoped it wouldn't be during the barbecue later. She had fancied Roger Daltrey since 'My Generation', in the days when she had been happily heading down the path of rebellion he offered.

She could remember practically screaming, '*Hope I die before I get old*' while dancing in the pubs and clubs she would go to with friends way back when, before Des, getting into trouble when she missed curfew or didn't go home at all. She wondered whether Roger had aged well, then laughed wryly. She felt as though she had aged at double speed over the last few years, whether it looked that way or not. The rebellious, wild young woman she had been was a distant memory now. She supposed she was old, or at least what she would have considered old back then.

THE BARBECUE AT NO. 9

She sat on the inoffensive, beige, former-showroom sofa and stared at the screen, momentarily captivated by the crowds of people packed into Wembley, their movements like waves in the ocean. The camera roved above them, the voiceover talking about this being 'the greatest show on earth', and Rita felt a pang of longing for the girl she once was. That girl would have been first in the queue for a concert like this. She stared at the hot, excited faces of the people there, when the camera settled on them. She imagined them telling their children and grandchildren that they had been at Live Aid, a bit like the women of her generation did about Woodstock. She had been married to Des and living in Australia by 1969, so there was no chance of her having been to that music festival, but she had been to the International Love-In Festival at Ally Pally in 1967 and seen Pink Floyd and The Animals with her best friend Alistair. It had been the most exciting day of their young lives so far.

She checked the *Radio Times* again to see if Pink Floyd would be playing in the concert and was thrilled to see they were, while also chuckling that she was doing so while sitting alone on her sofa with a cup of tea: very different circumstances from when she'd seen them before. Then, she'd been in a crowd of thousands wearing practically nothing, nicely buzzing on magic mushrooms which Alistair had procured from two hippies who had picked him up in their van when he was hitch-hiking to the venue. Still, she supposed that Pink Floyd had changed too. Hadn't everyone?

It had been after that concert in '67 when her parents had finally stepped in. She supposed it could be thought of as the beginning of the end. They had tolerated so much up to that point – the friends, the clothes, the smell of alcohol on her breath – but going AWOL for forty-eight hours, then being emptied out of a VW camper, delirious, by Alistair and the hippies, who then drove off, was more than the Stanleys could take. Rita had some sympathy with that. Elsie and Roger Stanley had not lived expansive lives and, as fully committed churchgoing, suburban-living Christians, had no idea how to manage their wayward daughter. By rights she should have been married or at the very least 'courting' by the advanced age of twenty-five, and they were baffled that she instead was choosing to 'throw her life away' in this manner.

Once she had sobered up, they had sat her down and made her a deal.

'We're concerned about you,' her dad had said. She'd looked at the two of them, sitting upright opposite her across the dining-room table, dressed smartly, and felt as though she was at a job interview she hadn't prepared for.

'Okaaaay,' she'd replied, elongating the word to try and slow down the inevitable scolding she was headed for. Her mum had looked at her dad, her pale face creased in an expression of anguish, her hand reaching up from below the table and squeezing Rita's father's arm.

'We hardly see you these days. If you're not out' – he'd paused, then said 'gallivanting', an almost imperceptible nod from her mother indicating he'd made the correct choice of word – 'then you're hiding away in your room doing goodness knows what.'

Her mum's nodding and squeezing had continued. Rita had looked at the two of them and stifled a giggle. She couldn't stop seeing them as a ventriloquist and dummy, though she'd never been actually sure which one was which.

The deal had been this. If she wanted to keep living in their house (she did), rent-free (having very little money, she definitely did), then she had to come home every night, no matter what time, and go to church every Sunday. She supposed her parents had hoped that if she went back to church something might rub off, and she might eventually heed the Word of the Lord and turn her life around, whereas instead she had met a visiting preacher from Australia who looked like Eric Clapton. Either way, it had worked. Her life did indeed turn around.

She did what they asked, calling Alistair to tell him they couldn't hang out for a while, much to his disappointment. 'No one else is as cool as you,' he said. 'When will I get to see you again?' And she realised he sounded genuinely sad. She was used to friendships and relationships as fleeting as her own attention span and was surprised by his reaction.

'It's just for a few weeks,' she replied, fully intending that life would go back to normal once her parents had forgiven her, which after all, as Christians, it was their duty to do.

The thought of her parents led Rita upstairs. Before she had time to question the decision or think about its consequences, she pulled down the battered tan suitcase she had travelled back to England with from the top of the wardrobe. It wasn't large, and for more than reasons of space, anything she had brought with her was practical, not sentimental, except the photographs. Tucked into the yellowing lining of the suitcase was an envelope containing a handful of prints, the most precious ones. She opened it and pulled out the one of her mum and dad. It was square, and as it was taken in the 1950s it was also sepia-toned, but it wouldn't have mattered anyway, as her parents were no more colourful in person than the beiges and browns of the photograph. Her dad, stiffly posed in a roll-neck jumper and dark slacks, was a full head taller than her mum. Her mum had a handbag hooked over her arm, like the Queen Mother, with her hands held together in front of her. Rita could imagine that just before the photo had been taken, she would have been clasping and unclasping them repeatedly, a nervous habit she had. Her face, though pretty, looked pinched and tight, more evidence of her perpetual anxiety. Her mum had been scared of her own shadow. This was a woman who needed to believe in the Lord's protection in order to have the courage to leave the house.

Rita wondered what age her mother had been in the photograph. She always thought of her as being old before her time, but now, having passed the age her mother was when she last saw her, she had more sympathy for the cares that had stooped her mother's back and furrowed her brow. Her father, on the other hand, stood tall and upright in her mind, unbending, his stature mirroring his morals. She had ended up becoming more like her mother than she liked to admit, and the thought made her put the photograph firmly back into the suitcase.

Rita had not seen them for seventeen years. When her mum had died, they couldn't afford the air fare for her to return. The photo was how she always remembered her mum looking anyway. Timid, faded. She allowed herself to wonder if her dad was still living in the house her parents had moved into when they were first married, and where she grew up: the little two-up two-down Victorian terrace that she had been so desperate to escape from. She knew it was no coincidence that she had moved to Delmont Close, only fifty or so miles away from the London suburb where she was born and raised. But she couldn't go and see him. For too many reasons to count. Not least the fact that she was sure by now he would have disowned her.

Her fingers itched to look at the only other photographs she had brought. But no good would come of that. She hadn't been able to look since she'd arrived. She put the photo of her mum and dad back in the envelope and the suitcase at the top of the wardrobe, deciding instead to have a shower and, although it was far too early, to change into her outfit for the barbecue, in the hope that if she wore it for a few hours, it wouldn't look quite so brand new. She experienced a little frisson of excitement at the thought of going out and dancing, then wondered if it was excitement or fear.

She was coming down the stairs, showered and in her new boiler suit and headscarf, when she heard the sound of 'I Don't Like Mondays' by The Boomtown Rats begin to play on the television, and the roar of the crowd as it went wild at the sight of Bob Geldof. She knew this song; it had even got as far as small-town Australia. Des had once done a whole sermon about it, this song about a young girl who carries out a shooting at an elementary school, killing two people, and it was shortly afterwards that they had agreed they would no longer play secular music in the house, and had got rid of their television. Rita found herself humming it anyway.

She stared at the figure on the screen. Bob hadn't exactly dressed up for the occasion and Rita allowed herself a brief middle-aged thought about how hot he must be in his shirt and jacket, then, in a moment of spontaneity she associated more with her younger self, she started to dance. Hesitant at first, she felt her limbs slowly but surely loosening and she began to enjoy herself, the noise of the crowd at Wembley singing along, their arms bumping the air in time to the words helping her lose any self-consciousness, until she joined in with the singing too. As she noticed her own temperature rise, she decided to take the dance outside, leaving the door open so that the music streamed out there with her.

She checked there was no one else there, remembering the dark figure she'd seen in the alleyway earlier. She felt a flicker of fear, but immediately dismissed it, reminding herself again that she had made sure that no one would, or could, find her. She was safe. Safe enough to lose herself in song and dance, and whirl around, until it felt as though the two parts of her, the girl she was and the woman she'd become, had merged – she ignored the years in between – and she felt briefly, truly whole.

She hadn't realised Bob had stopped the song for a moment, and she was still singing along when she noticed that not only were the crowd on the television whooping and cheering but so was someone in the next garden – and was that a howl? She stopped at once, as if she was playing musical statues, feeling her stomach rise to her throat at the thought that someone had heard her. A shock of blonde hair appeared over the fence, to the right-hand side of the house, followed by a wide-eyed face. It was a young girl, who must have been on tiptoes to see over. She was eleven at most, Rita guessed, but at least it wasn't an adult. No sooner had she had the thought than a woman's face appeared next to the child, her pillar-box-red hair atop the wooden fence pole momentarily making Rita think of a lit match.

'I'm so sorry,' the woman said. 'Don't mind my cheeky kids.' The girl giggled and her face disappeared, but the woman stayed, smiling at Rita in a disarmingly open way which Rita found herself mirroring, despite her mortification. 'I've been meaning to say hello,' the woman said, her red hair glinting in the sun. 'I'm Davina. I live next door.' She looked at the fence. 'Obviously,' she added and laughed.

Rita paused. She hadn't actually said her given name out loud in so long she had to pause first, to make sure she got it right. 'I'm Rita,' she replied, then couldn't think what else to add.

Luckily, Davina didn't seem to do awkward silences. 'Hi, Rita,' she said, still smiling. 'Welcome to Delmont Close. We'll stop interrupting you now, but maybe you might like to come over for a cup of tea or a glass of wine at some point?' There was a hesitancy there for the first time, Rita noted, her neighbour's eyes darting away, which Rita interpreted as momentary shyness.

Her reflex to rescue kicked in. 'Oh yes! I'd love that,' she said, her politeness and desire to make Davina feel all right about asking overriding any hesitancy of her own. Davina beamed at her, and Rita found herself adding, 'I don't suppose you're going to the barbecue later?' before she'd even realised she was speaking.

Davina's smile widened. 'Yeah, we are actually. Shall we knock before we walk down? You can go with us?'

Rita was already nodding with relief at the thought of arriving with someone else.

'Great, we'll drop by to collect you just before three,' Davina said. 'If that's okay with you? In fact, if you have time, feel free to come over beforehand. We'll be home all afternoon. I've already been to the shop to get some booze. It might say *no need to bring anything* on the invite, but you just know Lydia will disapprove if you don't,' Davina said with a wink.

'That would be brilliant. I'll come over then. Thank you so much,' Rita replied, and as the face disappeared from the fence, she felt as happy as she had when she was dancing, just from the briefest of friendly interactions. By necessity, she had been on her own far too much lately, and the trouble with being alone was that she had too much time to remember. It was like putting a magnifying glass up to the past and inspecting it from every angle. It only got bigger. It was time to make something of her present.

Back inside the house, she realised Davina was right about Lydia Gordon not actually expecting people to turn up empty-handed, despite what the invite said. She used to be so good at this kind of thing, always judging it correctly and being known for her graciousness as a hostess and a guest. But that was when she had a role to play, and Des to guide her.

She had no idea what her role was any more. It had always been so clearly defined for her before. With her parents, she had been the difficult child, the rebel, the black sheep of the family. With Des, she had been the dutiful wife. She couldn't quite work out who she was without someone else's eyes on her.

Maybe she would go over to the local shop and get something to take with her. Yes, she would do that. In an act of rebellion, she left the television on, The Boomtown Rats continuing to play rather tunelessly to her empty house. She half-walked, half-danced down the garden path. Roger Daltrey would have been proud.

Hour Four: 1–2 p.m.

Adam Ant, Ultravox, Spandau Ballet

Rita – No. 15

Rita had a spring in her step as she wandered around the local shop, picking up bits and pieces for the afternoon. She had decided she might even bake something to take to the Gordons. If there was anything she had learned during her years as a pastor's wife, it was how to bake a mean cake, and, despite the interminable heat of their Australian town, she had spent more mornings with the oven on and the kitchen door wide open than she could count.

For the first time since she'd arrived back in England, she felt as though she might be able to build a life here, maybe even make friends. It would never be the same, of course it wouldn't, but it was something, and would keep her going until, well, she didn't quite know until what. She said hello to the cashier behind the till, who had yet to smile at her, even though she'd visited the shop many times in her first few weeks here. The greeting was met with a slight raise of the eyebrows as the still straight-faced cashier started to ring up the items in Rita's basket. Undaunted, she decided to introduce herself anyway. 'Hi, I'm Rita, recently moved in nearby,' she said, the name now beginning to roll off her tongue. She waved her hand in the vague direction of Delmont Close. No point giving too much away.

'Aye, I know,' said the woman, without eye contact. 'Madge,' she continued, with no change of inflection, but it was a start.

'Just getting some last-minute bits for a get-together this—' she went on before Madge interrupted her with: 'Let me guess . . . the Gordons' barbecue?'

The word *barbecue* was said with some disdain, Rita noted. 'Er, yes, that's right.'

Madge muttered something along the lines of 'Who do they think they are with their posh barbecue; it's just burgers and sausages outside instead of inside' and Rita almost laughed out loud. It seemed that barbecues were a rarity here, and possibly the height of aspiration. In the town where she had spent the last seventeen years, a barbecue was as ubiquitous as a fridge, but she smiled politely and paid for her food.

She was just leaving and had turned to say goodbye to Madge when she almost ran into someone she recognised from the close. The man was tall and strikingly handsome in a very male way. She'd seen him outside a few times, cleaning and polishing his red sports car. He stepped back, waving her out of the shop with the mock formality of a bow. Before she thought to move, his brow furrowed slightly.

'Have we met?' he said. 'Delmont Close, right?'

THE BARBECUE AT NO. 9

Rita found her face suffused with heat under the man's gaze and nodded, her brain on autopilot.

'I thought you were familiar. I'm at number thirteen, unlucky for some. Michael Wilson.' He held his hand out for her to shake and she took it, the sensation something like an electric shock. 'But you can call me Mike,' he said, and held on to her hand for just a fraction too long.

'Rita,' she said, and moved to leave the shop again.

He smiled as he let her out and continued to watch her; she could feel his gaze as she walked down the street. He was the sort of man that people said had charisma, and she had to stop herself from looking back. Her body felt stiff, awkward, as though she was a teenager again, but she realised immediately that was probably because she hadn't experienced this kind of jittery, nervous excitement, almost adjacent to fear, for some years. The last time was when she first met Des.

She was still shaken by the time she got back to the house. The concert was playing from the television, Ultravox performing 'Vienna', and she let the melancholy of the music calm her while she unpacked the ingredients and prepared to make fairy cakes. Cake was community, she'd learned in her old home. It was also a great leveller. From mayor to mine worker, no one said no to a slice of cake.

It was the first time she had felt the desire to do anything associated with her former life in a while, and she realised as she beat the eggs and folded everything together that she had missed it; the act of measuring, sifting and stirring the ingredients was inherently soothing. No matter how much she tried to distract herself, however, her near collision with Mike meant she couldn't stop thinking about the first time she met Des.

Their initial meeting had taken place the first Sunday she had reluctantly attended church, as part of the new rules her parents had set. She had been missing having a social life, and seeing Alistair in particular, so much so that even going to church felt like a treat. Ever the rebel, Rita had been unable to stop herself from making it obvious that she didn't belong there, by lining her eyes in the dark kohl her father hated and wearing a pink mini-dress, her knees, shockingly, on full display.

'What?' she said to her parents' evident horror when she appeared in the living room, ready to go with them. 'I've done what you asked. I'm coming with you, and I've dressed up accordingly.' Her voice and expression were all innocence, and her dad, clearly weighing up the time and stress of making her change, gruffly acquiesced. 'Come on, then,' he said, and the three of them left the house, her mum scurrying closely behind her father, while Rita slowly strutted down the front path as though it was a catwalk.

When their usual vicar – a man so insipid he looked more like a ghost haunting the church than its leader –

introduced Des, or Pastor Hargreaves as she knew him then, the visiting preacher from the outback of Australia, Rita almost laughed with surprise as he stood up and stepped forward to the lectern. With his collar-length hair and beard, Des looked like a cross between Eric Clapton and the Hollywood version of Jesus. She sat up straight in her pew. He was gorgeous.

Des had conducted a rousing sermon about the consequences of sin; and Rita, completely mesmerised by him, was convinced his eyes had rested on her more than once as he spoke. His soft Australian twang made him all the more attractive and exotic to her. Although she was desperate to go outside and smoke, Rita waited with her parents after the service and queued up to shake the hand of the vicar and the visiting preacher, a practice she usually disdained as it reminded her of a wedding receiving line. She watched as Des smiled warmly at each person he spoke to and leaned forward to listen closely, even to the people Rita knew would have nothing interesting to say, which was most of them.

She had put on her most seductive smile as they drew near but was sorely disappointed when Des gave her the merest glance before focusing all his attention on her parents, who were practically simpering in front of him, her mum almost curtsying, her dad shaking his hand so vigorously and for so long Rita eventually had to put her own hand on his arm to stop him. Rita didn't know whether to seethe or cringe at his lack of attention towards her, so instead she settled on going outside for a cigarette after all, leaving them to talk.

On the way home, she was monosyllabic until her father mentioned that Des was staying in the UK for a month, and they had invited him for dinner after church the following week, at which point she immediately joined in the conversation while internally browsing through her wardrobe and choosing her outfit. She spent much of the next week daydreaming about him. The fact that she was no longer staying out late, plus her long hours of working in a shop, meant a lot of thinking time, which Des began to occupy. The culmination of all her fantasies was his eventual declaration of his love for her, where he would, in some anguish, talk of his inability to resist her.

In Rita's mind, it was her versus God, and – unlike the war for her father's approval and affection – this was a battle she was determined to win. Her thoughts went no further than that. She was aware enough to understand that this wasn't love, merely lust – plus a whole host of daddy issues, which she'd been informed she had plenty of by a psychology-studying boyfriend she'd had a brief fling with in her late teens.

When Sunday came, she got ready carefully, wearing a more modest skirt and blouse this time, with pearls borrowed from her mother, her make-up carefully applied to look as though she was barely wearing any. She was first in the car when it was time to leave, and she was so consumed by her thoughts she almost missed the satisfied look exchanged between her parents, who were presumably hoping against hope that their wayward daughter was finally turning around thanks to the healing hand of the Lord.

She studiously ignored Des when they arrived but made a show of speaking to the usual vicar, whose name she had never before taken note of, watching with satisfaction when she raised a blush from the man's pale cheeks with her mere proximity. She couldn't be sure, but she thought she could sense Des looking at her while she continued to talk to the poor man, who was eventually reduced to a somewhat breathless mumble under her gaze.

Des didn't preach that week; he sang instead. This could have meant the end of Rita's attraction to him, but it was only strengthened. His singing voice was powerful, and he imbued every note of 'How Great Thou Art' with meaning. This time she knew she wasn't imagining it. He was looking at her.

After the service, her father drove them all back to the house, with Rita and Des both on the back seat. This was the closest Rita had been to him, and she was finally able to inhale his scent. She knew she was making up the fact that he smelled of the beach, she hardly knew what beaches smelled like, and he didn't even come from the coast of Australia, but that's what she imagined, taking in the salty tang of him. She made sure no part of her touched him, and angled herself awkwardly towards the window, while remaining hyper-aware of his presence next to her.

As soon as they arrived at the house, Rita felt squirmy with hot embarrassment. It was as though she was looking at their home through someone else's eyes, and every aspect of it was found wanting, from how small and poky it was, to the dark, old-fashioned mismatched furniture it contained, much of it hand-me-downs from family. She was ashamed of her suburban parents and their suburban life and wanted to scream, 'I'm not like them!' before she realised that maybe that was exactly the kind of woman Des would be attracted to: suburban, submissive, quiet.

When they sat down at the table, laid with plates and cutlery Rita had never seen before but later found out were wedding gifts that were saved for 'best', the food was as bland and tasteless as she thought her parents were. Des, of course, was very appreciative, and kept up a steady stream of easy conversation while Rita simply watched him, saying little. When the meal was finished, Des made to get up. 'Let me help you clear away,' he said to her mother.

'Oh no,' she replied, 'please, stay seated, I insist.'

She nodded over at Rita, signalling that she should help instead, but Rita took the risk of ignoring her, the pull of being near this man too much. A conversation about biblical verses between her father and Des ensued, until, stuck on the exact wording of a particular quote from Psalms, her father went to retrieve his Bible from the living room.

The temperature in the room seemed to increase, and Rita practically fizzed with energy. She looked down at her lap in order to avoid looking at Des, but to her surprise, he reached for her hand, briefly holding it until her father bustled back into the room, flicking the pages of the battered leather Bible. Rita stared at the hand Des had touched, wondering if she'd imagined it, but when she finally looked up, he winked at her. That's when it all began.

Many years later, she was standing next to him at their church while he was telling a member of the congregation how he had 'saved' her, and she had found herself nodding along in agreement. It was true. He had saved her.

As the memories of those early days consumed her, in the kitchen of 15 Delmont Close, Rita let her tears for the innocence of their beginnings fall unchecked.

Steve – No. 20

It was only when he heard his mum call, 'I'm just popping out!' and the sound of the door closing that Steve remembered it was the day of his brother's fortnightly phone call. Unlike Steve, his mum was on the phone endlessly. He could never work out how she had so much to say to people, particularly the colleague who she worked with every weekday but often rang in the evening 'to catch up', as she would say.

The only time it rang for him was every second week on a Saturday afternoon. It was always his brother, Andy. Their mum made sure she was out of the way when he rang, knowing that if she was there, the two would use her as a buffer. Steve was pretty sure she spoke to Andy most days, but they still went through the charade of discussing Andy's news after his phone call, and she would feign surprise or interest.

They all knew Andy wasn't calling because he wanted to.

No, this was duty. He could imagine Andy's wife reminding him to call, and how he was presumably doing it to assuage the guilt he felt at not having visited for a while now; their mum always travelled to him instead. Steve didn't mind Andy not visiting though. It would have been worse if he had. The distance between them would have been made more obvious by physical proximity.

The phone calls felt like an awkwardly repeated set of lines from a play. The same questions asked, the same evasive answers, but Steve was always ready, sitting in his alcove with a fresh cup of tea and a cigarette, the wires looped through to his room so he could place the phone on the small table and position his chair to continue keeping an eye on the close.

Sometimes it had been so long since Steve had spoken to anyone, other than his mum, that he had to clear his throat and rehearse saying words to the empty room before the phone rang, so it wouldn't be too obvious that he was out of practice at polite conversation. 'Hi, it's Andy,' his brother always said, as though it might be someone else, as though there was a chance that Steve might mix him up with the numerous other callers he fielded throughout the week. The thought often made Steve chuckle.

The phone trilled. Having no idea what prompted him to break out of their routine, Steve picked up the receiver and, before his brother could say anything, said, 'Hi, Andy.'

There was a stunned silence. 'Oh. Hi. You knew it was me.'

'Well, given you ring at the same time every two weeks, I took a chance it might be.'

'Oh right, yeah, I suppose that's true . . . well, anyway, how are you doing?'

'Plodding on. You know, can't complain.'

They instantly settled into their well-practised roles.

Scene One was the exchange of meaningless, non-specific statements about their current lives, which would segue into Scene Two, a little light reminiscing, which would inevitably lead to Scene Three, an argument, followed by Scene Four, an abrupt apology, after which they would say goodbye and hang up until the next time.

'We've been invited to a barbecue,' Steve said, still in a rebellious mood, taking them straight off-script. He felt reckless, maybe because of the invitation. Perhaps because there was something different about the day, there could be something different between him and Andy.

'Oh,' said Andy, 'who by?'

Steve could tell he was trying to hide his surprise that his brother had been invited somewhere. 'By the Gordons at number nine,' he said. 'You might remember them from when we moved in. Couple with two children. Nice. But a bit up themselves.'

Andy laughed. 'Oh, I remember them. The wife – Linda, was it? – used to make thinly veiled comments about Mum's garden gnomes being at the front of the house. *You make such interesting decor choices, Christina. I would never have the courage.*'

Steve laughed. They had gone straight on to Stage Two, reminiscing.

'She's called Lydia,' he said, 'and she still insists on calling Mum by her full name. Clearly thinks Tina is too common. Mum always says she's as frosty as her lipstick.'

Andy carried on with his startlingly accurate impression of Lydia's haughty, judgemental tone: '*How on earth do you keep those net curtains clean, Christina? I'd be constantly worried about the dirt.*'

'It's supposed to be for Live Aid – the barbecue,' Steve said. 'Are you watching it?'

'We've got it on the telly, but, you know, we've stuff to do. I want to clear the garage out, then we've got work to do in the garden given it's a nice day, and . . .' Andy's voice trailed off, as though listing all the activities that went hand in hand with his full, 'normal' life might make the emptiness of Steve's more apparent.

'Well, will you go?' Andy asked. 'To the barbecue?'

Steve knew he would be expecting him to say no.

'I might, actually,' he said. And though he hadn't planned to say any of this, for a moment he really thought he might. To prove to himself, his mum, Andy and Madge that he could.

'Right,' Andy replied.

There was a long silence. Neither was good at improvisation when it came to their relationship. 'How's work?' Steve said, letting the tension up for a second. He could almost hear his brother's relief. They were back to Scene One.

'Fine. Good. You know,' he replied.

Steve was almost tempted to reply that no, he didn't know, but even telling Andy about the barbecue invitation had exhausted him.

'I think you should go,' Andy said. 'To the barbecue, I mean.' There was another long pause. 'It might be good for you.'

It was the same thing that his mum and Madge had said to him. Why did it bother him more when Andy said it? He sat up straight. He could almost physically feel the wave of defensive anger building up, his body tensing. He immediately wished he hadn't changed the nature of their conversation. Why not let things be as they had always been – well, as they'd been since the day after which nothing had been the same between them.

'What do you mean, *it might be good for me*?' he said, before he could stop himself.

'Oh, I mean, I thought we were . . .' said Andy, his voice low, resigned. 'Nothing. I didn't mean anything by it. Go, don't go, it's none of my business.'

'You're right, it is none of your business,' Steve said.

'Sorry,' said Andy, 'I'd better go,' and so the call ended in the same way it always did.

Steve sat in silence. He wished he could go back to the beginning of the conversation and not mention the barbecue. Especially as it meant that next time, Andy would ask if he had gone or not. Steve couldn't see that question leading to a comfortable chat, either way. And did he really think he might? Steve knew his anger at the question came from the knowledge that they were right. It would be good for him to go. Not for the reasons they were thinking though. They wanted him to get out of the house more. To be better, whatever that meant. Though no one ever said it directly, he knew they worried about him. His mum especially. That fact made him sad and angry, mainly at himself.

No, he'd read enough about covert intelligence to know that if he *integrated* more with the people who lived on the close, it would inevitably make his surveillance more effective. It would help him to corroborate what he saw and wrote down, as well as the things that Madge told him, meaning that she wasn't his only source of information, that he could rely on her less. He wasn't good at relying on other people. They all let you down in the end. Apart from his mum.

His thoughts went immediately to Cameron, who had taken pity on him and was kind after he'd been in trouble one too many times in initial training for not meeting standards, telling him in his strong Glaswegian burr, 'Even if you don't feel it, *act* like you're a soldier, man. Eventually your brain and body will catch up wi' you.'

Cameron had been right. That was a turning point

for Steve, and one of the most useful pieces of advice he'd received during his whole time in the army. He had even remembered it out in the Falklands, when his arms and legs regularly shook so much, he had barely been able to function. But he had managed to act as though he wasn't scared, and that had somehow helped him. He had often wondered since how frequently other people were acting as if they weren't feeling the things they were really feeling. How often the rest of the world was just playing a part.

So, Steve decided that he would act as though he was one of those people who went to local barbecues without thinking and bought 'Do They Know It's Christmas?' because they had room in their heads to worry about other places in the world. He would act as though he was the kind of person who watched Live Aid and knew all the bands and songs and could talk about them with his neighbours and say things like, 'I wish I was there,' and didn't start at every loud noise or grow panicky in crowds until he couldn't feel his hands or feet.

He turned on the portable black-and-white television that sat on his chest of drawers, angled so he could still keep his eye on the comings and goings of his neighbours, and started to watch. He so rarely had any noise in his room, the sound of the crowd and music was immediately overwhelming, and he felt his heart thud in his chest along with the drumbeat of 'Vienna' by Ultravox. Like him, Midge Ure hadn't let his wardrobe standards slip just because it was one of the hottest days of the year, and Steve marvelled at his composure while he sang, and sweated, in a long grey overcoat more suitable to cold Austrian winters than a hot summer's day in a stadium packed with seventy thousand people.

Steve had always thought there was something quite Soviet in the melancholy orchestration of the song. This was maybe because he associated it with his early days in the forces – 'Vienna' had been everywhere in 1981, his first year – and his burgeoning awareness of the reality of the threat that Russia represented. It was matter-of-factly referred to by officers, and expanded on by Cameron, who saw conspiracy everywhere, and urged Steve to 'open his eyes' for signs of espionage and attack.

It was after he had left the army, however, and they had moved to Delmont Close that he'd started writing everything down in notebooks, so he could look for patterns, signs, or anything out of the ordinary. It was incredible how much there was to observe in a close as small as this one, how much activity took place, how many lives were lived. After a while, Steve had started to feel oddly protective of the people he now saw it as his job to keep an eye on.

When he began all this, he'd been watching the people of the close for any suspicious activity – looking for signs of infiltration by the enemy – but his observations of what lay beneath the exterior mundanity of the lives of his neighbours had engendered a curious affection in him for them. Take the Chamberlains, for example. After Madge at the shop had mentioned that the family at no. 10 were having marriage difficulties, he had taken to keeping an extra eye on them, his binoculars trained on their impeccable house more often than not. He had noted Gerald Chamberlain's clothes getting smarter and slicker, his paunch getting smaller. Then he'd observed how his arrival home in the evenings had got later and later, and how he'd sit in the car for a while before he went into the house, just staring into the middle distance. There were no net curtains at no. 10 – Fiona Chamberlain deemed them to be 'common', as he'd overheard her saying one day in the shop and wondered what his mum would have made of such a declaration – so he could see Gerald's wife, while she sat alone in the living room, perched on their white leather sofa, her perfectly made-up face betraying no emotion while she stared out of the window for hours on end. It was the daughter – Antoinette – who cried.

A thump on the side window, loud enough to drown the concert out, startled Steve, and he dropped immediately to the floor for the second time that day, adrenalin coursing through him.

Silence followed, and he crawled over to the windowsill, holding on to it to peer out. A solitary football lay in the garden, and Steve let his breath return to normal. It was just kids playing football. He looked around to find them, this time seeing there was a figure out there, watching him. A teenage boy, dark sweatshirt tied around his waist. It was Ned Thomas, their next-door neighbour, staring up at Steve's window with a nasty grin.

Steve almost laughed at the sight. Ned fancied himself as Steve's tormentor – he was the originator of the admittedly amusing 'Lurch' nickname – but he had no idea that Steve was engaged with an enemy beyond Ned's comprehension, nor of Steve's strength if put to the test. Ned stuck two fingers up to the window, and, unable to help himself, Steve returned the gesture, watching the boy's eyes widen and his face twitch in surprise at the sight. Ned turned abruptly and went into his house, and Steve returned to his chair with a smile on his face, a smile which disappeared when he realised what Ned's silent, staring figure had reminded him of. Was he the person he'd seen watching the close? Had Steve missed something about this young man?

Hour Five: 2–3 p.m.

Spandau Ballet, Elvis Costello, Nik Kershaw, Sade

Hanna – No. 9

Hanna thought her mum might explode when the doorbell rang at five past two. 'If that's someone arriving early,' Lydia hissed, every word so crisply defined she didn't miss a syllable, 'tell them to come back at three, the time they were invited to arrive.' The two of them were in the kitchen, Hanna having been roped into putting various snacks in bowls, while her mum hyperventilated about the amount of food available for their guests, oscillating every five minutes between not having enough and having too much. She didn't want to be 'that woman' who didn't feed her guests – or overfed them, either, she told Hanna. It seemed to Hanna to be an exhausting way to live, constantly trying to second-guess the opinions of others.

Hanna went to the door, passing the living room on her way, where her dad and David were watching the concert under the guise of 'sorting out the video tapes' for recording. The two of them were sitting side by side on the leather sofa, staring silently at the screen, amazement on both their faces at the spectacle in front of them; Prince was dozing peacefully at their feet, despite the volume of the TV. It had been so long since she'd seen her dad so fully engaged in the moment, Hanna stopped to watch them, until the doorbell rang again and she hastened to answer it before her mum shouted at her.

'We thought we'd come round early and help,' Aunty Beverley said as she bustled through the door, carrying a tray of food covered by a tea towel. She wafted past Hanna, making her almost choke on a lungful of Poison by Christian Dior, a cloud of which seemed to accompany her aunt everywhere, like a perfumed version of Pig-Pen from Peanuts. Uncle Keith followed closely behind, his face red and forehead glistening, presumably due to the pale blue argyle sweater he was wearing, strained across his somewhat portly midriff. Uncle Keith always looked like he was on his way to, or from, a game of golf, which in fairness he usually was.

By the time Hanna had followed the two of them to the kitchen, her mum had removed the apron she had been wearing and was air-kissing Beverley, taking the tray from her and placing it on the side without looking at what lay beneath the tea towel. She was practically breathing fire as she caught Hanna's eye, seeming to imply that the ambush had been her fault. Hanna shrugged. Aunty Beverley looked down at herself – she was wearing a pale pink silk blouse and flowery skirt with a waist-nipping belt – then pointedly stared at Lydia, who was still wearing her aerobics kit. 'I feel quite overdressed,' she said, then waited.

THE BARBECUE AT NO. 9

Hanna's mum didn't miss a beat. 'You look gorgeous as always, Beverley.' Aunty Beverley was always Beverley, never Bev. 'I just haven't had a chance to get changed yet. You know how it is.' Aunty Beverley did not look as though she knew how it was. Hanna had never seen her anything other than perfectly turned out, and imagined that even at aerobics she would be fully made up, hair sprayed into an immovable helmet. She and Hanna's mum were both devoted fans of Princess Diana and emulated her look at every opportunity, whereas Rosie's mum called the princess 'the Patron Saint of Pastels', which made Hanna laugh.

'Where's that brother of mine?' Uncle Keith said, reaching for one of the sausage rolls laid out on cooling trays on the kitchen table. Before he could touch one of the offending items, Aunty Beverley was across the room and had slapped his hand away. David had once said she reminded him of an alligator with her speed and stealth, after she had whipped a Quality Street from his hand one Christmas before he'd even noticed she was in the room, apparently because it wasn't 'the proper time for sweets yet'. There was a proper time for everything in Aunty Beverley's world.

'In here!' came the call from Hanna's dad, and all four of them trooped from the kitchen to the living room, where he stood up to let the ladies sit down, and Hanna hovered awkwardly behind the sofa. David remained seated there, his eyes glued to the television.

'Nice bit of kit you've got there,' Uncle Keith said, pointing at the television and video recorder.

'Philips,' said Hanna's dad.

'Good choice,' said Uncle Keith.

'We've splashed out on a Bang and Olufsen, haven't we, darling,' Aunty Beverley said, from the sofa.

'Can't beat a bit of German engineering,' said Uncle Keith.

'Oh, I *do* love this song,' said Hanna's mum. 'Don't you, Beverley?'

It was Spandau Ballet, 'True', a song played during the slow section at the few discos Hanna had been to, and therefore deeply uncool. She froze with embarrassment as her mum and Aunty Beverley began to croon along with Tony Hadley, which even seemed to break her brother's trance. He stared at both of them, as though he had only just noticed they were there.

'He's a looker, that Tony Hadley,' Aunty Beverley said with a giggle.

'He looks a bit hot in that leather coat,' said Hanna's dad, and it was true: Tony was dripping with sweat and looked uncomfortable.

'It's *fashion*,' said Hanna's mum.

'It's boiling,' said Hanna's dad.

For a few minutes they all watched Tony sing while slowly melting, his melodic voice punctuated by the occasional loud snore from Prince, who was still asleep in front of the TV. Hanna had just decided to sneak

THE BARBECUE AT NO. 9

back into the kitchen to carry on dispensing crisps, nuts and Twiglets into bowls, when Aunty Beverley asked the question Hanna was always asked by adults and never knew quite how to answer.

'How's school?' she said, straining her neck round to make it clear she was talking to Hanna, not David.

'It's okay,' Hanna said, knowing this answer would not be satisfactory for Aunty Beverley, or indeed her mum, who jumped in immediately.

'She's doing better, aren't you, Hanna?' she said, sounding furious. 'Tell your Aunty Beverley about the award you won for the piece of music you wrote.'

Hanna felt herself stiffen. 'Oh yeah. I, er, yeah, I won an award for something I composed. A song,' she said, as though the words were being forced from her, syllable by syllable.

Her mum sighed and shook her head vigorously. 'Honestly,' she said, 'it's like pulling teeth. She wrote a beautiful song, and her music teacher put her forward for a competition, didn't he, Hanna?'

Hanna nodded, still unable to speak despite her mum's evident frustration. She had poured everything into the song she had written for her music assignment, had tried to express the feelings she found almost impossible to articulate otherwise. Writing and listening to music was the way she made sense of the world. She played Haircut 100 when she was happy, Joy Division when she was sad, and Queen when she wanted to feel safe. Music had become more than just her refuge: it was her whole vocabulary, she realised.

She was thinking of the moment in the classroom when her teacher had told her she had won something she hadn't had any idea she'd been entered for. Even Antoinette Chamberlain had been impressed. She had experienced a feeling of wonder and pride, not only that she'd won the competition, but that he'd thought the piece was good enough to be sent in the first place. Mr Allan had called it 'transcendent', a word she'd had to look up in the library afterwards. Her mum, on the other hand, had not asked to listen to it even once. Had shown no interest, except when it won the award.

'I don't know what it is about girls at sixteen, but they seem to lose the ability to articulate,' her mum said. 'Luckily, she can at least string a few notes together.'

'I blame that *Grange Hill*,' Uncle Keith chimed in, and Hanna, relieved that the subject had moved on, almost giggled at the thought of her uncle knowing who Zammo and Gripper Stebson were. 'Putting ideas in children's heads,' he carried on, without specifying what ideas, and how this implantation was taking place. It was time for Hanna to return to the kitchen. She knew that once her Uncle Keith had begun to express his disapproval of something small, that disapproval would widen and eventually encompass everything that a) wasn't invented in England (German engineering being a rare exception) and b) involved *young people*. 'I'm not against

THE BARBECUE AT NO. 9

(young people/the Irish/unemployment benefits) per se,' he would always pronounce, then go on to say something that made it clear that if he wasn't against them, he was doing a very good impression of someone who was.

He had just got on to the malign influence of video nasties and their corruption of young people's minds, when Hanna slipped out of the living room, murmuring, 'I'd better get back to the nibbles,' hoping no one would notice. The only person who did was David, who widened his eyes at her, presumably fearful that without her as a shield, Aunty Beverley and Uncle Keith's disapproval might land on him.

The relative quiet of the kitchen was a relief. It felt like breathing out after holding her breath for too long. Hanna often felt as though being around her family meant having to contort herself into an awkward shape; that she was less herself around the people who were supposed to know and love her than she was around strangers. She felt the baby kick and took it as a reminder that she would do the opposite for her child. She knew she would love them however they turned out, and gently patted her stomach as if to make that promise, beginning to sing softly to the child inside her. She always imagined her baby could hear her and know that the music was for them.

Her peace was soon shattered by the sound of her mum and Aunty Beverley. 'Just tell me what needs doing,' she heard Aunty Beverley saying as they made their way from living room to kitchen. 'It certainly looks like you could use some help,' she continued as they walked in and surveyed the room. Hanna actually felt some sympathy for her mum, watching her shoulders tighten and rise up almost to her ears. The two women began bustling around Hanna, who attempted to tune them out by starting the washing-up, but Aunty Beverley's judgements, even when not aimed at her, were like pinpricks on her skin, not easy to ignore. Hanna felt her aunt's eyes land on her.

'Shouldn't we just rinse those and pop them in the dishwasher, Hanna?' she said, and Hanna inwardly tensed as her mum barked out a laugh.

'Oh, we don't have one yet,' she said. 'I'm hoping my husband will take the hint at some point, ha ha.'

Hanna didn't look around, but she knew her mum's face would be flushed red, the lack of dishwasher another source of tension between her mum and dad.

'Gosh,' said Aunty Beverley, her voice dripping with sympathy, as though just informed about a death in the family. 'How *do* you cope?'

Lydia did not respond.

The three of them eventually settled into relatively harmonious industry, with only occasional remarks from Aunty Beverley: 'Do you not have any matching serving dishes, Lydia? . . . I'll just give this cutlery another clean.' Hanna had moved on to laying out lines of plastic wine glasses when she sensed herself under scrutiny again.

THE BARBECUE AT NO. 9

Aunty Beverley had stopped filling vol-au-vents with a disgusting-looking mixture of mushroom soup and sweetcorn and was observing Hanna closely. Hanna stood up straight and sucked her stomach in as far as she could, but it was too late.

'Are you still on the netball team?' Aunty Beverley asked. Hanna would have laughed if she hadn't been suffused with shame. She had to give it to Aunty Beverley: she was going to take the scenic route. Unable to speak, she shook her head. 'You might want to think about replacing it with something else,' Aunty Beverley said. 'Tighten things up a bit.' She waved the spoon she was holding in the general direction of Hanna's belly, and Hanna felt the hot smarting of tears.

Her mum steered the conversation, and Aunty Beverley's attention, away from Hanna, briefly touching her daughter's arm as she did so. 'Oh, that reminds me,' Lydia said, 'I saw Alison Prentice from number eighteen at aerobics this week. She was telling me about these shakes she's been using...' While Hanna's mum didn't hesitate to criticise her, she didn't think others had a licence to do the same, and Hanna was grateful to be out of the danger zone while the two women started discussing the benefits of the Green Goddess versus Mad Lizzie for their morning exercise routines.

She wasn't safe for long, however. Aunty Beverley was 'just tidying up' – meaning inspecting everything on the large pine dresser – when her eyes lingered on the shelf of St Michael cookbooks, the spines unbroken, free of any suggestion they had ever been opened. They were an annual Christmas gift from Aunty Beverley and Uncle Keith. Among them was a battered copy of *The Thorn Birds*, her mum's favourite book, hastily placed there while she was tidying up for the party, which meant putting anything embarrassing out of reach. Hanna could almost feel the disapproval radiating from her aunt.

'I've been reading an excellent book,' she said, and something about the pointed way that Aunty Beverley glanced at her put Hanna back on high alert. 'Do you remember that wonderful series on the BBC earlier this year? *A Woman of Substance*?'

Of course Hanna remembered. Her mum, along with the rest of the Neighbourhood Watch, and in fact the whole country, had become obsessed by the television drama, all sweeping landscapes, stately homes and class struggle, which Hanna had pretended to be bored by but instead had her transfixed. When the main character, then a maid, had got pregnant by the son of the owner of the house where she worked, Hanna had gasped, while her mum had expressed her views on the matter in her usual straightforward way. 'Consequences,' she had said, her voice flinty. 'What on earth did she think was going to happen?' It was the memory of Lydia's unforgiving, steely reaction that had informed Hanna's decision to leave when she found out about her own pregnancy.

THE BARBECUE AT NO. 9

'The novel is equally riveting, if not more,' Aunty Beverley was saying, still with her cold, blue-liner-rimmed eyes on Hanna. Did she know? How could she tell? She held her aunt's gaze for a moment, as though challenging her to say the words out loud, knowing she would never do so. Keeping up the pretence of politeness was more important to her aunt than exploding the grenade she clearly had in her hands.

The spell was broken by an oblivious Lydia. 'Oh, I must get that,' she said, coming between the two of them and handing Hanna a tray of nibbles to take into the men.

Hanna took the tray, robot-like, trying to force herself not to think too hard about the implications of Aunty Beverley having spotted her predicament, but the sight of her dad sitting silently in the living room, while Uncle Keith talked at him, only made her more aware of her parents' likely reaction to her news.

She remembered her dad – forced to watch *A Woman of Substance* by her mum, though Hanna suspected he was as swept along by it as the rest of them – had used the opportunity for a speech about 'boys' and their 'motives'. This was aimed in Hanna's direction, minus eye contact of course, and was a speech in which he managed to skirt around the topic of sex while also making it clear that he saw the act as something far, far in the future for Hanna.

She remembered feeling as though the entire room – inanimate objects and all – were cringing with embarrassment. Even her mum couldn't look at him. Thankfully, David was long in bed and probably fast asleep by then, exactly where Hanna wished she had been in that moment too. But what she remembered most was that this had been when her dad still regarded her as a precious jewel, when he still loved her without question. The thought of his reaction to her pregnancy now was almost more frightening than that of her mum's. You knew where you were with fury.

By the time Hanna returned to the kitchen, they were discussing which neighbours were coming to the party. The list contained plenty of opportunities for Aunty Beverley to channel her judgement, and Hanna heaved a momentary sigh of relief. There was Mr and Mrs O'Leary from no. 12, who for some unspecified reason were never referred to just as the O'Learys. 'We'll need to check their bags for bombs, surely,' Aunty Beverley said. And Davina and her daughters: 'I bet they're vegetarian.' Only the Chamberlains – '*lovely* family' – and the Wilsons – 'Is Mike still a handsome devil?' – met with her aunt's approval.

Hanna held her breath while the two women fawned over their handsome neighbour and was just about to let it out when Aunty Beverley said, 'Is your new boyfriend coming too?' Hanna's head began to throb. 'What's his name again? *Shane*, is it?' she carried on, disdain dripping from her words.

Hanna nodded and looked at her mum, a plea for

THE BARBECUE AT NO. 9

help in her eyes, but Lydia could only stare back, looking as trapped as Hanna felt. Hanna knew Aunty Beverley wouldn't think that Shane was good enough for their family. She quickly reminded herself that she had thought her mum would feel the same, and had been surprised when Lydia had welcomed him warmly the few times he had been to no. 9.

'And how did you meet him?' Aunty Beverley asked, clearly wanting to prolong the discomfort that had settled over the room.

'He's in my year at school,' Hanna said, her voice a mumble. 'We haven't been seeing each other long.'

'Is he another . . . what do you call yourselves? Another *goth*?'

Hanna was saved from answering this by two far worse questions.

'And where does he live? What do his parents do?'

There was nothing else for it. Hanna stood tall and spoke clearly as she said, 'He lives on the Blackthorn Estate,' her eyes alternating between her mum and Aunty Beverley, her expression a challenge. Her mum seemed to recover herself a little and stepped in. 'His dad works at the school,' she said and smiled at Hanna – a rare moment of solidarity between the two of them.

'Ah yes, isn't he the caretaker? Did I hear somewhere that he's a former miner?'

Hanna knew this fact would seal the family's fate in the eyes of Aunty Beverley, whose face had hardened as she said the word. Aunty Beverley had *views* on miners. Especially those involved in the recent strike. None of them complimentary.

'I always thought you'd go well with that lovely Ned Thomas,' Aunty Beverley said, and Hanna almost physically felt her toes curl.

'I think he's more interested in Antoinette Chamberlain these days,' said Lydia, and Hanna's eyes widened. This was news to her, though she was grateful to her mum for at least attempting to keep the conversation away from Shane.

'Is that the lovely girl from next door? Pretty? Petite?'

And with that, Aunty Beverley's eyes rested on Hanna's stomach once again.

Noise from the living room interrupted the three of them, with David appearing in the corridor, giggling and breathless, Uncle Keith following closely behind. 'Bob Geldof said the f-word!' David said. He looked as though he might explode with excitement, every limb was jiggling, and his eyes were huge. 'He actually said it on the telly.'

'Unbelievable,' said Uncle Keith, his expression one of grave sorrow. 'On the BBC as well. It's just a lack of respect. This country's going to the dogs.'

'Well, what do you expect?' Aunty Beverley said, reaching for his arm as though to soothe him. Hanna, now in the mood for a fight, was just about to ask what she meant by that when the doorbell rang.

THE BARBECUE AT NO. 9

'Oh, for goodness' sake,' said Hanna's mum. 'Everyone civilised knows that three o'clock means three-thirty. I'd better get changed. Hanna, could you answer the door, please.'

As Hanna made her way to the front door, she glanced into the living room where her dad was still sitting, perfectly still, staring at the television screen, his face blank. For just a moment, Hanna felt the urge to go over and wrap herself around him, like she used to when she was small. But he had long been somewhere she couldn't reach, so she carried on.

Through the glass pane of the front door, Hanna could see that Shane and his mum and dad were standing outside. Taking a deep breath, and drawing her lips into a smile, she opened the door.

Rita – No. 15

Rita sat perched on her sofa, the bottle of wine she planned on taking to the party on the coffee table in front of her, the fairy cakes still cooling on the side. She had been sitting there for at least half an hour, marking time until she felt it was somehow reasonable to go round to her neighbours, while not really knowing when that was any more. She wondered at how quickly she had lost any sense of what the social rules and protocols were, when once she had been the perfect adherent to them.

She half-watched the concert, only really focusing when she found herself singing along to Elvis Costello's rendition of 'All You Need is Love' with the hot, wilting crowd, who seemed to move as one as they sang along too. The more she sang, the more she found her throat tightening. There was something about the spectacle that she found incredibly moving, though she couldn't identify exactly what it was. She decided she would go around to Davina's once the song was over.

There was no reply to her first ring of the doorbell – unsurprisingly, as Rita could almost feel the bass of whoever was onstage next reverberating through Davina's house and out of the upstairs window. She rang again, and this time Davina answered, barefoot and in a pair of worn-looking dungarees. 'Come in, come in,' she said, and Rita followed her through to the back garden, taking in every detail as she went. She could hardly believe that their two houses were essentially the same. Where hers was bare, beige and nondescript, Davina's was colour and clutter.

There was hardly any free space on the primary-coloured walls, which were covered in large works of art, mainly abstract batik prints in shades of blue and green, which gave a sense of fluidity and motion. The kitchen was dominated by a battered wooden table, covered in mugs and plates, none of which matched. A large earthenware pot with a ladle in it sat on the stove, emanating a rich, spicy smell. The house felt alive. Full of energy, as though it existed by itself, separate to its inhabitants. All the newness had been worn in already. Rita felt immediately at home.

Outside in the garden, a small patio contained a hotchpotch of seating, from a stripy wooden deckchair to metal foldaway ones, to an ornate cast-iron seat, with an overturned packing box used as a makeshift table. Weighing up the chances of being able to get out of the wooden deckchair with any elegance, Rita sat on one of the foldaway chairs.

'Excuse the rather make-do-and-mend nature of the house,' Davina said, smiling. 'I would pretend it's because we've not long moved in, but that would be a lie, I'm always like this.'

Rita wondered what it must be like to be so free.

'Would you like some wine?' Davina said. 'Or orange juice? I have both.'

'Juice, please,' Rita replied. Though she was desperate for a glass of wine, she knew she mustn't let her guard down this early. There was some dangerous territory to navigate first. Davina disappeared inside the house and the girl Rita had seen over the fence earlier appeared instead, plonking herself next to Rita on the deckchair and staring unabashedly at her. Her upturned nose gave her a somewhat impish look, and her blonde hair, which looked as though it hadn't seen a brush for a while, was like a halo of yellow curls around her cherubic cheeks. There was none of the painful shyness Rita had experienced at her age. She looked as if she had no fear.

'Hello. I'm Rita,' she said, forgetting they had already met over the fence. The words felt wooden, as though she was a maiden aunt from the last century. How had she forgotten how to speak to young people so quickly?

'I know. You're our next-door neighbour. I'm Emmeline,' said the girl. 'I'm ten and three quarters.'

'What a pretty name,' Rita said.

'It's not pretty,' said Emmeline. 'It's strong and powerful. I'm named after Emmeline Pankhurst,' she continued, as if making an announcement; the words had clearly been said many times before. The expression on the girl's face was so fierce and serious, Rita found herself on the verge of laughter.

'Is that right?' she said.

Emmeline nodded, her face sombre. 'Do you know who Emmeline Pankhurst is?'

'I do,' Rita replied, 'and you're absolutely right that it's a strong and powerful name.'

'She was a suff-ra-gette,' Emmeline carried on, as if Rita hadn't spoken, pronouncing the word slowly and clearly.

'Emmie, I hope you're being polite to our neighbour,' Davina called, from the open kitchen window. 'Come and help me carry, will you?'

'So, you've met Emmie,' Davina said, once they were settled down with drinks: wine for Davina, juice for Rita and Emmeline, who barely took her eyes from Rita while she drank hers noisily. 'The rest of the brood are Galina – my middle girl, who's upstairs watching the concert – and Persephone, or Percy, the eldest, who's off with her boyfriend God knows where, doing God knows what.' Davina smiled as she said this, and Rita thought how attractive she was – her face bare of make-up, her eyes deep brown. The only artifice about her was her scarlet hair and the cascade of earrings following the line of one ear.

'And I may as well get it out of the way before the Delmont Close gossips tell you: there's no Mr Davina, and the girls all have different fathers.' Davina spoke the words in a dry, matter-of-fact way, her gaze steady, her eyes clear. There was no defensiveness there, and no challenge either. Rita was fascinated. What would it be like to be just as unbothered by the weight of other people's opinions of you as this woman? She wondered how old Davina was, and what her parents were like. She wanted to open up Davina's mind and root through it, searching for the secret of how she came to be so freely, authentically herself.

'Oh,' Rita found herself saying into the long silence that had been left between them, which she felt she ought to fill. 'Where did you move here from, then?' she added, switching into the kind of small talk she was better practised at.

'London,' Davina said. 'It had just got too expensive. Sadly. We loved it there. What about you? Where are you from?'

'Dorset,' Rita said. 'Lyme Regis.' She had already erased the slight Australian upswing from the end of her sentences that she had adopted over the years, and had rehearsed the answer to this question in front of a mirror so many times that the words fell from her mouth with liquid ease. She had chosen a place she knew well from annual trips there as a child, a place she could navigate around in her mind if asked any questions.

She knew the next piece of information would be difficult but decided to offer it before she was asked. Crossing her fingers, she said, 'And it's just me. I used to be married but, well, you know.' She could feel her eyes filling up at the words, but she knew she had to say something. She felt Davina's hand rest on her arm, her touch soft.

'Separation is hard, whatever the reason,' she said, and Rita felt relieved that Davina had read her sadness as being about a non-existent divorce. 'I never actually got round to marrying any of mine,' Davina carried on, a smile in her voice, though Rita couldn't yet look at her face through the tears that had formed a film over her eyes.

'Mum's got terrible taste in men,' Emmie said, from the rug she was now lying on, on the parched lawn.

'To be fair, she's absolutely right,' Davina said, and raised her glass. 'To terrible taste in men,' she said, and all three of them raised their drinks and laughed, the sadness of the moment broken. A head appeared from one of the upstairs windows. A younger version of Davina, minus the red hair but just as striking, was peering out at them. 'Nik Kershaw's on, Emmie,' she said. 'Hello, I'm Galina.' She waved at Rita, who shyly waved back. Where did this family get all its confidence from?

Emmie took her drink and ran inside, then ran back out again. 'I love Nik Kershaw,' she cried, her arms wide as she stood in the middle of the lawn, as though announcing it to the whole world before she disappeared inside once more. The two women smiled at each other, then leaned back in their chairs, their faces turned towards the sun.

'You can tell me about it . . . about him, if ever you want to?' Davina said, her eyes closed, her expression relaxed. Rita knew that – lovely as this woman seemed to be – she would never, ever tell her the truth about Des.

Des and Rita's early relationship was entirely chaste. The celibacy had lasted for three weeks, but this represented a record for Rita, given she had once been with a particularly handsome guitar-playing songwriter and the length of time from meeting to sex was approximately forty-three minutes. By the time they came to Des's last day before he flew back to Australia, Rita was practically feral with desire.

Those three weeks had been a series of the kind of outings she would have laughed at had they been with anyone else. There had been many walks in the countryside; one trip to the pub, where Des had a pint, and Rita a lager shandy – not wanting to give the impression that she could handle anything stronger than that; and more visits to more churches than she had paid in her short life. But Des somehow made them thrilling. She felt almost hypnotised by him and watched as other people were too.

There wasn't a subject she could name that he didn't have some knowledge of and opinion on. Rita had always felt like she was a blade of grass, constantly being blown this way and that, never really knowing what she thought or felt about anything. There was something about how sure Des was of his place in the world that she found compelling. He was like an oak tree, and as she stood in his shadow, she felt stronger just by being associated with him.

She told Alistair this the one time she saw him again. No longer trapped by her parents' disapproval, she had met him in their usual pub and told him all about Des and his magnetic pull, unable to talk or think about anything else. Alistair had been quiet in response, which Rita had put down to misplaced jealousy for her affections. 'He'll never replace you!' she had said, putting her hand out and touching his arm gently. 'He's far, far too good,' she had added, intending to lighten the moment, which felt dense with meaning.

She had been suddenly gripped by a fear that Alistair might be about to make some sort of declaration, and the knowledge that this might break the spell of happiness and desire made her want to head him off at the pass. Instead, Alistair just smiled. 'All I want is for you to be happy,' he said, and she felt relief at having escaped something she didn't want to face or feel.

The day before he had to fly home, Des came over to her parents' house to say goodbye. Rita had planned this final visit with precision, making sure she invited him over at a time she knew her parents would be at Bible study. Having dressed more like a middle-aged librarian during the previous weeks, she put on the shortest skirt in her wardrobe, with a flowing, almost transparent blouse and no bra. She loosened her hair and kept her feet bare, intending to imply she was late in getting ready, and had rushed to the door.

Her shock when she opened it put paid to Rita's plans. Despite his profession, Des usually dressed fairly casually. It was part of his charm, and his lustrous hair, which reached his shoulders, was one of the first things she had noticed about him. Standing in front of her now was a man she barely recognised. Des was wearing an ill-fitting, brown three-piece suit, presumably borrowed from someone as she couldn't imagine he had brought it with him. The hair was all but gone, replaced with a short back and sides that would not have looked out of place on her own father, and he was carrying an enormous bunch of flowers – chrysanthemums in shades of pink and lilac – that made her think of English country gardens. His shock was equal to her own, his eyes wide and staring at her braless chest.

Rita instinctively put her hands in front of her chest to cover up, suddenly ashamed of herself like some modern-day Eve, but Des reached for her arm and slowly moved it back down again, not taking his eyes off her. She hardly had time to register what that meant before his lips were on hers. The kisses they had exchanged before were nothing like this. If Rita had wondered whether Des desired her, she had her answer now, and she let herself be led by him as he gently pushed her back into the house and began removing what little clothing she was wearing.

'I came over to propose to you,' Des said, as they lay on the living-room floor afterwards. Rita's head was so scrambled that it took a moment for the words to sink in.

'Marriage?' she said, as though there was another option.

Des laughed. 'Marriage,' he said, and stared intently at her.

It was on the tip of Rita's tongue to laugh too; to say, 'it's too soon' and 'we barely know each other', but under his gaze she found her mind went slowly blank, as if he was hypnotising her again, erasing her resistance.

'I know you don't believe,' Des said. 'In God, I mean,' he added, and before Rita could say anything he carried on, 'But I think, in time, you might come to find Jesus, especially through our work at the church.' He was lying on his side now, and his body was as magnificent as she had imagined all the many, many times she had imagined it over the past three weeks. Rita blushed, feeling as if he could see inside her, all the way past her heathen soul to her carnal, craving heart.

They had never talked about her beliefs, or lack of them. She had listened to Des talk about his unwavering faith and felt envious of his certainty, but she had nodded and smiled in response and mistakenly thought she had hidden her agnosticism behind her charming face and sparkling green eyes. She still hadn't come up with any coherent thoughts or a response before Des continued speaking. 'And I know we haven't discussed much about our pasts, but I don't think that's important to our future together,' he said, and Rita felt a sense of relief, wondering if he'd heard things about her and was sparing her the embarrassment.

'Isaiah sixty-five, verse seventeen, says: *The former things will not be remembered, nor will they come to mind.* It's all about starting anew,' he said, and his already dark eyes seemed to deepen, as he looked at her with an expression of such meaning and significance that she realised he knew all about her. All about the men, the music, the drinking and the drugs. Her entire body felt drenched with hot shame, and tears began to burn their way down her cheeks.

'Don't cry, my darling,' Des said, and he reached out to wipe the tears away with his thumb. 'God doesn't care, and neither do I.'

She made her decision in that moment.

Her parents arrived home about an hour later and were full of the glory of God. So great their joy and so fulsome their approval of Rita and Des's betrothal, neither showed any upset at the announcement that they would be moving back to Australia after getting married. Rather a virtuous daughter living on the other side of the world than one gallivanting on their doorstep.

*

The silence between Davina and Rita stretched on. Despite her discomfort, Rita kept her mouth firmly closed, as if the words might fall out involuntarily if she opened it even the slightest bit. Eventually, Davina saved her. To Rita's enormous relief, still with her head back and her eyes closed, Davina said, 'Equally, if you never want to talk about it, you don't have to. I'm just nosy. And I'm glad you've come here. It's nice to have someone on the close I can chat to. I sense a kindred spirit in you, if that's not too forward a thing to say,' and she laughed a little, as though to lighten the moment.

'I feel that too,' Rita said, surprised by the swell of emotion inside her.

She wondered how it was that Davina had seen anything in her at all. She pictured herself arriving in the close, and all she could see was the faded outline of an almost entirely broken woman, but maybe she still retained a glimmer of the person she had once been? Maybe that's what Davina was responding to.

'Tell me about you,' Rita said. 'I mean, whatever you want to tell me, that is,' she added, sitting back in her own chair and closing her eyes. She wanted to listen closely. She wanted to soak up the story of Davina and her daughters like it was the rays of the sun.

'I suppose much of my life is the girls,' Davina said. 'I had Percy pretty young. I was only seventeen.' Davina paused and Rita wondered whether she expected a reaction of shock, though Rita didn't have one. 'I met her father, Johnnie, at a Ban the Bomb march in 1965. He was terribly rich and terribly posh and had fallen out with his parents over something or other. I ended up being his biggest rebellion.' She laughed, but it was a hollow sound. 'By the time he got back on the aristocratic track and married a very lovely woman called Cressida, I'd already left him. Percy was a year old. I'm lucky, I suppose, in that he adored her. Still does.'

'Why did you leave him?' Rita asked, wondering what it must have been like to make that decision and then carry it out. 'I mean, if that's not too personal a question,' she added, knowing she was asking things of Davina that she wouldn't answer if asked about them herself.

Davina sat up and reached for her wine. 'I was too young to even think about marriage,' she said, with a visible shudder, 'and that's what his parents really wanted us to do. They were horrified that their precious son and heir had had a baby out of wedlock and so wanted to rescue the situation as quickly as possible, even if that meant him being married to me.'

Rita pictured her own parents sitting across from her the day they gave her the ultimatum about her way of life. She had often wondered how much they had been driven by worry, and love for her, and how much by reputation and expectation. She wanted to believe it was the former but had always feared it was the latter.

'What about your parents?' she asked, and an expression

of pain passed across Davina's face. 'Oh, I didn't mean to . . .' Rita started to say, fearing that she had stepped over a line without realising.

Davina shook her head. 'They were wonderful,' she said. 'All they ever wanted was for me to be happy. They were so excited about the prospect of being grandparents, however it came about. When I left Johnnie, I went back home to them, and Mum pretty much helped me raise Percy.'

She took a deep breath in before she said, 'I lost them both, last year. Mum died of cancer and Dad of a broken heart.'

Rita held her body entirely still, forcing herself to concentrate on Davina and not let her mind drift back to the death of her own mother, and the consequences of that loss. This wasn't about her. 'I'm so sorry,' she said.

Davina took a sip of wine and stared inside the glass. 'Anyway, I just knew me and Johnnie would never last. And I was right, by the way, we never would have. Johnnie now goes shooting most weekends and is looking to stand as a Tory MP at the next election.' She cocked an eye at Rita, who couldn't help but laugh at the thought of scarlet-haired, bare-faced and -footed Davina as a Sloane Ranger, wearing Hunter wellingtons and a Barbour. She was too colourful for that world, in every sense of the word.

'But his family is very wealthy,' Davina continued. 'So they can afford to be generous, and they really are, which is how I get to live here. They bought this place and let us live in it. It's not somewhere I would have chosen necessarily, but I can hardly complain. This way I get to pursue my art and send the girls to the kind of school I want for them.' And there it was, Rita realised. The key to any woman's freedom was, as always, money. She almost felt resentful of Davina for a moment, until she remembered it had been the key to her freedom too: the money that her mother had secretly left her. What would have happened to her without it?

She recalled the beautiful batik prints she had seen on the walls on the way in. 'Are the ones in there yours?' she said, indicating the house. Davina nodded, turning her face away as though suddenly shy, even after revealing so much about herself.

'You're incredibly talented,' Rita said, 'and brave, for leaving Johnnie when you had a baby, and you so young.'

'Brave? Stupid? Depends which way you look at it,' Davina said. 'But for me, it was the right thing to do. I would have withered and died in Johnnie's world, do you know what I mean?'

Rita knew exactly what Davina meant.

They were interrupted by the sound of Galina and Emmeline inside the house singing 'Wouldn't It Be Good' at the tops of their voices, and they both turned as Galina's face appeared at the bedroom window. 'He's so amazing,' she said, her expression one of adoration, and disappeared again almost immediately.

THE BARBECUE AT NO. 9

The two women carried on looking up at the window, as if hoping she might appear again, eventually turning their attention back towards each other. 'The next two men were considerably more feckless,' Davina said. 'But they gave me Galina and Emmie, so even though neither of them are in my life any more, I will always be grateful to them.'

Rita found herself unable to speak. There was so much she wanted to ask, and as much that she wanted to say. She wanted to know everything about this beautiful woman and her confident, thriving daughters, but her throat felt like it had sealed up entirely. It was almost as though she was being given a glimpse into the life she might have led, had she not met Des. She was overcome with yearning for something she had only ever briefly glimpsed.

Freedom.

Hour Six: 3–4 p.m.

Sade, Sting, Phil Collins, Howard Jones

Hanna – No. 9

Hanna's breath caught at the sight of Shane. He was now taller than his father and had recently seemed to grow into himself, his gangly frame developing into something altogether lither and more athletic, and his once shy smile now cheeky. He was becoming more comfortable in his own skin, while she felt itchy in hers.

'Hello,' she said, her eyes wanting to linger only on him, but reluctantly moving on to his parents out of politeness. 'Thank you so much for coming, Mr and Mrs Mitchell,' she said.

His usually warm, easy-going mum shoved a box of Black Magic into Hanna's hands, as though she was a great-aunt at Christmas. 'Here,' she said, her tone abrupt, 'for your mother.'

'Oh, you didn't need to bring anything . . .' Hanna began to say, but trailed off when Shane stared at her, a meaningful expression on his face. 'Thank you,' she added quietly.

Mr and Mrs Mitchell nodded in unison, and they all stared at each other on the doorstep, Hanna feeling suddenly self-conscious, as if this was the first time she had met them. It wasn't, of course. She had been round to Shane's many times, including long before they were boyfriend and girlfriend. She had always felt comfortable around them, even trying them on as imaginary parents, as she often did with her friends' mums and dads.

Then she noticed what was different. Bob, Shane's dad, was wearing a tie and had shaved his beard off. It made him look younger and less sure of himself, less like his usual bear-like, affectionate self. His mum, Sandra, was wearing a burgundy velvet dress, which looked uncomfortable in the heat, instead of a T-shirt and jeans, and consequently looked older, more formal. Together, they gave the impression of guests attending the wedding of someone they didn't know very well, and the effect was unsettling.

'Sorry, I mean, come in,' Hanna said, and stepped back to let Bob and Sandra come inside, while Shane looked at her with a somewhat confused expression.

'You okay?' he said, and briefly held her hand as he stepped into the house himself.

They had been brought together by science. As with all her lessons except music, Hanna struggled with chemistry and had been assigned Shane as a lab partner to help her. Though at first she had imagined they would have nothing in common and had groaned with Rosie about their forced pairing, they had eventually bonded over a Bunsen burner. Their friendship developed slowly, going from the classroom to post-school homework sessions in the library, to his house in the evenings, to being invited for dinner at the Mitchells, and all watching television together with their plates on their knees, something Hanna would never be allowed to do at home. *We are not savages*, her mum would have said. Hanna's interest in school, never particularly strong anyway, had waned in the last year, but Shane had kept her going by sharing his notes and refusing to let her fail. It was his kindness that had turned their relationship into a romantic one.

One morning Hanna had arrived at school late, after an almighty row between her mum and dad, before her dad went to work, had escalated into a further row between Hanna and her mum about her wearing eye make-up. 'You look like the bride of Frankenstein!' Lydia had screamed. 'Maybe that's who I want to look like!' Hanna had screamed back. Hanna had refused to get into the car and insisted on walking the two miles to school.

Ironically, the tears she had shed along the way had messed up her eye make-up anyway, and she was attempting to wipe her face on the street around the corner from school when she realised that Shane was sitting on a nearby wall. As she got closer, he held a tissue out to her and she took it, using it to wipe underneath her eyes, where black mascara was streaked in trails. She didn't ask him what he was doing there; there was no need. She knew he was waiting for her, no doubt asking Rosie where she was when she didn't appear at registration. She also knew he would wait for her forever if she asked him to. She had known this for quite some time, in the way that teenage girls sense things about teenage boys, having studied them closely, often more closely than their textbooks, and so she leaned forward and kissed him gently on the cheek.

'Thank you,' she murmured.

He blushed scarlet and opened his mouth as if to say something, then closed it again. Hanna sat down on the wall next to him, positioning her hand so that her little finger was just touching his little finger.

They sat in silence for a few minutes, the only sound a tuneless clashing of musical instruments from a distant lesson. 'Do you want to go in?' he said, and though she knew he was anxious about getting to class, she said, 'Can we wait for another minute?' and they continued sitting on the wall, fingers touching.

'I really like you,' Shane said, without looking at her, his cheeks still flushed with her kiss. 'And I know I might not be your type, but . . .'

'You are exactly my type,' Hanna said, knowing that though this wasn't strictly true, she wanted it to be, and sometimes wanting things was a way of making them happen.

'Really?' Shane said, now turning towards her, the smile on his face so wide it was contagious, and she found herself smiling too.

THE BARBECUE AT NO. 9

'Really,' she said, and they held hands as they walked into school together.

As Hanna and the Mitchells made their way along the hall, Lydia chose that moment to waft down the stairs in the manner of a 1950s Hollywood starlet, having gone upstairs to quickly change. She had attempted to model her look on Krystle Carrington from *Dynasty*. The grey drudgery of *Coronation Street* and *EastEnders* was not for Hanna's mum; she preferred her drama to be sparkly, American and rich, and Krystle was her favourite character, second only to Princess Diana in feminine grace. Lydia seemed almost to levitate in her floral chiffon dress, which gave just enough of a hint of her Jane Fonda-toned limbs underneath.

'Welcome!' she said as she got to the bottom of the stairs, extending one arm as though to signal the extent of a vast palace and grounds, not a five-bedroomed detached on a new-build Wimpey housing estate. Sometimes Hanna admired her mum's level of aspiration. Sometimes she thought it was delusion. She certainly seemed to possess extraordinarily little shame.

'It's so lovely to finally meet you,' Lydia said to the speechless Bob and Sandra Mitchell, who had virtually turned to stone under the gaze of the sparkling woman before them. If Hanna hadn't known better, she might have believed that her mum was telling the truth, but she knew all too well that this version of Lydia could be switched on as easily and brightly as a spotlight on a stage and would be switched off just as soon as someone more interesting was in front of her. Scanning Bob and Sandra's frozen faces, Hanna decided to rescue them.

'Mr and Mrs Mitchell brought you these,' she said, holding out the box of Black Magic. Lydia looked at the box, then back at Hanna without taking it.

'Do you want to pop them into the kitchen, my darling?' she said. Lydia never called Hanna 'darling' unless people from outside the family were present. She turned her glittering gaze back to the Mitchells. 'Thank you *so* much, you shouldn't have. Now, please make yourselves at home while I just finish making the final arrangements.' With that, she floated off in the direction of the kitchen, leaving Hanna, Shane, Bob and Sandra in her wake, the Mitchells still not having said a word.

'Right,' Hanna said, with an overly jolly voice that reminded her of a children's television presenter, 'I'll just pop these away, then I can show you around. Would you like a drink?'

'Do you have any beer?' Bob said.

'A cup of tea?' Sandra said at exactly the same time.

'I'm not sure they'll be serving tea,' Shane muttered in his mum's direction, his face flushing its customary raspberry colour. It immediately reminded Hanna of when they had first got together, when it had seemed he was a permanent shade of pink. Hanna watched Sandra's face flush too. 'Don't worry, I can make you one. One tea and one beer coming up,' she said, still in the same overly enthusiastic tone as before. She would be exhausted by the end of the day if she kept this up. 'Why don't you go into the living room? The concert's on in there.'

Shane gently manoeuvred his parents into the living room, where David was sitting cross-legged in front of the television, watching Sade perform 'Your Love is King'. As they walked away, Hanna felt her body deflate, as if she had expended all the breath inside her on the effort of appearing chirpy. She wished she could just sit with Shane and David and watch the concert, but she took the chocolates into the kitchen, where her mum was now installed with Aunty Beverley, wine glasses in their hands. She put the box down on the side and switched the kettle on.

'What on earth are you doing?' Lydia asked.

Hanna sighed. 'I'm making Mrs Mitchell a cup of tea,' she replied, without looking to see the inevitable eye rolls from her mum and aunty at the idea of someone asking for a cup of tea at a do like this.

'We never did finish that conversation,' Aunty Beverley said, her voice smooth, her tone innocent. 'What does Mr Mitchell do at the school? A caretaker, is he?'

Hanna felt the baby move inside her, as though it shared her fury. She didn't answer the question, knowing no reply was required, and continued to make the tea, all the while reminding herself that soon she wouldn't have to put up with any of this, that she would be free.

The doorbell rang, and they all turned to look in the direction of the front door. Before Hanna's mum had the chance to tell her to answer it, she held up the cup, as if to say, *I'm busy*, and watched as her mum flicked the switch on the spotlight once more and sashayed off in the door's direction. Hanna went to the fridge to take out a can of beer for Mr Mitchell, feeling her every move being scrutinised by Aunty Beverley.

'Your mum and dad have a lot going on at the moment,' Aunty Beverley said, after an uncomfortable pause. 'I wouldn't want to add anything to their worries.'

Did she mean the arguments? Hanna wondered. Or was there something else going on? And what was she trying to insinuate? She almost considered asking her aunty straight out, but realised that there was no need. Even if Aunty Beverley had realised she was pregnant, she would be gone by tomorrow, so what did it matter.

Back in the living room, everyone was glued to the concert, where Sting was singing 'Roxanne', the crowd bellowing the name back at him like a football chant. Shane was discussing with David whether Sting was better with The Police or without. Both decided with. Hanna handed Bob and Sandra their drinks – they were sitting on opposite sides of the sofa, still as stiff as wooden bookends – then sat on the arm of Shane's chair. Listening to the music, she felt a sense of calm wash through her as she allowed herself a moment to get lost in it.

THE BARBECUE AT NO. 9

Their next-door neighbours the Chamberlains, minus Antoinette, bustled into the living room, with Lydia unseen but bringing up the rear: Hanna could tell she was there from the fragrant cloud of Anaïs Anaïs, a sickly-sweet floral perfume her mum loved.

'Sorry we're late, the traffic was terrible,' Mr Chamberlain said, a recurring joke which Hanna's dad would have appreciated, but, given he wasn't in the room, fell flat among the current audience. 'Oh,' he added at the sight of people he didn't know.

Lydia squeezed around him and Mrs Chamberlain. 'This is Mr and Mrs Mitchell,' she said, indicating Bob and Sandra. Bob nodded, and clumsily stood up, his bulky frame almost stuck in the soft cushioning of the sofa. The room suddenly felt full of people, airless and awkward, then the melancholy sound of The Cars playing 'Drive' turned everyone's attention to the television, where there was a shot of a wide-eyed child with a distended stomach, a fly crawling across their face.

Mrs Chamberlain burst into noisy tears and immediately left the room.

'She's been like this all day,' Mr Chamberlain said, both frustration and resignation in his voice. 'One glimpse of an African child and she's off.'

'Why don't we go outside?' Lydia said, holding her arms wide as though attending to sheep, and the doorbell rang again. 'Could you go and answer that please, darling. And direct everyone outside,' she said to

Hanna, her voice getting higher and tauter with each sentence. 'And David, can you turn the television down please?' David glanced at Hanna, rolling his eyes, before getting up and turning the volume button a smidgeon.

On her way to the door Hanna passed Mrs Chamberlain, who was patting her eyes with a handkerchief. 'It's the children that get me,' she hiccupped through her tears, and Hanna nodded and carried on, feeling the same yet unable to add anything more to the list of things she knew she needed to worry about today.

It was Davina and the woman from no. 15 at the door, with Galina and Emmeline. Davina smiled warmly at Hanna, handing her a bottle of wine, while the woman held out a tray of fairy cakes. 'I'm Rita,' she said. Hanna found herself smiling back, more genuinely than she had all day. Her mum would be furious that these two women had made friends. 'I'm Hanna,' she said. 'Come on in.' She directed Davina and her daughters through the house to the cluster of people now in the garden, and Rita followed her to the kitchen with her tray. The doorbell went again.

'You answer it,' Rita said. 'Don't worry, I'll clear some space for these.'

It was the Thomases at the door. Ned, tanned from their holiday, wearing a pale blue polo shirt and neatly ironed grey Farah trousers, stood behind his parents, his blond hair artfully arranged to look casual, and his green eyes locked like lasers on Hanna.

THE BARBECUE AT NO. 9

She kept her gaze firmly on his mum and dad, not allowing his obvious stare to unsettle her, though she could feel her stomach churn as she let them in and directed them straight through to the garden. This time she kept the door open, as she could see another couple of her parents' friends pulling up in their car.

After greeting more guests, Hanna went to the kitchen and was surprised to find Rita still there, arranging food and sorting out drinks. 'Force of habit,' she said, which Hanna neither understood nor questioned. She was already exhausted from smiling and being polite, and the party had barely begun. She got cans of Fanta for herself and Shane and a bowl of crisps to take to David, who she assumed would still be glued to the television, before planning to go and find Shane in the garden, but he was waiting for her in the hallway. He nodded at the growing throng of people standing stiffly outside, like the plastic garden ornaments Tina at no. 20 had in front of her house and which Lydia disapproved of deeply.

'Shall we leave them to it for a bit?' he said, his eyes indicating upwards, to Hanna's room. Hanna nodded, feeling enormous relief at the thought of a brief respite from the party. This was followed almost immediately by a lurch in her stomach. This was her opportunity to talk to him about the baby, and she had no idea whether she had the courage to take it. The two left David still glued to the television and went upstairs to her bedroom, where Hanna turned on the radio and Shane sat back on her bed, his head on her pillow. He held out his arm for her to curl up into, their usual position, but Hanna stayed perched on the edge.

'Are you okay?' Shane said, his forehead creasing. Hanna nodded. She just wanted to have a few more minutes with him where things were normal, where he didn't know, because when he did, it would change everything between them.

'It's been a stressy day,' she said. 'You know what Mum's like.'

Though Shane didn't come over to hers that often, both of them preferring the more relaxed atmosphere of Shane's home, he knew enough of Lydia to know how things were. Hanna had never spoken to him about her dad. As was so often the case, she didn't have the language, and somehow it felt that saying it out loud might make her worries about the change in him more real.

'You should've seen mine getting ready. You'd think they were going to the Royal Wedding,' Shane said with a laugh, but Hanna could tell it was forced, that there was an edge to it. 'I think Mum was actually nervous,' he said more seriously, and Hanna felt a tug inside at the thought of Shane's lovely mum feeling anything other than confident and comfortable.

'She spent all morning telling Dad what he can and can't talk about,' Shane went on. 'No politics, no religion and no swearing, apparently. If he can't weave "that bloody Thatcher woman" into a conversation, I'm not sure what he's left with, to be honest.'

Hanna laughed at Shane's affectionate impression of his dad, then realised with a rush of emotion that made her skin flush how much she would miss Shane's family. Almost as much as she would miss him. Everything was straightforward with them, you never had to work out what anyone was thinking or feeling, it was all there, laid out like the little market stalls she and Rosie used to hold when they were little, selling their mismatched wares from a tablecloth on the front lawn.

At home, Hanna felt as though she was playing a sport where no one had explained the rules. There were things that could be said, and emotions that could be expressed, and you only found out which ones when you got it wrong – which in her case was frequently. She hated to think about Mr and Mrs Mitchell downstairs trying to play the game and feeling the same shame she did when she misjudged it.

'Maybe we should be down there,' she said, suddenly wanting to look after them, to protect them from her parents.

'I'm sure they can look after themselves,' Shane said, shrugging, his expression puzzled, clearly wondering why she wanted to get back downstairs. 'They're all grown adults.'

Hanna didn't know how to explain to him that some adults were more straightforward than others. She didn't like what it said about the adults in her family. Or about the people they spent time with, all of whom were down there now. She could imagine them surrounding Shane's mum and dad, closing in on them as they got the unspoken rules wrong over and over.

'Can we have some time, you know, on our own?' Shane said, then paused, opened his mouth and paused again before saying, 'I don't feel like I've seen you at all lately . . . you seem like you're . . . somewhere else. In your head, I mean. I, I miss you.' He looked down at the bed, cheeks pink. This was her moment, Hanna thought, this was when she should tell him, but then he reached into the back pocket of his jeans and brought out a cassette in a box.

'I've been waiting to give you this,' he said. 'I made you a mix tape.'

He sat up and held it out to her, and Hanna took it, hoping the tremor in her hands wasn't showing. Opening the box, she could see that the songs had been neatly listed on the cover in Shane's handwriting, including their song – 'I Wanna Know What Love Is' by Foreigner – though Hanna would never have admitted she liked the song to anyone but him. They'd had their first proper kiss to it, after a school disco. Tears pricked in the corners of her eyes. How could she possibly tell him what this meant to her? He'd given her music. He was speaking in *her* language.

'Thank you,' she almost whispered. 'Shall I put it on?'

THE BARBECUE AT NO. 9

Shane shook his head. 'Listen to it later on your Walkman,' he said. 'If we put it on now, I'll lose your attention again. I know what you're like with music. Come on, come over here.' He held his arm out for her, and this time she gave in, curling up and under his arm. 'That's better.'

They lay there for a moment, until Shane turned to kiss her. She leaned into him, letting herself float off into the feeling of the kiss and away from the situation she'd found herself in. Despite being his first proper girlfriend, she'd always thought Shane was the best kisser. His kindness and gentleness were both present in his lips. There was no way she could tell this not-yet-man about the baby she one hundred per cent knew wasn't his because they'd never slept together. It would break his heart.

Rita – No. 15

Rita felt more comfortable in the kitchen, even one as floral and fussy as this. It reminded her of her role in parties gone by. She would be the one making sure everyone had food and drink, and ensuring the smooth running of events, while Des held court, informally preaching to members of his congregation or charming the rare potential donors to the church.

After getting drinks for herself and Davina and popping briefly out into the now busy garden, she had found herself asking Lydia and the woman she was introduced to as Beverley if they wanted a top-up or any nibbles and sorting out Galina and Emmeline with soft drinks. She retreated to the kitchen afterwards almost automatically, as though she was a homing pigeon, out of sorts among all the exotic birds in the garden in their colourful finery. The navy boiler suit she had thought so cool earlier in the day now felt shabby and dull. She couldn't seem to regulate her temperature either, swinging from pleasantly warm to furnace-like from moment to moment.

She watched on through the kitchen window as

Davina seemed to chatter away with ease to everyone in her orbit, and wondered if she could ever be like that or if it was just too late now. Maybe her role was always meant to be in the background. In order to avoid going out into the garden again, she headed for the living room to see if there were any glasses or plates to collect. 'Hi,' she said to David, who was cross-legged in front of the television. He didn't respond; perhaps he hadn't heard her. A sob turned her attention to the woman sitting curled in a beige leather armchair. It was another neighbour, Rita realised, from next door in fact.

'Are you okay?' she said. 'Do you need me to get someone?' The woman shook her head and brought a handkerchief to her eyes. She pointed at the television, where they were showing lines of small children queuing for food in a desert camp. 'It's just . . . It's just the children,' she said.

'Oh God, I know,' said Rita, and she sat down next to the woman, feeling a creeping sense of shame. Her worries seemed so trivial in the face of this. She could imagine Des pointing this out; he cared deeply for those less fortunate. She should be grateful for the life she had, she thought. No matter what she had lost.

The doorbell rang once, then again, and Rita realised the music and chatter meant that no one else had heard it, so she patted the still crying woman's hand and went to answer it. At the door was the O'Leary family, who she knew lived at no. 12. Mrs O'Leary – Tara – had come round when Rita first moved in to drop over a shepherd's pie: 'For you to pop in the oven. You'll not want to be cooking when you've just moved in,' she had said, her plump face a picture of maternal kindness. Rita felt herself flush at the sight of them. She had returned the dish the shepherd's pie had been in a couple of days later, under cover of darkness, with a little note saying thank you, and hadn't spoken to them since. She hadn't felt able to in those early days. She welcomed them in regardless, forgetting this wasn't her house as she slipped into hostess mode, and was further embarrassed by the warm smile Tara gave her as she came into the house.

Rita was just about to close the door when a woman she recognised from a few doors down walked, or more accurately tottered, somewhat hesitantly up the drive. She was dressed in an electric-blue ra-ra dress with stilettos to match, blonde hair teased into a pile on top of her head, a bag with bottles in it clinking against her twig-like legs. She looked like a Christmas decoration, incongruous as that was in the middle of July, and something about her meant Rita couldn't help but smile and express her admiration. 'You look spectacular,' she said, and the woman did a wobbly twirl on the path.

'Thanks, doll,' she said, 'I like to make an effort!' Rita stood and watched as she made her way to the door. 'I'm Tina from number twenty,' the woman said, her face suddenly crumpling with confusion. 'Aren't you . . .?' she

THE BARBECUE AT NO. 9

questioned as she looked around for the house number, presumably to check she'd got the right one.

'I'm Rita from number fifteen,' she said. 'Just answering the door.'

'I thought I recognised you!' Tina said, her voice as expressive as her clothes. 'I've been meaning to pop round and say hello, but you know what it's like.' She waved her arms around, bottles clinking dangerously now, as if to express the busyness of life.

'I know exactly what it's like,' Rita said. 'Shall I take those to the kitchen for you?' she added, pointing at the bag of bottles, nervous for their future in this somewhat chaotic woman's hands.

'Thanks, doll,' Tina said. 'You're an angel.' She handed over the carrier bag of bottles and then took a cigarette from the handbag she had over her shoulder and lit it. 'I'll follow you in, shall I?'

Rita resisted holding out a hand to lead the precariously balanced Tina as they went through to the kitchen. 'Ooh, that's fancy,' Rita heard Tina say about something they had passed, then: 'I bet that cost a pretty penny.' Rita had already decided that she liked this brash, apparently fearless woman enormously.

In the kitchen Tina continued to comment on the things she saw, this time the size of the fridge and the deliciousness of the snacks she immediately filled a plate with. She poured herself a glass of her own wine. 'Fancy some Blue Nun?' she said, holding the bottle out to Rita.

So far, Rita hadn't indulged, not wanting to let her guard down, but she couldn't resist Tina's open smile. 'Thanks,' she said, holding an empty glass out, which Tina filled to the brim.

'I'd better go and say hello to Lady Di,' Tina said, nodding at the garden. They both looked out at the perfectly manicured lawn, where Lydia could be seen in the centre, holding court, one hand elegantly clasping a glass of wine by the stem, the other waving theatrically. She was easily identifiable; something about her stance reminded Rita of a peacock displaying its feathers. 'But I'll be back,' Tina said. 'I want to know everything about you!' With that she patted Rita on the arm and wobbled off in Lydia's direction. For reasons she didn't yet understand, Rita wasn't scared of Tina's questions. Not that she would answer them honestly. But she somehow sensed that Tina was the kind of woman who had her own story to tell.

Rita took a sip of her own wine, wincing at its sharpness, then followed Tina out into the garden. She'd intended to find Davina again, but then spotted Peter Gordon standing at the barbecue alone. She was about to go over and speak to him when the expression on his face gave her pause and she slowed, taking in his drawn, pale skin, out of place in the hot sun. She remembered the image she'd involuntarily conjured of him with his head in his hands, then watched as another man tapped him on the shoulder, and, like a waxwork coming suddenly to life, Peter smiled his charming smile, and the anguish she thought she had seen disappeared.

Rita turned and found herself among a group of unfamiliar people. A large man with a look of Peter around his face, wearing a golfing jumper which was wholly inappropriate for the weather, was talking about football hooligans to a seemingly rapt audience. 'Thuggery. Pure and simple,' he was saying, the red of his cheeks glowing like a Pink Lady apple. 'Lock them up and throw away the key. Same as the miners. I'm not against the miners per se, but the strike got completely out of hand.'

Rita felt the couple standing next to her tense. The woman held on to the arm of the man so tightly her knuckles went white. She turned towards them. 'I'm Rita,' she said. 'It's lovely to meet you.'

The woman shot her a grateful look. 'I'm Sandra, and this is Bob,' she said, tugging on his arm, forcing his attention away from the opinionated man. 'It's lovely to meet you too. Isn't it, Bob?'

Bob nodded, his expression starting to relax, though his mouth remained firmly closed.

Rita moved slightly to the left of the group, hoping to encourage Bob and Sandra to follow her, which Sandra did, half-pulling Bob out of earshot of the man who was still talking and had returned to the topic of hooligans. Rita wasn't sure why she felt the need to rescue this couple, or indeed what she was rescuing them from, but some finely tuned instinct had kicked in, and she had almost smelled the potential for an explosion, like a whiff of smoke. Rita was an expert in defusal.

'Shall we go and get some food?' Sandra said to Bob, who was still staring at the man as he spoke, at volume and without pause, seemingly oblivious to the fact that someone may have had a different perspective. Rita often wondered what it would be like to be so sure of oneself and one's views on things. She was never so convinced of her rightness that she would state an opinion with as much surety as this man seemed to have. He didn't seem to notice anyone else, let alone Bob and Sandra's reactions to his words. He was on transmit only.

As Sandra led Bob away, she turned back to Rita and smiled, an expression of gratitude on her face. Rita smiled back, a moment of almost ancient solidarity between two women who had sensed and averted danger, and the potential for violence, between men.

A queue of people with paper plates was now forming at the barbecue, with Peter at the grill, his good humour apparently restored. Rita was about to go and join the people waiting for food when her ears tuned into the sound of Lydia's voice. She was almost at the end of the garden by now, but her voice was filled with such drama she could be heard over the rest of the chatter, and the radio, the opinionated man having briefly paused for a break to light a large cigar. Lydia

THE BARBECUE AT NO. 9

seemed to be telling the story of an intruder in their garden earlier that day.

'I mean, I screamed blue murder,' she said with a dramatic flourish, to accompanying gasps from the women surrounding her. 'Which seemed to scare him away, and he made a run for it.'

Rita remembered the person she had seen earlier, in the alleyway. Was it the same person? She moved closer to Lydia and her friends, wondering whether to join them and tell them that she too had seen someone. Just as she reached the group, a particularly bird-like woman dressed in a candy-striped dress, agog at Lydia's story, turned to look at her, then back at Lydia, presumably deciding that Rita was of no consequence. The woman's hand fluttered up to her chest in horror.

'What did he look like?' she said.

'I couldn't see him properly,' Lydia said. 'He was wearing a baseball cap and the sun was too bright.'

The woman looked around to see who else was listening before saying, 'So you didn't see the colour of his skin?' in a low voice. Lydia shook her head before replying, 'It certainly wasn't anyone I recognised, though of course it wouldn't be.' This time Rita smothered a laugh. These people were so sure of themselves that they imagined they knew what everyone in their circle was like, and what everyone outside their circle was capable of. Their notions of right and wrong were so clear to them. Just like the church.

'Peter is going to put a padlock on the gate,' Lydia was saying. 'And we're going to get an alarm installed,' she said almost proudly, a pride well-founded judging by the oohs and ahhs of the gaggle surrounding her.

Rita took a step forward, intending to tell the group about the person she had seen earlier in the alleyway. As she did so, the women's eyes all alighted on her, and one of them held their now empty glass out. Rita took it automatically. 'Oh, your timing is perfect. I'd love another one,' the woman said.

'Rita, you're a wonder,' Lydia said, slightly flushed. 'Ladies, this is Rita, who's just moved into the close.' Rita stood there while the women appraised her. 'Oh, I'd love another glass of white if you're going,' said the candy-striped woman and held her glass out too. Rita took it, turned around and headed back to the kitchen.

At first, she thought that no one else was in there and she put the glasses in the sink, leaning over it for a second. She felt winded, like she'd been punched. It wasn't just them casually treating her as though she was staff, it was the all-too-familiar feeling that she'd been put, rightfully, in her place. She would get the drinks for these women, and either find Davina or Tina or go home, she decided.

She turned to go to the fridge, realising as she did that there was someone there already, peering inside it. Whether they had been standing behind the open fridge door when she came in, or whether she'd been so wrapped up in her thoughts that she hadn't noticed them arrive, wasn't clear. It was a boy. A teenager, to be precise.

It was when he turned around and she got a closer look at his features that her knees buckled. For a moment she thought she was hallucinating at the familiarity of the face in front of her. Though she knew it wasn't him, couldn't be him, he looked so like him she felt faint. She managed to hold on to the side before she almost fell and only just managed to steady herself.

The boy smiled, ruffling his almost white-blond hair with his hand. 'You caught me,' he said, and looked down at the can of beer he was holding before he glanced back up at her, his green eyes wide, eyelashes extraordinarily long, almost girlish. He didn't seem as though he felt guilty at all; in fact, he looked amused, which quickly turned to bemused as he took in her expression of shock. It must be all over her face, she thought.

'Are you all right?' he said, starting to edge towards the door. The expression of concern, whether genuine or fearful, made the tears begin to trickle down Rita's face.

He took a step towards her then, but she held out a hand to stop him. 'I'm fine,' she managed to say eventually. 'Sorry, I, sorry, it's . . . nothing.'

'Okay,' the boy said, 'I'm going to . . .' And he headed off in the direction of the front door, beer still in hand, and as she watched him, Rita leaned against the sink, the tears continuing to fall.

He looked just like Jacob. Her boy. Her precious son.

Steve – No. 20

Steve had talked himself out of going to the barbecue by the time his mum left to go. He went downstairs anyway to admire her outfit, sensing rather than seeing her disappointment that he wasn't going with her. He knew how careful she was about sparing his feelings. It often made him feel sick with guilt.

'Give us a twirl, Anthea,' he said, and she spun around like her favourite glamorous assistant on *The Generation Game*, while he gave her a round of applause. The jewel-like colour of her dress made her look like a Quality Street with legs. 'You'll do,' he said, and she stuck her tongue out at him with affection. She looked so tiny that Steve suddenly wanted to wrap her in his arms and hug her tight, protect her for once, rather than the other way around. Instead, he said, 'You look great, Mum. Have a lovely time,' and she smiled down at herself. 'Do you think I'll pass muster with her ladyship's friends?' she said, her eyes giving away a nervousness he more than understood.

He nodded. 'You'll outshine them all.'

'Sure I can't tempt you? There might be some lovely

young ladies there.' Though her face expressed doubt. They both knew that any young lady who was an associate of Lydia would not be interested in the likes of Steve. He shook his head.

'Well, think about it. You can always change your mind later,' she said. 'I've left some dinner for you in the fridge.' She tottered off, like a circus entertainer on stilts, Steve watching her go. He felt the familiar discomfort at letting her down. He should go with her, look after her, but he just wasn't sure he could. The thought of being among all those people made his throat close in panic, a panic that was always there but lay dormant in the pit of his stomach most of the time, because he made sure he kept his life small and easy to navigate.

He trudged upstairs to his alcove armchair, picking up his cigarettes, notebook and pen from the table. He drew four columns on a page, heading them with *Name*, *Time*, *Description*, *Observations*, then lit a cigarette, watching the close as he took slow, deliberate drags from it. His mum was still making her way over to no. 9, but now he felt somehow detached from her, writing down on his pad what time she arrived, alternating his cigarette with the binoculars, noting in the *Observations* column that the door was opened by the woman from no. 15, which was interesting given his earlier sighting of her with Peter Gordon.

He couldn't resist a smile though as he watched his mum replicate the twirl she had performed for him in the kitchen, and the wonder on their neighbour's face as she did so. Once she was inside, his expression became serious once more; he knew that he needed to keep his wits about him. He wondered about the person he'd seen watching the close earlier. Whoever they were and whatever they wanted, surely it would be unlikely for them to turn up to the barbecue. Certainly not dressed as they had been before. But if it *was* Ned Thomas, then no doubt he would be in attendance.

He continued to watch as the Gordons' driveway and the bottom of the close got fuller with cars, making a note of each registration number and every person. If someone wanted to infiltrate the close and harm them in any way, this was the perfect day to do so. No one would notice a stranger among them. Steve tensed, and wondered what he was doing, sitting there alone. Maybe he should be down there with his mum after all.

Steve's fears about the enemy had crept up on him. In the Falklands it had been clear who they were fighting for, and who against. It was straightforward. But Cameron had been in his ear, reminding him that there was a bigger, altogether more powerful enemy than the Argies and to keep an eye on how the Soviet government were responding to the conflict, pointing out an article in the paper about their abstention from the UN resolution calling for the withdrawal of Argentine forces from the island.

THE BARBECUE AT NO. 9

'Don't think they're not watching our every move, mate,' Cameron had said one night when they were on guard duty. 'They'll be assessing us, weighing up how well we do in this war. We're a lot smaller, closer, and easier to invade than the US,' he said.

Steve was always impressed by how much Cameron knew about things he had never even considered. Before joining up, his experience of the world had been limited, his understanding of politics even more so. Cameron opened his mind. He also made him feel protected. Though Cameron was shorter than Steve – wasn't everyone – he was stocky and thick with muscle, which made him appear overall like a big man. Steve found their conversations oddly reassuring. There they were, in the centre of actual live conflict, yet talking about an enemy that was somewhere else, somewhere less visible and altogether more nebulous. Cameron made the war in front of them less frightening and more manageable. At first, Steve looked to him as he used to look to his big brother when he was at home. Then, later, he saw Cameron as something else entirely.

It was after the war was finished and Steve had been discharged and therefore had a lot of time on his hands that he became more acutely aware of the dangers. The trial of Geoffrey Prime, the Russian spy who worked for GCHQ, had taken place in November 1982, and Steve had devoured the papers every day, recalling Cameron's words and realising that this seemingly unassuming man had not only fooled his family and friends but also the British government. He was a sex offender too and was eventually convicted of those offences along with his espionage. Steve became obsessed with the thought that someone like this man could be hiding among them, and became more and more vigilant.

Then came the film *Threads*, which had tipped the balance even further. His mum normally chatted through every film or television programme they watched together, but they had both stared at *Threads* almost unblinkingly, in uncharacteristic silence. What Steve found most frightening about the prospect of nuclear war was the unseen enemy, so he had stepped up his surveillance in response. He might not have a role in the forces any more, but he could play an even more important role in the community: keeping those around him safe, watching out for the kind of danger no one else would be aware of. It had become his sole purpose. It was only every now and again that he wondered whether he had been mistaken about who the real enemy was; whether his mind and body had been infiltrated to such an extent that his main battle was with himself.

Steve tensed as he watched Ned Thomas coming out of the Gordons' front door, carrying a can of what looked like beer. The boy was looking around him, as though checking to see if anyone else was around. The close was empty of people, most of its residents currently in the

THE BARBECUE AT NO. 9

Gordons' back garden. Ned walked a little way from the house, enough so that he wouldn't be seen by anyone leaving or arriving, and leaned against a parked car, taking surreptitious sips from the can. He drew out a packet of cigarettes from his pocket, lit one, and smoked it as if he was a dodgy character from *The Bill* – holding it between his thumb and first two fingers, and pulling on it like an inhaler.

Even though it was clearly an act, there was something curiously adult about him in that moment. Steve had brushed off Ned's name calling – he'd experienced that his whole life – but he wondered now if there was something more to him. Something darker . . .?

There was an intent in the boy's eyes that reminded Steve of some of the men he had met in the army. The small minority who would have fought whether they were in the forces or not. Ned had that same look about him. Steve continued to watch as Ned put his cigarette out on the Chamberlains' lawn, kicked the empty can under the nearest car, then popped what Steve assumed to be a piece of chewing gum into his mouth before sauntering back to no. 9. He had just rung the doorbell when he turned around, looking back down the close.

Steve followed Ned's line of sight with the binoculars and felt his posture straighten involuntarily as he recognised Ryan, also heading in the direction of no. 9. Ned was immediately forgotten as Steve followed Ryan's progress. He looked smarter than Steve had ever seen him, wearing what looked like freshly ironed blue jeans and a crisp white T-shirt. He still had the look of a mad professor about him, thanks to his round glasses and curly blond hair, but had clearly tried to make an effort. By the time Steve had trailed Ryan to the house and confirmed that he was indeed going to the barbecue, he had decided that maybe he would get ready and go too, the desire to finally be near Ryan, maybe even meet him, temporarily outweighing his fear of being among people.

He couldn't observe the barbecue from their house and what if he was needed, he reasoned. It wasn't just about Ryan. It was about keeping an eye on Ned and looking for the person he'd seen watching the close. It was about protecting his mum. He imagined her face when he appeared, how pleased she would be to see him. He thought about telling Madge and Andy afterwards. They would both be shocked. He tried to imagine himself being introduced to Ryan, but he couldn't quite picture it, so he checked that his shoes – neatly laid out under the bed – were shined (they always were, whether he was leaving the house or not), opened his wardrobe and chose an outfit instead. He was really doing it. He was going to the barbecue at no. 9.

Hour Seven: 4–5 p.m.

Howard Jones, Bryan Ferry, Paul Young

Hanna – No. 9

Hanna was lying in Shane's arms, still debating the right course of action, when Prince nosed his way around her bedroom door. The little dog took a running jump at her bed and landed in the middle of them, stubby tail wagging, to both their laughter. They sat up as David appeared at the door too.

'Mum wants you downstairs,' he said to Hanna. He pulled a mournful face. 'Mrs Chamberlain keeps crying at the television and I want to listen to Howard Jones. Can I stay in here?' Hanna's room was usually off-limits to David, and the thought of her packed bag stuffed under the bed crossed her mind for a second, but Shane would keep an eye on him, she thought, and she'd regret it tomorrow if she said no to him today. She didn't want to add any more guilt to the already heavy load she was carrying.

'Come on then, I'll be back in a bit,' Hanna said as she got up off the bed and patted the space she had created. She kissed Shane on the cheek and left the two of them tickling Prince, much to his delight. On her way out to the garden Hanna passed the living room, now empty apart from the still weeping Mrs Chamberlain. She glanced at the television, expecting pictures of the famine to be the source of her neighbour's tears, but was surprised to see that it was in fact Howard Jones on-screen. She wanted to stop to watch him perform but felt uncomfortable about intruding on such unexpected emotion from Mrs Chamberlain, so carried on.

Outside, the garden was full. Hanna could see that the whole close seemed to have arrived while she was upstairs, along with the golf-club members and the Neighbourhood Watch. The sound of chatter was now louder than the music blaring from the various speakers, set up to play the concert. The party was in full swing. Hanna knew her mum would be thrilled, and at that moment was probably crowing to Aunty Beverley about their popularity and influence on the close. She knew that the people her mum had turned her nose up at only that morning would be welcome guests if it meant proving something to Aunty Beverley.

She couldn't see her mum in the crowd, however, so she started to make her way through the throng, stopping while women handed her their empty glasses, and men looked at her in ways that made her feel uncomfortable. She smiled as she passed Shane's mum and dad, who appeared to have teamed up with Mr and Mrs O'Leary and Tina, Lurch's mum. It brought her pleasure. She liked seeing the people who didn't fit in, the outsiders of the group, find each other.

THE BARBECUE AT NO. 9

Tina was telling them a story which involved wild gesticulation, the cigarette she was waving coming dangerously close to Mrs Mitchell's hair, but the four of them were agape and didn't seem to notice. Hanna felt relieved that they seemed to be having a good time, having worried about how they would fare among her mum's friends. The thought made her look for her dad, who she was worried about too. He was behind the barbecue, beer in one hand, tongs in the other, and was chatting to Uncle Keith. He seemed to be in great spirits, and suddenly aware of her own hunger, she headed towards him.

'All right, princess?' he said when she got to him, and her throat tightened as he came over and threw an arm around her. She flinched slightly as she caught the powerful, sour tang of alcohol on his breath. He was drunk of course, but he hadn't called her 'princess' for so long, she stayed where she was, hungry for more.

'What can I get you? Burger? Sausage?'

He put a cremated-looking burger in a bun on a paper plate for her and ruffled her hair as he handed it to her. Despite how famished she was, Hanna found herself unable to move her arm to take a bite. She wanted to stay glued to her dad's side, with his arm around her, and drink in his affection. She had missed it so much. Maybe he was back? Maybe all it had taken was this party to shake whatever shadow had fallen across him in recent months.

'Now, if you don't mind, love, me and your Uncle Keith were just having an important business discussion,' her dad carried on, but Uncle Keith was already heading away.

'I'm sure there's no rush, Pete,' Keith said. 'We can pick it up later, or another day,' and he disappeared into the crowd. Peter seemed to visibly dim, as though a bulb had just blown.

'Dad?' Hanna said, as he closed his eyes and placed a clenched fist to his forehead. 'Are you okay?' But it was as if he had forgotten she was there.

Two friends of Lydia's fluttered over, each asking for a sausage with an accompanying giggle, and the moment passed, her dad turning his smile back on and serving up the required wink along with the food. Hanna took a bite of her burger and stared back into the party, searching for her mum, finally spotting her standing near the bench at the end of the garden. For a moment she watched her mum dispassionately, as though they weren't related, and marvelled at the spell she cast on those around her.

The group of people surrounding her seemed to be gazing up at Lydia, as though she was an angel, bathed as she was in the glow of sunshine. She was still immaculate, despite the slightly scorched appearance of many of the others, who were wilting in the heat. When Hanna observed her from a distance, she could see what people admired about her mum – her confidence and

THE BARBECUE AT NO. 9

style – but as she got closer she couldn't help doing what she thought everyone else did, which was to measure mother against daughter, and find herself wanting.

She wondered whether her mum would miss her. There would no doubt be histrionics and drama when she was discovered to be gone – Lydia was nothing if not aware of what was expected of her in any and all circumstances – but underneath it all would she secretly be glad?

Hanna looked down at herself and her unwieldy body, sighing at the sight of the large blob of ketchup she had managed to spill in the middle of her black top. No wonder she was a disappointment. The contrast between them was stark. She blotted the stain with her serviette – *It's a napkin, darling*, her mum would say – then set the burger to one side and made her way in the direction of Lydia's group. It was only as she got closer that she realised who it was her mum was standing with. She immediately froze.

The rest of the occupants of the garden seemed to fade away along with the noise, and all she could see were Lydia, Mike and Mrs Wilson (Hanna didn't know her first name) and, inexplicably, her music teacher Mr Allan, standing with a woman she presumed was his wife. The juxtaposition of her teacher and Mike together, gazing at her mum as she talked, created a complex set of responses in Hanna, all of which were uncomfortable. She had an almost overwhelming desire to run, to be as far away from this moment as possible.

Mike was wearing a denim shirt, unbuttoned further down than her mum would consider decent, chest hair curling out of the top of it. On anyone else it would have been ridiculous, too much, but Mike was different, Hanna thought. He looked tanned and perfectly at home in the sunshine, unlike most of the people Hanna knew. His wife, on the other hand, seemed camouflaged with the garden, thanks to the earthy tones of her wrinkled clothes, which looked as though they had shrivelled in the heat. Her expression was dour.

Hanna remembered the Neighbourhood Watch discussing the fact that Mrs Wilson couldn't have children. It was spoken of in the hushed tones they usually reserved for cancer or poverty. According to Aunty Beverley, their lack of offspring had 'made her bitter, not that she was a bundle of laughs before'. It was one of the few times Hanna could recall her mum not joining in with her usual gusto, instead withdrawing from the conversation with an unreadable look on her face.

Next to them, her teacher and his wife looked closer in age to Hanna than the company surrounding them, dressed as they were in jeans and a Smiths T-shirt (him) and a flowery, vintage-style dress (her). What were they doing here? Why on earth had her mum invited them?

Someone stumbled into Hanna, knocking her elbow. 'Sorry, love,' she heard a man say, making her realise she had stopped moving. She was about to turn and walk in the other direction, away from here, away from her

THE BARBECUE AT NO. 9

mum, Mike, her teacher and his wife, when somehow Lydia spotted her in the crowd. 'Hanna, darling!' she called. 'Come and say hello.' Mike and Mrs Wilson turned around to stare at her, Mike's expression one of amusement.

It will be over in a minute, she told herself. You just have to smile and nod, then find a reason to leave as soon as possible. She would go back up to Shane and David and spend the remainder of her time here on the close with them. None of the people in front of her now were her people.

'Look who's here,' her mum said in an overly loud voice, waving a hand at Mr Allan and his wife as Hanna joined them. Lydia stepped forward and took Hanna's arm, pulling her into the circle as she whispered in her ear, 'I've discovered Mr Allan's father is the chair of the City of London Opera, so try and be impressive.'

Raising her voice for the benefit of the rest of the group, she continued, 'I just wanted to thank your lovely teacher for entering your song into the competition you won.' Mr Allan blushed, looking uncomfortable. Lydia was staring meaningfully at Hanna, her rictus grin presumably an entreaty for Hanna to smile back, which Hanna tried and failed to do. At least she knew now why her mum had invited her teacher. The family connection would be one she was keen to exploit. Anything to enhance the Gordon family status.

Hanna wondered whether this information plus Mr

Allan's role as her teacher would outweigh her mum's disapproval of his casual attire. Having never gone beyond secondary education, with scant few O levels to her name, Lydia had a disproportionate respect for those she saw as educated and allowed them more eccentricities in their style than the average person, as if she believed their brains were too busy thinking clever thoughts to consider what they were wearing.

One of them at least seemed to sense Hanna's deep discomfort and stepped forward. 'I'm Laurence's – sorry, Mr Allan's – wife, Natasha,' the woman said. Hanna felt glued to the spot, not knowing if she should shake her outstretched hand or not. A hesitant smile stretched across Natasha's face as her hand went back down to her side, and Hanna realised how pretty she was, and trendy, with her red lips and freckles and her vintage dress. She was everything Hanna wanted to be when she grew up.

'Nice to meet you,' Natasha said.

Hanna was never comfortable with too many eyes on her, and there were too many eyes on her now. Her mum's expectant ones, Mike's amused, knowing ones, Mrs Wilson's cold, narrowed ones, Mr Allan's somewhat embarrassed ones and Natasha's sympathetic ones. She forced a smile on to her face, knowing she needed to get away as fast as possible.

'Nice to meet you,' she said, though the words came out with no expression, making it sound as though 'nice' was the last thing it could be described as. This was a situation in which Hanna wanted more than anything to be perceived as an adult, and knew she was coming across as a truculent child. She couldn't help it though. A way of escape sprang to mind, and she grasped it like a life raft. 'Would anyone like a drink? Some food?' she said, cringing at how much her tight, high-pitched voice reminded her of her mum in her more tense moments, when trying to remain polite.

She was saved by – of all people – Mike. 'I'd love a beer,' he said with a wink, and she was so grateful to him for giving her a reason to leave, she could have hugged him, until she realised that it meant she would have to return. No doubt he knew that. She wondered for a moment if he was deliberately taunting her.

No one else wanted anything, so she headed for the kitchen with the intention of handing Mike his beer then leaving immediately. She even thought about whether to leave altogether, while the party was in full swing, but, remembering that Shane and David were still upstairs in her bedroom, decided to wait a little longer.

The kitchen was quiet, and Hanna leaned against the sink for a moment, letting her breath out in an audible sigh. Her legs ached and she could feel her pregnancy in a way she hadn't done before. She understood the expression 'carrying a child' for the first time, as that was exactly how it felt, its weight heavy and burdensome.

She closed her eyes, willing herself not to cry, when she heard a movement at the other side of the room.

Surprised, she swung round, realising as she did so that there was someone sitting on the floor in the corner of the kitchen, leaning against the pantry door, their head between their knees.

'Are you all right?' she said.

They were curled up so small it was hardly a surprise that Hanna hadn't spotted them.

As their head came up slowly, Hanna realised it was Rita, the woman from no. 15 who she had met earlier. She seemed to stare at Hanna without seeing her at first, then as her glassy, red-rimmed eyes focused, she almost jumped to her feet.

'Yes, yes, sorry,' she said, her voice high-pitched and harried. 'I was just . . .' She seemed to run out of steam, and Hanna felt moved to reassure her.

'Oh, don't worry, I came in here for a break too,' she said, waving her arms in the direction of the garden. 'I just wondered if you were okay or if you needed anything?'

They were interrupted by Ned Thomas, who wandered in slowly, his gait slightly lopsided. It felt to Hanna that the room tensed, though she knew it could only be her. This party was like a minefield, she thought. No sooner had she escaped from one person she didn't know what to say to, than she ran into another.

'I'd better find Davina,' Rita said, with an abruptness which startled Hanna. Before she could say another word, Rita left the room. Ned went up to Hanna by the sink. He was a tad too close, and she felt herself draw back. 'She's weird,' said Ned.

His voice was low and thick, the words woolly. His eyes, normally sharp and predatory, seemed half-closed, and his breath smelled of beer. Hanna took another step away from him, sensing the danger in his drunkenness.

'She freaked out at me earlier,' Ned carried on, shrugging his shoulders as though baffled. Hanna was almost tempted to say that she understood why Ned might have that effect when the doorbell rang and once again she had an excuse to leave. She was starting to wonder if the whole of her last day on the close would be spent running away from men she was avoiding, though at least this confirmed that she was doing the right thing in leaving.

It was Antoinette Chamberlain at the door.

The two girls appraised each other as they always did, with a quick up and down, taking in clothes, hair and make-up. Hanna breathed in the cloying smell of hair lacquer, a layer of which glistened in the hot sun, keeping Antoinette's flicked fringe frozen in place. She no longer knew why she still compared herself to her next-door neighbour, considering she had bigger and more pressing things to focus on, but it was a long-instilled habit with Antoinette and she couldn't seem to break it.

'Come in,' she said, while at the same time Antoinette said, 'Are my parents still here?'

'Your mum's watching the concert,' Hanna said. 'I think she's a bit upset by it,' she added. Antoinette stared at her, as if she expected Hanna to find her mother's distress amusing. She didn't find the reaction she was looking for.

'Okay,' she said and went straight to the living room, where Hanna watched her grab hold of her mother's hand and draw her, still weeping, from the armchair into a long hug. Hanna looked away. She felt a pang of something deep inside her, almost like a craving. She and Lydia never hugged.

She went back to the kitchen and was relieved to find that Ned was no longer there. The room was empty. She steeled herself and walked back outside with Mike's beer. The brightness and volume out in the garden had increased even more in the time she'd been inside, as though someone had turned the dial up to the max. To Hanna, every voice seemed to be clamouring for her attention, wanting something from her, though no one was speaking to her; all she wanted to do was get her bag and go. She wished she could put her headphones on and disappear but instead tried not to catch anyone's eyes, particularly Mike's as she handed him his drink. He barely glanced at her, and she was grateful for that. Her mum and Mr and Mrs Allan were no longer standing with him, and she could have cried with relief. Mike was in the middle of telling a story involving the horsepower of his car to some people she didn't recognise, so she managed to escape without anyone noticing.

She immediately retreated to the bench in the shade at the bottom of the garden, hoping her dark clothes might help to blend her into the background. She wanted to take a few minutes to settle herself before she went back upstairs. She could imagine Shane asking if she was okay the moment he saw her, and she didn't want to lie to him any more than she had already.

She surveyed the crowd in front of her. The laughter and conversation of adults. She wondered whether one day she might feel easy in company, be able to chatter away with little thought or self-consciousness, whether it was just to do with her age. She hated to admit that she wasn't an adult yet, but at moments like these she was painfully aware of being a teenager. Then she happened to spot Antoinette Chamberlain again, who had come out of the living room and was now talking to Uncle Keith and Aunty Beverley. She was all poise, and Hanna could almost hear the tinkle of her laugh as she smiled and gently shook her head, making her hair cascade down her back like a Timotei shampoo advert.

Hanna often felt like she and Antoinette were entirely different species of girl, and never more than in that moment. She wondered where Ned had disappeared to, and when Rosie might arrive, hoping that she could keep her friend away from him, then froze with a movement from inside her belly. Soon none of this would matter.

Soon it would be just her and this baby. And then she would *have* to grow up. She had already changed beyond recognition in the last eight months.

It was eight months ago that she realised the crush she had been harbouring was reciprocated, though it felt like another lifetime. It was almost as if it had happened to an entirely different person. The realisation had dawned after the first long conversation they'd ever really had. Before then it had just been short interactions. Of course, they didn't really run in the same sorts of circles, but she saw him often enough for her to be hyper-aware of the effect he had on her. They were feelings she had only ever experienced in the abstract before him, starting with Nick Rhodes from Duran Duran, who she still adored, despite having left their music behind in her early teens. She found the combination of discomfort and desire she felt in his presence wholly intoxicating.

She knew he would never look at someone like her, but that didn't stop her from being overtaken by a squirming self-consciousness whenever he was in the vicinity, a desire to impress that made her clam up even more than usual – or, at the other extreme, begin to fixate on whatever the topic under discussion was, no matter how trivial. It was the latter that day. They'd somehow got on to the topic of The Cure, and she was making an impassioned plea for Robert Smith's vocal ability. She'd made some long declaration about the deceptive power of his simple lyrics when he started to smile widely and shake his head.

'What?' she'd asked, wondering if she had said something wrong, or gone on for so long he was trying to shut her up.

'I was just noticing how much you light up when you talk about music. You actually smile.'

Hanna felt herself flush, could even sense her ears had turned pink.

'Oh, I'm sorry. I didn't mean to embarrass you. I shouldn't have said anything,' he said, though he continued to smile so that she started to question whether he was sorry at all. It was a smile that made her entire brain fizz.

'No, no, I mean it's fine,' she said, feeling her words desert her.

He continued to smile at her, saying nothing, and she became suddenly aware of every part of her body in a way she wasn't usually, unless it was to criticise it. It was as though she was pulsing with energy. Eventually she broke the spell, looking down at her feet and breaking eye contact, the intensity too much for her. She felt like she might explode or, even worse, say something silly that would remind him of who she was. Her surprise when he reached his hand out and lifted her chin back up, so that she had no choice but to look at him, struck her completely mute.

'Don't hide your face,' he said, 'you're beautiful.'

When she thought about that moment now, she wondered whether she should have – or indeed could have – made a different decision. At the time it had felt like there was no stopping the momentum. There was an inevitability to everything that followed which made it difficult to imagine another outcome. As she sat there on the bench, her hand moved instinctively to her stomach and she wondered what he might feel if he knew about the baby, whether he might wish it hadn't happened. Or whether he would feel anything at all.

Steve – No. 20

It took Steve a while to get ready. Every time he looked in the mirror, he would notice something awry – a smudge on his shoes, a hair out of place – which would send him back to the beginning of his elaborate grooming routine. Eventually he ran out of excuses, and though he felt the same trepidation as he had as a child on his first day of school, it was now or never. He was ready. He found himself almost marching over to no. 9, as if on patrol or going into battle, which in a sense he supposed he was. The last time he had attended a party of any kind it had been his own: the one that his mum threw the night before he left for basic training.

His mum had long accepted that at least one of her sons would go into the Guards. It felt inevitable. Her husband, Steve's father, had served, and his father before him. Unspoken within the family was the fact that she would have preferred it to be her eldest son, Andy, rather than her 'baby', Steve, who joined up, but on the day he left for training she threw him a going-away party that spoke of her love for her boy regardless.

It had taken place in their old house in Scotland, where they had moved when Steve's dad got ill, to be closer to family. After his father had died, and the shadow he cast over them had dissipated and they could breathe properly, they had been happy there.

The whole extended family had come to the do: a blur of uncles and aunties and cousins and nephews and nieces, as well as hangers-on who everyone had long forgotten their connection to. Tina's new boyfriend, Trevor, was there as well. The fact that his mum might have found love again made Steve feel less guilty for leaving her, even if 'Tina and Trevor' sounded like a couple from a sitcom. Anyway, Andy wasn't going anywhere, a thought which Steve found comforting.

Tina had put on an amazing spread. Their kitchen table, covered in a paper tablecloth, had groaned under the weight of sausage rolls, and cheese and pineapple on sticks (for the vegetarians), and sandwiches cut elegantly into diagonal quarters, a nod to the importance of the occasion. She'd made Andy draw up a banner with *GOOD LUCK* emblazoned across it, and everyone had toasted to Steve's good fortune.

'Your dad would've been so proud of you,' Tina had said in her impromptu speech, given after a Babycham or three, her voice slightly louder than would have been comfortable had everyone else not had a few too many as well. There was a pause, and Steve immediately pictured his father sitting on the sofa, watching the football.

THE BARBECUE AT NO. 9

Would he have been proud? Steve wondered. Or was that something people said to make other people feel better about their choices?

As far as he knew, he had mostly been a disappointment to his father, who had frequently expressed his concern about his son being 'soft' whenever he showed any sort of emotion. But maybe he would at least have approved of Steve going into the forces. Perhaps he would have thought that Steve was becoming more like him. Tough. Driven. When the real reason was that Steve didn't know what else to do, that the idea of routine and following orders appealed to him, that he hoped joining up would mean he wouldn't have to think for himself, as his thinking only seemed to get him into trouble.

He quietly prayed that what his mum said was true, before his Uncle John began a rendition of 'Danny Boy', a confusing choice of song given that to Steve's knowledge his dad's family were Scottish, and his mum's cockney. The rest of the party had joined in immediately, Tina swaying as she sang the words – entirely tunelessly – waving her cigarette in the air, eyes closed and the black of her mascara streaking down her face as she was swept away with emotion. He had never loved her as much as he did in that moment and would have done anything he could to feel as though he deserved it.

In the early hours of the following morning, after

all their guests had left and Tina and Trevor had staggered off to bed, Andy had attempted to give Steve some fatherly advice. At least the kind of advice he thought a father should give, their own never having been much of a role model to either of them. The two of them had just finished cleaning up the debris from the party, throwing empty beer cans and paper plates into big black bin bags, when Andy put his hand on Steve's arm. 'Sit down for a minute,' he said, his voice still slurring slightly, but his eyes focused and intent. They both sat on the rickety chairs at either side of the kitchen table. 'I know the last few years have been hard,' Andy said, 'with Dad dying and everything, but it's time for us to go and live our lives.' He leaned his elbows on the table and held his hands out as though reaching for Steve but not quite: they rarely touched each other, except during rough and tumble.

By that point Steve was beyond tired and still very drunk, so he'd just nodded and mumbled something, even though what he'd wanted to say was 'I love you, brother.' He knew beyond a shadow of a doubt that if Andy had not metaphorically held his hand through his short life so far, he would have gone under.

Steve had left later that morning, hungover and groggy after only a few hours' sleep. But as he watched, from the back window of the bus, the two people he cared about most in the world wave frantically at him until he was out of sight, he had felt the kind of strength that comes from knowing you are loved. He hadn't appreciated then just how precious that was, and how quickly it could disappear. He still had his mum, of course, but everything else had changed, including the person he had been then. That strength had disappeared, along with his naive beliefs about good and evil being clearly recognisable, and somewhere along the line his brother's love and protection had faded too, though that was entirely Steve's own fault.

No one answered the door at no. 9 at first, and Steve had to force himself to stand there and ring the doorbell a second time, his feet itching to turn around and go back to the comfort of home. Eventually he heard the thumping sound of feet on stairs, and David, the youngest of the household, hair mussed and breathless, answered the door, his little dog at his feet. Steve suddenly realised he had no idea what he was supposed to do, and without really thinking it through, found himself giving a little bow to the boy.

    David stared at him, his eyes wide. Steve couldn't read if his expression was one of fear or astonishment. After a few awkward moments, during which Steve felt himself visibly sweating, David stepped to one side and let him in. Steve nodded in thanks while David just stood there, his body rigid as a sentry, his eyes and those of the dog not moving from Steve's face. The two of them seemed to be staring at Steve in wonder.

'I'm Steve from number twenty,' Steve finally croaked, his mouth dry.

'Hello,' David practically squeaked in response.

The dog began to weave its way around both David's and Steve's legs in a figure of eight, sniffing at Steve's trousers with interest as he did so. Something about the action seemed to settle the boy, and his shoulders dropped a little.

'Do you like dogs?' he asked.

Steve nodded, then bent to stroke the Jack Russell, wanting to somehow show the boy there was nothing to be afraid of. The dog leaned into his touch and turned its head to gaze at him. 'His name's Prince,' David said. 'He likes you.'

Steve was inordinately thrilled at this and found himself beaming. David beamed back, the two of them having reached an unspoken understanding.

'The barbecue is in the garden,' David said, pointing through the house, as though Steve knew where he was going, then ran off back upstairs. Steve looked down at Prince, who seemed to be debating who to stay with, his doleful eyes still on Steve, until he turned on his heel and disappeared after the boy.

Alone again, Steve took a deep breath and headed down the hallway. Unlike their home, everything at the Gordons' looked as if it was from a Wimpey show home. From the paint to the pine surfaces, to the perfectly positioned pictures on the walls, there was a glossiness to the place which made Steve want to check the soles of his shoes for dirt. He wondered what his mum had made of it. He could imagine her expression as she said, *But it's not a* home, *is it?* For her, home meant comfort, personality and, most of all, *stuff*. Even though, thanks to him, they very rarely had visitors, she wanted everyone to feel welcome. For the Gordons, it clearly meant a sheen of perfection and being a source of envy.

He peered around the half-open living-room door, surprised to see Mrs Chamberlain there, watching the concert, hanky in hand and sniffling loudly, her swollen face and red eyes making it clear that she had been crying for some time. He was momentarily startled at the display of emotion from this person he had observed, for months, showing none. Her eyes stayed steadfastly glued to the screen in front of her, not appearing to notice his presence in the doorway, and he made a mental note of the place and time, having decided that bringing his notebook and pen to record events might not be the way to blend in with the other barbecue guests.

He felt the stirrings of discomfort, a tightness in his belly. Up until that point he had managed to justify his observations from afar as being somehow his job and purpose in life. He was detached from the subjects of his scrutiny. He watched them for professional reasons only. But this felt different, like he was spying, encroaching on the pain of another human being. What was he doing?

He shook his head as though to dislodge the thought

and decided to go via the kitchen next. He felt like a child dipping their toe into a cold sea; he had to acclimatise himself to this amount of people slowly. Glancing out into the garden through the window, he could feel his breath quicken. It was some time since he had been around this many people in one place, and the prospect was almost overwhelming until his eyes alighted on the sight of his mum, her bright blue dress standing out among a sea of pastel. She was standing with a group of people, her face animated as she talked and laughed, whirling the cigarette she had in her hand around, as if to emphasise a point. She would keep him safe.

He decided to make his way around the outskirts of the garden so he could get a feel for the terrain. A reconnaissance, if you will. That way he would be able to keep to the shade of the trees and fence, camouflaging himself with the dark brown of his clothes. It was hard to be unnoticed when you were as tall as him, but everyone seemed to be intent on food, drink and impressing each other. He would take the risk, he decided, and slipped out of the patio doors and into the shadows.

He kept his eye on the guests, looking for anything out of place, or anyone who might fit the description of the person he'd seen in the close earlier, but everyone was starting to blur into one. He couldn't seem to differentiate people close up. It was hard to record what was happening when he was part of it, and when his heart was thumping so loudly it almost drowned out any other sound. Once he got to the barbecue itself, he paused, allowing himself to stand still for a few moments to breathe, as Cameron had taught him to do whenever he was overwhelmed by sights and sounds.

Cameron didn't just teach him about the Russians. Alongside the history books he kept in a pile by his bedside in the barracks were the entire works of Shakespeare and books by a philosopher called Alan Watts. He would frequently quote things Watts had said and read passages out loud from his books whenever he sensed Steve needed distracting. Often Steve would drift away while Cameron read the words to him, not making sense of them, just losing himself in the sound of Cameron's voice, which was soft and hypnotic, belying his burly frame. But something about the idea of being in the moment had stuck, and he found himself using it whenever he felt unsettled, no longer able to ask Cameron for help.

There was no one serving, so he picked up a paper plate from the side and added a hot dog in a bun from the piles of food laid out on the picnic table next to it. He was too nervous to eat, his throat closed just at the thought, but he would use the food as a kind of prop or disguise, he thought, hoping it would make him look more normal. While he served himself, he tuned into a nearby conversation between two women who looked as though they were attending a wedding or a royal garden party.

'I'm not exactly clear how this is *for the children* of Africa,' said one of them, a note of indignation in her voice. The other one looked around her, checking for who was in earshot, Steve thought, her neatly coiffured hair remaining in place as her head moved, as though she was wearing a helmet and was ready for combat. Steve took a step back into the shade to avoid being spotted, but her eyes seemed to skim over him as if he was of no consequence. 'What do you mean, Denise?' she said to her companion in a low voice. 'I thought the famine was in Ethiopia, anyway.'

Denise gave her companion a withering look. 'Same difference,' she said. 'On the invitation, it said that the barbecue is *for the children*, but how? How is it for the children? Is anyone collecting money?' she said, her voice now so loud that other people around them briefly turned in their direction. Her friend flapped her hand, to indicate that she should keep her voice down.

'I'm not exactly sure. Maybe it's about raising awareness,' she said.

'But we're all aware already. That's what the concert is for,' Denise said, not willing to give up her argument. 'I feel like we're a bit *too* aware, to tell you the truth. You can't turn around these days without being assaulted by photos of starving children. As if it's our fault or something.'

'Maybe Lydia just wanted to do *something*, you know? I mean, it is very distressing.'

THE BARBECUE AT NO. 9

They both turned to look at Lydia Gordon, who was at the centre of the garden, swaying slightly while she chatted to Gerald Chamberlain and a younger couple Steve didn't recognise, smiling and nodding emphatically from one to the other, as though she was watching a tennis match at Wimbledon. She looked entirely unbothered by anything, though Steve knew that the insides and outsides of a person didn't always match.

'Hmmmm,' said Denise. 'She looks *very* distressed indeed.'

Steve carried on around the perimeter of the garden, plate in hand, passing the families he recognised from his observations of the close until he got near enough to his mum to be able to make his way to her with minimum disruption. She hadn't spotted him yet: her refusal to wear the glasses she needed meant she couldn't see very far in front of her.

He was just working out the shortest route to get to her when he realised that sitting on a wrought-iron bench was another individual, also camouflaged, her dark clothing blending her into the background.

'Hello,' said Hanna.

She looked at him with such familiarity – as if she saw and spoke to him every day – that he was momentarily wrong-footed.

'Hello, Hanna,' he said, then winced as he realised he had given away the fact that he knew her name. She showed no reaction, however, and he looked at her more closely, seeing faint grey tracks of mascara down her cheeks. She saw him looking and wiped her eyes. Steve turned away, spotting the wooden garden gate, which seemed to be hanging lopsided on its hinges.

'Oh, it's broken,' Hanna said, her voice quiet, muffled by the sleeve she was using to clean her face. 'Someone did that earlier.'

Steve froze, his skin prickling. 'Today?' he said.

'Yes.'

Steve looked at her, working out his next question. He didn't want to give away his interest, nor the fact he had been watching. 'What happened?' he asked, trying to inject a note of nonchalance into his voice, though nonchalance had never been his strongest suit.

'I don't really know,' she said, staring straight ahead. 'It was Mum who saw them, then she screamed and me and David – my brother – came downstairs to see what was wrong.'

'Did she recognise them?' Steve said, aware of his stiff formality, wishing he knew how to sound like a neighbour having a conversation with another neighbour. Hanna paused, looking around the garden.

'No,' she said, so quietly he could barely hear her.

Steve sensed that she had more to say when her eyes alighted on something in the garden, giving him a moment to register the fact that he had been right. There was someone watching. He hadn't made it up. His instincts were correct. The relief of that was almost equal

THE BARBECUE AT NO. 9

to the urgency he felt to protect this girl and her family. He was just about to ask more when the little dog from earlier, Prince, bounded up to the two of them, giving Steve a cursory sniff, then leaping on to Hanna's lap, vigorously licking away what was left of the tears on her cheeks. Steve watched as her face transformed with the giggle she couldn't help but let out.

Prince was followed by David, along with another boy that Steve recognised as being Hanna's boyfriend, and then her best friend, Rosie. Rosie said to Hanna, 'I've been looking for you everywhere,' and seemed about to carry on when she stopped abruptly on spotting Steve, taking in his appearance with an expression of wonder. It was time for him to leave Hanna with her friends.

Steve had the sense of each group he passed stopping and slowly turning to watch him, like dominoes falling, as he made his way over to Tina. He was all arms and legs and had no sense of how a normal person walked any more. He found himself marching again, to give himself some semblance of control over his limbs, but was conscious this only made him look weirder to his growing audience. He felt like a circus freak-show exhibit. He knew his height didn't help but was also aware he had got his outfit badly wrong. For some reason he'd assumed that Lydia and Peter Gordon would be all about smartness, and so he had dressed accordingly, but his suit was clearly out of place here. He knew he looked funereal in his formality.

When his mum turned around, alerted to his presence by the stares and mutters of the crowd, he felt a measure of pain at the joy on her face. He knew she would be reading the fact that he was here as a sign he was 'getting better', whatever that meant. It was a phrase she used often about him and to him, suggesting all kinds of things that might 'make him better', from going to the pub for a pint, to applying for jobs he knew he would never get. He could imagine her telling Andy that he had come to the barbecue on their next muttered phone call, but the thought caused a wave of irritation he knew wouldn't help him navigate the next stage of his mission, so he focused on the people she was standing with instead.

He recognised the O'Learys, had in fact met them once when they came round to introduce themselves after moving in. They hadn't seemed to notice his awkwardness and discomfort, had only treated him with warmth and kindness, which made him feel guilty about his initial distrust of them. Since then, Mrs O'Leary always stopped to say hello whenever she saw him on his way to or from the corner shop, whether he acknowledged her presence or not.

According to Cameron, while the Irish weren't on a par with the Russians, their proximity and the ease of their assimilation into Britain made him cautious. This was before the bombing of the Brighton Grand – when

THE BARBECUE AT NO. 9

the IRA came close to assassinating a sitting British prime minister – and Steve had often wondered whether the IRA were more of a threat to Delmont Close than he'd realised. He'd met Mrs O'Leary enough times to sense it was unlikely that she was a member of the IRA, but in his darker moments he reflected that if she was, that would be exactly what she would want him to think. The mental knot this tied him up in had led to one of the rare times he had ever had a flash of insight into the trap he had created for himself. Seeking hidden motivation and capacity for evil in everyone he met made for a lonely life.

Along with a couple he wasn't familiar with, the rest of the small group consisted of red-haired, dungaree-clad Davina from down the road and a woman he recognised as Ryan's mum, who was dressed in a strange hodgepodge of floaty garments draped rag-like around her, making her look like a middle-aged Kate Bush.

The sight of Ryan's mum made him light-headed. There was no sign of Ryan himself, and Steve felt a tug of disappointment in his chest. Taking them all in, he had the thought that this group was essentially the odds and sods of the party, none of them quite blending in with the Laura-Ashley-meets-golf-club feel of the rest of the guests. The idea made him smile briefly; he would at least be at home among them.

'Well, if it isn't my boy,' his mum said as he reached

them, her face beaming with pride and cheap white wine. 'You decided to come.'

Steve nodded, internally begging her not to introduce him to everyone, a message he was relieved she seemed to receive or intuit, as she moved directly on. 'We were just discussing vegetarianism, and Davina here was telling us about all the choices you can get nowadays.'

She took a deep drag from her cigarette and nodded over at Davina as if to allow her to continue, and Steve was unsurprised to see that it looked as though Davina had been waiting for permission. His mum was always in charge of the conversation. As Davina began speaking again, his mum looked over at him with an eyebrow raised and a sparkle of mischief in her eyes. Steve knew they would laugh about this conversation later. His mum was deeply suspicious of vegetarianism. 'It goes against the laws of nature,' she used to say. Steve was about to smile in return when he spotted a figure weaving in and out of the guests, precariously carrying too many drinks, and blowing his curls off his glasses as he wobbled and spilled his way over. Steve felt himself go rigidly still, his eyes laser-focused on Ryan, the rest of the garden blurring into the periphery.

'Let me take some of those, Ryan,' Mr O'Leary said as the young man got nearer.

Ryan let him take two of the drinks and visibly exhaled as he handed out the rest, presumably relieved

THE BARBECUE AT NO. 9

that they, and he, had made it back to the group intact. He stopped as he got to Steve.

'Oh,' Ryan said, 'sorry, I didn't get you anything. I mean, you weren't here when I went, so how could I? But still. I'm sorry. Shall I go and get you a drink now? What would you like?' The words tumbled out of him while he blinked rapidly, as though also communicating via Morse code. Steve almost smiled, realising that Ryan sounded exactly like he looked: intense, scatty and, above all, kind. Suddenly aware of every aspect of his being, from his height to his hands to the desire to swallow, Steve felt overwhelmed with choices of how to respond. He couldn't ask for a drink, as that would mean Ryan leaving again, though that might release the tension in the silence that was growing with every second he didn't speak. He wanted to say, *Please don't apologise, I'm fine*, but found his mouth was so dry he suspected it would come out as a croak. He shook his head instead, hoping that would communicate something similar.

Ryan handed him his own glass.

'Would you mind holding on to that for a second?' he said, and took his now misted glasses off, wiping them on his T-shirt. Steve kept his eyes trained on the top of Ryan's head and away from the skin between his jeans and T-shirt that this action had revealed.

'Oh,' Ryan suddenly said again, looking back up at Steve. 'There's me giving you my drink to hold before I've even introduced myself. You must think I'm so rude.

I'm no good at parties, as is evident. I just, anyway, I'm Ryan,' he said, putting his glasses back on and holding his hand out to shake Steve's, then laughing as he realised that Steve was holding the drink in his right hand. The sound was infectious. More of a giggle than a laugh, and Steve found himself laughing too.

'Steve,' he said, amazed that he had managed to form the word.

'Hi, Steve. And who's your little pal?' Ryan said, bending down to stroke Prince, who, unbeknown to Steve, must have followed him.

'He's not mine,' Steve said; then, conscious of his abruptness, added, 'He's called Prince, he belongs to the Gordons.'

'Well, it looks like he's taken a shine to you,' said Ryan, and they both watched as Prince rubbed himself against Steve's legs, more cat-like than dog-like. Steve half-expected him to purr. Steve bent down to stroke Prince, and Ryan sat on his haunches to do the same. They were so close, Steve could feel Ryan's breath on his face. There was just the briefest moment of eye contact before Steve snapped back upright again, wondering if it was possible that Ryan had felt it too, the jolt of electricity so strong it winded him. He stood up so fast they knocked heads and Ryan immediately began apologising, then laughing, but Steve couldn't summon any amusement now. This was too much, the overwhelm threatening to cause an episode. He felt almost consumed with the need to escape.

'I'm going to get myself a drink,' he said, then practically staggered away from the group, gasping for air as he headed inside the house.

Hour Eight: 5–6 p.m.

Paul Young, U2

Rita – No. 15

Rita had considered leaving the party after seeing the boy who looked like Jacob. She imagined running back to her house, locking the door behind her and disappearing into herself, not even attempting to make friends or build a life here ever again. But she knew that if she was alone with her thoughts, it might be dangerous, so she stayed, floating around the people in the garden, collecting glasses, serving food, as though she really was the hired help. But it kept her busy, the familiarity of domestic tasks like a well-worn groove.

At one point Davina found her, her expression curious. 'What are you doing? Are you okay?' she asked. Her new friend was staring at her with concern, and Rita wondered how she must appear to her. For the second time that day she felt the desire to reveal the truth of who she was to Davina but managed to stop herself. She gave a small nod. 'I'll be okay,' she said, her voice almost a whisper. Davina let her be, saying only, 'Come and find me if you need me,' then gently touching Rita's arm before disappearing back into the crowd.

Everyone was getting into the swing of the party. Rita

watched the stiffness leaving people's limbs, their bodies and tongues loosened by alcohol, their faces growing pinker as their voices got more animated. The next time she saw the boy it was less of a shock, but she still had to take a step back and steady herself, holding on to the cool brick of the house. He was standing with the pretty young girl from next door – Antoinette, was it? They were close enough to suggest a casual intimacy between them, though Antoinette's face was expressionless while he talked at her, his head bowing to bridge the height gap between them. He was swaying slightly, clearly drunk. She felt the sudden urge to step in. Where were the boy's parents? she wondered, acutely aware of the irony of her judgement of them.

She stared at him for longer this time, able to study him unobserved. The more she looked, the more she saw how different he and Jacob actually were. This boy's nose was long and sharp; Jacob's was fuller. Jacob's hair was almost white-blond from the sun and had more of a natural curl to it, compared to this boy's more coiffured style. Rita couldn't imagine Jacob gelling his hair, he was all rough and tumble, whereas there was something more considered, more artful about this young man. It was a relief to notice these differences, and she felt her body settle out of the blind panic she had been in earlier. She was glad she had stayed.

Looking out into the garden, she watched the groups of people chatting to each other, finding herself invested in their imagined lives and relationships. It was so long since she had been among people, she found herself thirsty for their stories, wanting to drink them all in. She smiled as she saw Tina, cigarette in one hand, plate of food in the other, talking without pause to a rapt audience, but there was also a young couple who caught her eye with their style: him in a band T-shirt, her in a dress that wouldn't have been out of place in the 1960s. Rita watched them with interest as the intensity of their conversation increased, the man holding on to the woman's arm so tightly you could see marks. The woman pulled away and stormed off and Rita wanted to cheer her on.

Next, her eyes were drawn to a heavily pregnant woman, wearing a patterned dress with ruffles at the neck. Rita remembered being made to wear the same sort of dress during her own pregnancy: designed to detract attention from the bump, as though it was an embarrassment, a visual reminder that women have sex. The woman was standing with two men who were deep in conversation, their attention firmly on each other. She was moving from foot to foot, her heeled shoes clearly uncomfortable as evidenced by her swollen ankles, her face flushed and flustered. Rita felt a rush of empathy, remembering her own discomfort when she was pregnant with Jacob, and Des's insistence that she 'keep standards high' and continue to wear her Sunday best when accompanying him to church.

Rita went to the kitchen, feeling anger start to bubble up deep inside her. She filled a glass with ice cubes and cold water, went back out into the garden and silently handed the glass to the woman, who shot her a grateful look. Though they didn't say a word to each other, Rita could sense her relief. She wanted to take this woman away, sit her down somewhere quiet and remove the painful-looking shoes, like some topsy-turvy Cinderella story. She knew though that if she did that, she would upset some delicate balance, imply some slight against the man she assumed was the woman's husband, who had not even glanced in his wife's direction since Rita had spotted her.

As she walked away, Rita let herself indulge in a fantasy where she interrupted the two men – who appeared to be debating the relative benefits of fixed- versus variable-rate mortgages – and tipped the water over them; imagining their spluttering beetroot faces, and her mischievous, triumphant joy at standing up for this woman she didn't know and would probably never see again. It was the woman's husband the anger she felt was directed at. Him and all the men like him. She had to breathe slowly to contain the fury. She had only managed to stand up to Des once during her own pregnancy, of course. She didn't risk it a second time.

They didn't tell her parents, but she was pregnant before they left for Australia, Des having delayed his return until they were married. Rita had been shocked at the discovery, but Des was thrilled, and she had come round to the idea, helped by his obvious delight. Her shock wasn't naivety, she knew where babies came from, but she'd assumed due to the many, many risks she had taken already – sleeping with multiple men with neither contraception nor a resulting pregnancy – that she was safe. She had loosely relied on him pulling out but had been so hungry for him at that time – a hunger she realised later was exacerbated by the sneaking around, finding places to have sex, falling into each other the moment her parents left the house – that she hadn't insisted on it. She learned too late that Des had always seen the purpose of their union to be the bearing of children.

For the first few days in her new home, Rita couldn't tell what symptoms were created by pregnancy and what was jet lag; they seemed to merge into one. She was sick, dizzy and disorientated, not helped by the number of people trooping in and out of the house daily to meet 'the new Mrs Hargreaves', none of whose names she could remember. All she could recall was the vague sense of the men looking her up and down, and the women staring hard, as though trying to discern from her face what it was about Rita that had finally ensnared their precious preacher.

It hadn't taken long for her to realise that Des had something of a god-like status in their small town.

Whenever they walked down the dusty main street, people would stop, or lean out of their cars, or even wave from behind the counter in shops. The only person who didn't was a small, pretty woman they sometimes saw out and about, who would blanch and scuttle away every time she spotted them. Des explained that he and the woman had once 'stepped out' together, as he called it, and she was probably jealous that he had chosen to marry her instead. She was a 'troubled' woman he had taken pity on and she had mistaken it for love, he said.

At first, all the admiration made Rita giggle – after all, she was intoxicated with him too – and it made her feel important to be the woman he had chosen for his wife. As her belly grew, however, the constant attention began to make her self-conscious, and she started to feel as if she would never be able to measure up to her husband's perfection in the eyes of his congregation. Then finally, much later on, it made her afraid.

Des was patient with her in the beginning. His early adoration of her body extended to include the child she was growing inside it. He would lie in bed, his head on her belly, talking away to his son – he was convinced it would be a boy, even before he was born and they knew for certain – telling him all the things he had to look forward to when he arrived in the world, and he included Rita in that. 'You'll get to meet the most wonderful woman in the world,' he would say. 'Your mother. Rebecca.'

THE BARBECUE AT NO. 9

Des had suggested the name change on the journey from London to Sydney, during one of their many stopovers, this time at Kuala Lumpur airport. They had been sitting on hard plastic chairs, watching hordes of people pass by them, and Rita had felt as though she was watching them all on-screen. She felt hypnotised by the journey. It was as if she couldn't remember where they had come from or where they were going to. There was only where they were now.

But it wasn't an unpleasant experience; in fact, the opposite. Rita was enjoying this strange, liminal space; she really had left the past behind, in a very physical way. She wasn't worried about leaving home in the slightest. The only person she would miss was Alistair, and their friendship had become strained due to her relationship with Des. Alistair thought he sounded sanctimonious and so she had never introduced them. She had barely even said goodbye to him, telling him on the phone that she was leaving, unable to face his sadness in person. Alistair didn't seem to understand that Des represented the chance to rewrite who she was and become someone her parents might actually be proud of.

It seemed to her that Des was feeling the same when he said, 'I was thinking about how we might really make this a new start – symbolically, I mean.'

Rita had nodded, loving how in tune they were with each other.

'And given we've already talked about giving our boy

a biblical name, I was wondering how you might feel about taking one too.'

At this she had woken up slightly, turning to him, a distant alarm bell ringing in her mind that she promptly dismissed.

'Change my name, you mean?'

'Yeah. I know you've struggled with your faith, and I really understand that. This might be a way to make a commitment. To our new life. And to God.'

She thought about it and wondered if he was right. She did want to make a change. To herself as well as her circumstances. She wanted to be the wife that Des wanted her to be. A thought came to her, and she spoke it out loud before she had the chance to censor it.

'And you? Will you be changing your name?' she said, a small smile on her face as she spoke, knowing the answer. His brow furrowed. 'Well. No. Everyone already knows me as Des. That would be confusing. They don't know you at all yet.'

'And what would my name be?' she said, going along with it now, like a game of make-believe.

'Rebecca,' he said. 'Mother of Jacob.'

His answer was immediate and sure. He'd clearly been thinking about this, and she had a glimmer of how little she knew about him, and how vulnerable she was, moving to the other side of the world with this person she had known for a matter of months. Rita blinked at him slowly, as though seeing him for the first time.

'Rebecca,' she repeated, trying the name out for size and finding it clunky in her mouth.

And so it came to pass.

Rita had wondered at first if it was the name that had stopped Des from wanting to sleep with her once they arrived in their new home. It was as if he now saw her as a biblical character. While her appetite for sex seemed to increase during pregnancy, his diminished. She also wondered if it was her changing body. She wished she had someone to talk to about it, to ask if it was normal and if it would change once the baby was born. She didn't feel able to express to Des how much she still wanted him, needed him, and wondered whether that was down to her new name. Rita was the old her, full of wants and desires and appetites; Rebecca was goodness and purity. So she stayed silent.

Des became quieter too, letting her know just with the set of his mouth how he wanted her to behave. It was an adjustment, of course, being the wife of a man of God. 'You're not only representing me; you're representing the church too,' Des had said to her one day when she'd worn a dress made shorter by the now sizable bump on her front. And he had a point, didn't he? She had always wanted to belong, but of course belonging came with rules. Even the world she had been a part of before Des had its own unspoken doctrine and dress code, no matter how easy-going and cool they had all pretended to be. She just needed to adjust to this new way of being.

It was the day she made the Victoria sponge cake that changed everything.

One of the only pieces of advice Rita's mother had given her before she left was that she should learn to bake. It was a skill she would need as the wife of a pastor, and 'I can always win your father round with the promise of a Battenberg,' she had said, and she'd pressed a small notebook with red and blue flowers on it into Rita's hands. Inside, she had written all the baking recipes she used, from fairy cakes to date and walnut loaf.

Rita had started to use baking to fill up the long days while Des was out 'tending to his flock', and found the process soothing and the outcome magical. Des's approval of her efforts was the best thing of all. She practically hummed with pleasure every time he took a bite and nodded his head in approbation. She'd not tried a Victoria sponge yet though, and on another searingly hot day at the end of a seemingly never-ending series of hot days, towards the final stage of her pregnancy, Rita decided to make one for the church's bake sale that coming weekend.

She was hot, the house was hot, even with all the windows and doors wide open, and whether it was that, or the fog in her brain that seemed to be constant in those days, she didn't follow the recipe correctly. The cake, when it came out of the oven, was flat and dense. Rita knew it wouldn't pass muster at the bake sale, but given that she and Des had already had a conversation about how waste was 'ungodly', she decided that the two of them would eat it instead.

After dinner that evening, they sat opposite each other at their makeshift dining table. The furniture in their small place was donated by the not-at-all wealthy congregation of the church, meaning that their dining area consisted of a small square table with two chairs that matched neither the table nor each other. Des had at first offered her the higher of the two chairs, but as she and her body had become heavier, she had swapped to the lower one, which meant that Des was now looking down on her in more ways than one.

She had served Des a slice of the flat-looking cake, laughing nervously that it hadn't gone quite as she'd imagined. His expression didn't change as he took a bite, then opened his mouth and let the piece fall back on to his plate, shoving it away from him and towards her.

There was a silence.

Rita got up and took the plate over to the sink before leaning over it to let her tears drip down into the plughole. They weren't tears of upset this time – she had shed enough of those quietly at night, while Des slept peacefully beside her – they were tears of fury. All the pent-up feelings she had managed to swallow down in her efforts to be a new and different person in this new and different place seemed to ignite a fire in her that moment, and when she turned back to him and said, 'Was it really necessary to do that?', her voice sounded higher than usual, the words clipped.

His forehead creased in confusion. 'I'm sorry, what?' he said, as though he might have misheard her.

'Did you have to do that? With your mouth? Just then? You couldn't just be nice for once, couldn't just pretend it was okay?' Rita said, knowing that she was already beginning to gabble, feeling the power being sucked from her by his unwavering gaze. 'It's just, it's just, hard,' she said. 'This, all this . . .' She waved her arm to indicate the house, him, emigrating to the other side of the world, marriage.

Des got up slowly, his movements gentle as if he didn't want to spook her. Rita breathed out, the tears now dripping from her eyes and nose, the anger gone, replaced by sadness and relief at having spoken. She felt her shoulders give, and was readying herself to relax into his arms, when he hit her.

Her head whipped back with the force of the slap, and she staggered backwards, her hands moving automatically to her face, touching the sharp sting of her cheek.

'Oh!' she said, as though this was a surprise.

As her knees began to give way, she became aware of a give between her legs too.

She slowly sank to the floor and looked down at the puddle of water she had created, then back at Des.

'Oh,' she said again, more softly this time, with the realisation that the baby's journey into the world had begun.

Rita had thought back to that day many, many times in the years since. Had wondered whether, if she had done something different, maybe even made the Victoria sponge perfectly, there would have been a different outcome. Every time she played the story out in her mind though, they always ended up in the same place. He was always going to hit her. The only way to change that would have been for her never to have met him, which meant that Jacob would not have existed, an idea she could not tolerate for even a second.

Rita scanned the garden, hoping to find the boy who resembled her son once again. When she found him, she watched him carefully, drinking in every bit of his likeness to her beautiful Jacob. He and Antoinette Chamberlain appeared to be engaged in a heated discussion now, and Rita watched the young girl stalk away from him, leaving the boy standing alone, his face impassive, his eyes expressionless.

Hanna – No. 9

Surrounded by Shane, David and Rosie, who had arrived to rescue her like a ramshackle teenage cavalry, Hanna let herself briefly relax. They crowded on to the bench to watch the world – or at least the party – go by, and Rosie put her little transistor radio on so they could hear the music more clearly. They all bobbed their heads along to Paul Young. David had picked up a packet of Nik Naks from the kitchen and they shared them, passing them up and down the row. Hanna felt something like happiness as they did so. Just briefly.

'Where's Prince gone?' Hanna said, suddenly noticing the dog's absence as he loved cheesy snacks and would have been sniffing around, salivating, had he been in the vicinity.

'He went after Lurch,' David said, as though that was the most normal thing in the world.

'Don't call him that,' Hanna said, feeling somehow defensive of the man now that she'd talked to him. There had been something unexpectedly gentle about him, and she felt a kinship with his awkwardness.

'What's his real name, then?' said Rosie. Hanna

realised to her shame that she still didn't know, but luckily Rosie carried on in her usual fashion, not waiting for an answer.

'Oh. Oh. I love this song,' she said, whispering to Hanna that it was Ned's favourite, before tunelessly singing along to 'Sunday Bloody Sunday' by U2, placing her hand on her heart and swaying, her eyes now closed.

The rest of them rolled their eyes at each other, used to Rosie's dramatics, but they all began to sing along too, and Hanna felt tears start to well with the knowledge of how much she would miss them all. How had she strayed so far from the people she loved? She knew her actions had separated her from them forever. They would hate her when they knew, especially Shane.

'What were you talking to Lurch about anyway?' Shane said.

Hanna realised she hadn't told him about the person in the garden and found she didn't want to. She didn't know why exactly, except that she didn't want to be the focus of everyone's attention, or speculation, or interest. Even Shane's. He would want to talk it through. He might even be worried for her. She wanted this day to be *normal*, or at least as normal as life got these days. She wanted to soak up every last drop of her ordinary life before she left it.

The decision to run away had been gradual. As was the realisation that she was pregnant. With the acceptance she was having a baby came the end of her infatuation with the person who had made her so. Every time she thought about telling him, she imagined him receiving the news with horror. The circumstances under which she imagined telling him were different each time, and she'd pictured many scenarios, but his horror was always the same. In those imaginings she saw a truth that had evaded her before: he couldn't possibly love her.

Rosie, ever the romantic and still a fan of the photo-stories of love and romance they used to pore over together, might have told her, *You never know, what if he surprises you by being happy and says he wants to be with you forever?* But the thought of that response revealed a truth about her own feelings.

This time the imagined horror was hers.

She'd also thought about telling her parents, then remembered the headlines on her father's *Daily Mail*, proclaiming single mothers and so-called broken families to be the source of all the ills of the world, or, as one article put it, 'the scourge of modern society'. She remembered her mum's tuts and head-shakes as she'd read the many columns decrying teenagers who had got themselves into the same situation she had. 'Where are the parents?' she would ask, which Hanna thought almost funny considering what was taking place under her very nose. No, there was no way she could tell them. She had found solace in music instead. Any music, though the melancholy of bands like The Smiths and Joy Division seemed to speak to her particular sadness.

Eventually she realised she could no longer ignore the fact of her pregnancy, and she made a plan. One that involved a long letter and various calls from a phone box on the nearby Blackthorn Estate to her long-term pen pal, Amanda. Amanda was a few years older, and they had met through music, Hanna having won a scholarship to attend a summer school in London a few years before where Amanda was also a student. She was impossibly cool. She looked like Siouxsie Sioux and worked in a vintage shop in Camden, cash in hand, while claiming the dole. She was in a band and wrote songs, mainly consisting of swear words, about overthrowing the government, but she was also the kindest, least judgemental person Hanna had ever met. She also happened to love to crochet. She had already made a blanket for the baby, made of squares of multicoloured yarn sewn together, in contrast to the black she always wore.

Amanda shared a cavernous, colourful squat that seemed to be populated by various waifs and strays, including a single mum with a baby. She understood. Hanna was going to work in the shop until the baby came, and then, according to Amanda, 'We'll figure something out.' It was the conviction with which she declared this that made Hanna decide that this was the right move, and with some relief she realised that she had a way forward that didn't involve her facing the wrath of her mother and the disappointment of her father. She was so out of tune with her family, she would make a new one, she would compose her own.

'Uh-oh,' David said, nudging her, and she looked up to see their mother's wrath heading in their direction. To anyone else she was a smiling vision in florals, but Hanna and David knew just by the set of her mouth that Lydia was furious.

'I've been looking for you everywhere,' she said, her attention squarely on Hanna. 'Mr Allan wanted to say goodbye to you, as he and his wife had to leave, and here you are, lolling about, when I distinctly remember asking you to make sure that people had food and drinks and that things were cleared away.' She paused briefly for breath. 'And instead I find our *neighbour* is doing it instead.' She waved her arm out across the garden, where Hanna could see Rita carrying a glass of water and handing it to a tired-looking, heavily pregnant woman. 'Honestly. She'll be telling everyone that we're *that family* who invite people over, then make them do all the work.'

'Sorry, Mrs Gordon,' chorused the rest of the bench at the same time as Hanna said, 'Sorry, Mum.' Lydia had a way of rousing collective guilt. 'We'll all help, Mrs Gordon,' Shane said. 'What do you want us to do?'

'There's no need for you to do anything. You're a guest in this house, Shane. Hanna can collect all the empty plates and glasses, inside and out, and make a start on the washing-up.' Lydia didn't look at Hanna as she said this, maybe anticipating a fight, but Hanna got up off the bench. 'See you later,' she said to the others, knowing there was no point in arguing.

She decided to go inside first, so that she'd at least have a chance to watch a bit of the concert while she cleared the living room. There were more people in there now, their attention fully on the TV while Bono sang to a mesmerised crowd. There was a quietness in the room, apart from the television, while all the flushed faces stared at the spectacle in front of them. 'Gosh. This is really quite something,' said a friend of her parents to murmurs and nods from the rest of the guests.

Hanna wished she could stay and lose herself in the music, but she didn't want her mum to find her there so she carried on moving things from living room to kitchen, mouthing the lyrics quietly to herself. On her second trip she noticed that the door to her dad's study was ajar. He'd closed it himself before guests started arriving and he'd asked them all to make sure it remained that way. 'I don't want anyone spilling things in here or making a mess,' he'd said.

Her dad's study was his sanctuary. It was the only room in the house where he had any say about the decor, opting for plain walls and dark colours with a desk and a black leather chair behind it. They all called it his *Mastermind* chair, and in happier days he would sit Hanna and David opposite and ask them questions about their 'chosen specialist subjects' in the style of Magnus Magnusson. David's chosen specialist subject was *Danger Mouse* and Hanna's the Top 40 charts, 1980 to 1984. They would both shout 'Pass!' with glee when they didn't know the answer, and sometimes even if they did.

She and David had stopped going in there at all lately, whereas their dad spent more and more hours in the room with the door firmly closed. Hanna often thought it was where he went to escape her mum's instructions and requirements to do things. In the same way that Hanna went to her bedroom, her dad retreated to the study. She had no idea what it was he did in there, except that he would play 'his' music, which was how she knew the words to every Queen song. It was where he had put his brand-new stereo system, stacked high with a state-of-the-art CD player on top. David and Hanna had strict instructions that they weren't to mess around with it.

Hanna moved to close the door when she became aware of voices coming from inside. It was her dad and Uncle Keith, their voices strained.

'So, you won't help me out?' her dad said.

'I just don't think it's a good idea,' Uncle Keith said, his voice firm.

'But I'm your brother! Are you saying you'd rather

see me, Lydia and the kids out on the street than lend me some money?'

'I'm not against lending you the money per se, I'm just saying that you might need to be realistic about your chances of getting another job at your level in the current economy, and it might be worth thinking about changing your lifestyle accordingly instead of borrowing more.'

'I just need to buy myself some time. That's all.'

'Pete. It's been months. Have you even had an interview recently?'

There was a silence.

'What about me getting a job at your place? Working for you?' her dad said, and she winced at the high-pitched desperation she could hear in him. He never sounded like this. His voice was typically low, not emotional like this.

Uncle Keith audibly sighed. 'Pete, that's just not going to happen. We're feeling it as much as anyone. I'm going to be making redundancies myself. Be realistic, man.'

'Well, thanks for nothing, *brother*,' Peter said, the words sounding more like they were spat than said.

Hanna stepped back and hid on the stairs at the sound of her uncle getting up to leave, then watched him walk down the hallway into the living room before she went back to the now closed door. She was standing as close to it as possible, deciding whether to knock and go in, when she heard a muffled sound, almost like a yelp. At first, she thought it was Prince, but when it was repeated, lower this time, she realised her dad was crying. Not just crying, sobbing.

Hanna closed her eyes, wanting to shut out what she'd heard. She felt her entire body slump, as though all the air had been taken out of it. When she opened her eyes again, she was surprised to find that she was still upright. She felt hot tears roll down her own cheeks.

His pain and anguish felt as real to her as if it was her own. Her dad sounded lost and alone, which was exactly how she had been feeling, except somehow this was worse. The change in his mood and the slow withdrawal from the family made sense now. Why hadn't he told them? What had he been doing all day when he got up and put his suit on and 'went to work'? He'd been carrying this alone. And now they didn't have any money left and Uncle Keith wasn't going to help. Maybe they could have helped if they'd known? Maybe they could have made a plan together?

For a moment Hanna thought about whether she should go to him. Whether she should tell him she had heard the conversation. Whether she should tell him that she had messed up too, and that maybe they could tell the truth to Lydia together. But the idea of making things worse for him was too much. Better he thought that she had run away to London to make music than that she was pregnant and had *thrown her entire life away*, a phrase that she could imagine her mum liberally throwing her way if she ever found out. If her dad could keep the truth hidden to protect his family, then so could she.

Steve – No. 20

Steve sat on the kerb outside no. 9. He had made his way out there after the moment with Ryan, needing to be away from other people to settle himself. He folded his gangly limbs into the space between two parked cars at such an angle that no one could see him from the house, while also giving him a full view of Delmont Close. He was used to finding places where he could see but not be seen. He'd learned that in the army. He had also found that this was the position where he could breathe, unobserved by anyone else yet able to scout out any danger.

The place he really wanted to be was at home, in his alcove, but the knowledge that if he went there, he wouldn't go back to the party, and might never have the chance to speak to Ryan again, had stopped him. This would have to do. He could sit here for a while, watch the still, silent street and wait until he felt normal again. With each thump of his heart against his chest the words *I . . . have . . . met . . . Ryan* beat like Ned Thomas's drums, reverberating inside him.

He forced himself to take in the details of Delmont Close, like Cameron had taught him to do whenever he

THE BARBECUE AT NO. 9

got panicky. 'Just be where ye' are,' he used to say, in his wise and frequently annoying way. Steve noted the faint sound of the concert and the chatter from the Gordons' back garden behind him, and in front, the deserted uniformity of the houses in the street. As his breathing began to calm, he chuckled wryly to himself at the memory of Tina watching the first episode of *Brookside* on the TV a few years before. That was when the idea of moving here had first started to take shape.

It was after that terrible day. He'd been on leave after the Falklands, and it was in the hazy time when he hadn't known which way was up, and she had nursed him back to himself, or at least as close to himself as he was ever going to get. The two of them had existed on a diet of Pot Noodles and endless soap operas, from *Coronation Street* to *Emmerdale Farm* and back again.

He found it comforting, watching people's issues play out in familiar-looking places – terraced streets with houses and people crammed together – but *Brookside* was new and different. Tina had kept up a steady stream of chatter while watching it, commenting that she 'wouldn't like to live somewhere like that. No character.' But of course she became, and remained, a devoted fan.

When the adverts for this real-life version of Brookside Close in this new town with its new housing estates and opportunities for new starts had also appeared on the telly, she had gently suggested that this might be what they needed. To get as far away from everything as they could and start again. She had given up her life, and all her friends, and living close to Andy, all for him. The trouble was that all the issues she had hoped to leave behind in their old house had followed them to this new one. Because all the issues began and ended with him.

He was distracted by the sound of the front door of no. 9 opening and turned to see who had left. It was Antoinette Chamberlain, her eyes filled with sadness. His breath caught when he realised that Ned Thomas was close behind her, grabbing for her arm and missing in his unfocused drunkenness.

'Leave. Me. Alone,' Antoinette said, without turning, preventing Ned from seeing the pain clearly etched on her face. 'How could you? With *her* of all people.' Ned shrugged, his shoulders lopsided, his expression unchanging, looking bored if anything.

Ned's eyes followed Antoinette as she walked away, upright and strong at first, but then seeming to almost fold in on herself with each step. Steve watched too, to make sure that she got into the house safely, only whipping his eyes back to no. 9 as the door was slammed, presumably by Ned returning to the party. The sound made his whole body start, as if jolted into life. Once more Steve's mouth felt as parched as the grass of the front gardens. His fists were clenched hard, and his heart felt like a pinball machine, ricocheting around his body.

He had to remind himself once again that he wasn't in a war zone. There was no danger here. No risk involved in sitting on this pavement, or even in being at the barbecue. He was so tired of his body constantly reacting as though there was. It was one of the reasons he hated being out in the world. Back in his alcove, everything was safe, manageable. Out here, he felt bombarded from all sides, on constant alert for what, he wasn't sure.

Before the Falklands, he had never been in hand-to-hand combat. Everything had been like a game of pretend. A training exercise. Even then his body had responded as if it was real, and Cameron had often had to calm him down at the end of each day, the two of them taking long walks around the base together. But the adrenalin hadn't stayed with him, he hadn't carried it like the rucksack filled with bricks they also used on those training exercises, not at first. No, it was only when he had found himself face to face with his first dead body that things changed.

The landscape on the Falklands was barren and bare, reminding Steve of the Highlands. He and Cameron were a two-man team. Cameron would fire while he would be manoeuvring, using grenades to expose where the Argies were hiding. It was after one successful assault that they had come across the dead soldier. Steve had felt like a boy again, like he was in a science class at school. He had stared at the body, which was slumped against a hillock, observing it closely as though he was supposed to write it all down, drawing arrows to point out his knowledge of anatomy.

Now he wished he hadn't recorded the details so closely. Because now he saw it all the time. The sinews and bones of it. It had been a young man, just a boy really. Just like him. It was after that day that he had started seeing images of the body everywhere, flashes of the boy's expressionless eyes at inopportune moments: on the street, in the supermarket, going about his day. It was also that day that Cameron had held him for the first time and rocked him while he sobbed.

Something about the intimacy of that moment had changed their relationship, and where once Cameron had been the cure for his pounding heart and light-headedness, now his presence had begun to cause it. It had made Steve start to withdraw. A withdrawal he now regretted with every fibre of his being.

Yet here he was, withdrawing again. He had felt something between himself and Ryan, some tiny fraction of the feeling he had felt for Cameron, and he had run away once more. He thought of Andy's and Madge's words about going to the barbecue: 'I think it would be good for you.' No doubt they meant something entirely different, but somewhere deep inside himself Steve knew that the smaller he made his life, the lonelier he would be, until it would be just the four walls of his bedroom and nothing else. Maybe it was time to take a step back into the world.

Steve turned his attention to the street and had just

settled into silence, readying himself to return to the party, when the door to no. 9 opened. At almost exactly the same time, he thought he glimpsed a person at the end of the street. Not knowing where to look first, he instinctively chose the threat closest to him, and turned towards the door. It was the woman from no. 15. She was standing on the short pathway from the house to the gate, her eyes glazed with tears. He stood up slowly, not wanting to startle her.

'Are you okay?' he said, injecting a softness into his voice, like you might use on a wounded animal. She didn't seem to hear him at first, but then she glanced at him and he noted how pale she was, almost blanched, her eyes filled with something he couldn't name. He wanted to tell her not to be afraid of him, that he wouldn't harm her, but he knew enough about social interaction to understand that wasn't the sort of thing you said to your neighbours in Delmont Close. That it would in fact be weird, though of course most of them probably thought he was weird anyway.

'Do you need anything?' he said instead. 'Do you want to sit down?' he added, indicating the kerb where he had been nestled, as though it was a comfy armchair.

'I'm okay,' she said, 'it's just . . . it's a long story.'

'I'm Steve,' he said, employing Cameron's distraction tactics. 'I live at number twenty.'

'You're Tina's son, right?' she said, though it wasn't really a question. 'I'm Rita, just moved into number fifteen.' Steve nodded, unsure what to say next, not being used to polite chit-chat, especially not with someone who looked as shaken as the woman in front of him.

'I will sit down actually,' Rita said. 'Just for a minute.' She slowly walked over to Steve, then sat on the kerb. He sat back down next to her and the two of them stared out at the close.

'So, what made you move to Delmont Close?' Steve said, trying to flex his underused conversational muscle. He wasn't sure whether the question might be considered nosy, or whether this was an accepted level of neighbourly curiosity, but either way, he expected one of those replies that is full of words but says nothing. What he got instead was a long silence.

'It's funny. I moved here to start again. To build a new life for myself,' Rita eventually said, then paused once more, the silence so long this time, Steve wondered whether that was all she was going to say. He was just about to open his mouth to respond when she carried on.

'Yet everywhere I look I see reminders of the past, and I seem to spend more time thinking about the past than I ever did when I was living in it.' She followed this with a short barking laugh. 'Sorry,' she said. 'I have no idea where that just came from. It's been ... well, it's been quite the afternoon.'

Steve nodded. He knew what she meant. It had been quite the afternoon for him too.

'I thought I'd be safe here,' she said, and Steve

THE BARBECUE AT NO. 9

wondered what had been unsafe about where she had come from. 'But it turns out when you've been afraid for long enough, you take the feeling everywhere you go.' She laughed again, the same barking sound with very little humour in it.

'Wherever you go, there you are,' he murmured, which was another thing that Cameron used to say. Then, before he'd even thought about it, he added, 'You're about as good at small talk as I am.'

This time they both laughed, really laughed, Rita's face transforming as she did so, the sadness or fear he had sensed earlier dissipating. With that, Rita seemed to take him in properly, unashamedly studying his face while they sat there. He wondered what she was observing; what kind of person she thought he might be.

'I don't see you very much, do I?' she said eventually. 'Around the close, I mean.'

'I don't come out that often,' he said.

'Like Boo Radley,' she said, her voice almost a whisper, though he didn't know who that was.

'The kids call me Lurch,' he said.

'I mean, it's not as applicable, but it works, I suppose,' Rita said. 'But you came out today.'

Steve sensed the question mark at the end of the words. 'Yes,' he said. 'I'm not even really sure why.' He found he could no longer work out why he had come to the barbecue. He didn't know whether it had been in the hope of finding the person watching the close, or pleasing his mum, or meeting Ryan. He wasn't even sure it mattered.

The thought of the watcher reminded him of the figure he had glimpsed earlier, and he looked towards the end of the close. There was no one there of course, and he wondered whether there had been anyone there at all. Maybe he was seeing things that weren't there? Maybe, like Rita, his head was still in the past, and in dangers long gone. Then he remembered what Hanna had said about the person in the garden. Could his instincts be right? How was he supposed to know when to trust them and when not to?

'Well, I'm glad you did,' Rita said, leaning her body over to his and giving him a little nudge. Steve felt himself flinch at the touch of another person but managed to stay where he was. He liked this woman. It was okay to be leaned on.

'It's good to finally meet someone on Delmont Close who's as awkward as I am,' Rita said, and they smiled widely at each other. The door to no. 9 opened again and his mum appeared in the doorway, blue dress glistening in the sun like a sapphire. Prince ran around her and down the path towards Steve and Rita.

'Oh no!' said Tina. 'Stop, you damn dog!' But he scampered on and landed between the two of them, spinning like a whirling dervish from one to the other as though he couldn't choose which to be closest to. Steve got to his feet. There was a vulnerability in his mother's

THE BARBECUE AT NO. 9

eyes as they exchanged glances. She'd come looking for him, of course she had.

Steve held his hand out to help Rita up. 'We're coming back in,' he said to his mum, whose expression changed to one of curiosity when Rita appeared from between the cars. The three of them trooped back inside no. 9, Prince following at their heels.

Hanna – No. 9

Hanna suddenly wanted to see Rosie more than anyone else. She felt frantic with the need to unburden herself; everything she had been carrying felt too heavy for her to hold for a moment longer now she had overheard the conversation with her dad and Uncle Keith. She looked around the living room for her friend, then peered outside the patio doors. She couldn't immediately see her, so wandered into the garden, scanning the glowing pink faces and glazed eyes and listening out for her friend's chatter. She passed Shane and David, who were now standing with Shane's parents. 'You seen Rosie?' she said as she passed, but Shane shook his head and David shrugged.

She had just got to the bench at the end of the garden when she heard Rosie's voice, coming from the direction of the alleyway. Though it was muffled by the fence and the noise of the party, she immediately recognised the edge to it, her hearing attuned to the nuances of her friend's emotions. They had been in enough scrapes together for her to know that Rosie was frightened.

'Stop it,' she heard Rosie say, her voice now clearly

anguished, and all thoughts of everything that had happened in the last hour were replaced by a fierce need to protect her. She moved straight to the lopsided garden gate and wrenched it open, then looked down the alleyway. At first, the tangle of limbs against the fence made no sense, and she couldn't see who was with Rosie until Ned Thomas turned around, allowing her friend to wriggle out from under him, pulling her open blouse back together again, and scrambling over to Hanna.

Ned smiled lazily at Hanna, slowly buttoning up his jeans without trying to hide the fact. 'Hey,' he said to her, as though they were just passing each other in the street.

'Leave. Her. Alone,' Hanna said, her arm going around Rosie's shaking shoulders. 'Leave her alone,' she repeated, feeling a surge of fury at this boy, alongside a twisting knife of guilt that she had not warned Rosie about who he was. Ned's expression did not change as he sauntered away from them down the alleyway, his fingers moving to his forehead in a salute. Rosie slumped against her.

Hanna held on to her friend and the two girls sat down, their backs against the fence, side by side. Hanna could feel her whole body vibrating. Rosie, on the other hand, was still and pale. Her usually noisy, vibrant friend looked small and frail.

'Did he . . .?' Hanna began to ask, then stopped and steadied her voice. 'Did he . . . hurt you?' She didn't have the words for what she was really asking, only hoped and prayed that he hadn't got that far, while knowing that however far he had got, her friend would be changed. Because she had been changed too.

Rosie shook her head vigorously, the pink in her cheeks coming back.

'He didn't get the chance,' she said. Hanna felt some relief.

'I just, I don't understand what happened,' Rosie carried on, averting her gaze. 'I mean, we came out here, and we were kissing, and it was . . . okay, nice even . . . and then it was like he switched. I don't know how to describe it. It was like a glaze came over his eyes and he . . . disappeared.' She stopped and took a shuddering breath. Hanna could see that a single tear was trickling down Rosie's cheek. 'Then he just wouldn't stop.'

Hanna nodded. She knew exactly what Rosie was talking about. She'd seen the same expression on Ned's face only a few months before.

When Ned had invited her to listen to his band rehearsing and maybe join in with them, she had absolutely believed that was his intention. She had felt flattered that he had even noticed her, believing herself too weird and quiet for the most fanciable boy on the estate to even look in her direction. It wasn't that she liked him that way particularly. She knew that everyone else fancied him, but all that mattered to her was that he could play the drums and was in a band. That he loved music too. This alone was enough for her to say yes.

THE BARBECUE AT NO. 9

Her mum had insisted that she take Prince out with her, so that she could clean the house 'and maybe keep it like that for more than five minutes', and the two of them had made their way down the same back alley between the houses where she had just found Rosie and into the shed at the bottom of the Thomases' garden. She had been surprised but not at all worried when she'd discovered that only Ned was there.

'The others will be here soon,' he'd said. 'They're always late.'

He sat at his drum kit, gently tapping out a rhythm on the cymbals while she perched on one of the stools set out for the rest of the band and relieved her sudden awkwardness by watching Prince as he sniffed around the corners of the shed, presumably on the hunt for Garfield, the Thomases' ginger cat.

'Do you play?' Ned said, nodding at one of the guitars leaning against the wall.

'Not the guitar,' said Hanna, 'but I play violin and piano. And I write music and sing sometimes.' She stopped abruptly. She rarely told people she sang.

Ned picked up the guitar and walked over to her, placing it in her hands. 'Have a go,' he said, as she held it awkwardly. Hanna gave the strings a half-hearted strum, while Ned adjusted her hands and arms so that she was holding it correctly. She strummed again and he moved so that he was behind her and positioned her fingers over the frets. She was acutely aware of his proximity and the smell of him, a mix of boyish sweat, spearmint and the faint tang of cigarettes.

'Now,' he said, and it was only then that she realised she had stopped playing. He moved her fingers in an intricate sequence while she continued to strum, creating the vague outline of a tune she couldn't have named. Her brain felt scrambled by his closeness and by her acute discomfort. Oh, how she'd wanted to be the cool girl in front of this cool boy, but in that moment Hanna's overwhelming desire was to run.

She stopped playing again and coughed, but Ned's hand stayed on hers, and his other hand settled gently on her waist. Hanna jumped at his touch, but she didn't move away, a fact that would haunt her in the days after, when she would replay the scene over and over to work out what it was she did wrong. Was it that moment that told him it was okay to go further? Was it her subsequent silence as his hand moved lower, down the front of her skirt? Did he see that as encouragement to touch her like he did? Pressing hard in ways that hurt. She felt as though she had split into two. Outside she was frozen, statue-like. Inside she was a tumult of emotion and her head was screaming, 'No, no, no!' as his hands, and his breathing, felt heavier and heavier.

It was Prince who saved her. Bored of hunting for the non-existent cat, and having explored the shed and all its smells, he turned his attention back to Hanna, running over and jumping up at her, in the way that drove her mum insane, and led to screeching about how 'someone needs to train this bloody dog!' Prince broke the trance Hanna had seemed to be in, and she bent down to pick him up, moving her body out of the reach of Ned's grasping, insistent hands. 'I need to go home,' she said and left, Prince in her arms. Ned didn't say a word.

She hadn't told Rosie about that day; in fact, she hadn't told anyone. What was there to tell? That a handsome boy had touched her and she didn't say anything? She'd worried that Rosie might have thought she secretly wanted him to, knowing how her friend felt about him. And was what he'd done bad? Or wrong? It hadn't felt good, but she hadn't stopped him. Could she blame him for carrying on? Thinking about it made her head go fuzzy, so she stopped thinking about it at all.

Prince stayed close to her in the days afterwards, and she would stroke his silky head, finding the action soothed her, allowing her brain to float free. In the weeks after, when she had got together with *him*, she'd felt similar feelings at first, remembering that day in the shed and how she had felt. But she had told herself it was different. Because *he* loved her. Didn't he?

'You okay, Han?' Rosie said, and Hanna realised her friend was staring at her, concern across her face, even though she was supposed to be the one in distress.

Hour Nine: 6–7 p.m.

Dire Straits, Queen

Peter – No. 9

Peter hadn't even considered that Keith would say no to his request for help. Asking his brother for money had been the last of a very long list of options, all of which he had made his way through over the months since he had found himself unemployed. His reason for avoiding doing it sooner was more about pride and the knowledge that not only would he be beholden to Keith, but that Keith would no doubt frequently remind him of the fact. He had not thought for a second that Keith might say no.

The refusal stunned Peter. His body felt stuck, heavy, separated from his brain, which was in a dream-like state anyway, unable to hold on to any thoughts for more than a fleeting moment. In some ways he was grateful for this, as almost every single one was either a prediction of the inevitable doom he had sentenced his family to, or a reminder of his many failures. He had felt exactly like this on the day they had told him that his twenty-year career was over.

He had been called into Malcolm's office by Janice, his secretary, for a meeting on a Friday at 4.30 p.m. This in itself should have raised his suspicions immediately. He and Malcolm, his boss, had started at FW Savage & Company on the same day. They had attended each other's weddings, and their wives had brought presents on the births of their respective children. They played golf together. They drank pints at the end of long working weeks. They were pals. They didn't only communicate through their secretaries, and they were more likely to be at the bar in the Bull and Butcher at that time on a Friday afternoon than in a meeting.

The second sign should have been the fact that Suzanne, the young girl who made up their newly formed Personnel department, was also present, looking more childlike than usual, and ill at ease in one of Malcolm's huge rotating leather chairs. Prior to that moment Peter had not been sure what exactly Personnel was for, but he had a suspicion he was about to find out.

He could remember very little about the conversation now, but two things about it *had* remained with him. First, that Malcolm – usually a ribaldly funny, always smiling, red-faced man – seemed to have been replaced by a robot. He not only sounded as though he was reading from a script, he really was. His eyes kept drifting down to the piece of paper in front of him, when they weren't looking over at Suzanne for approval. There were no smiles, and Malcolm's normally ruddy complexion looked grey. Under normal circumstances Peter might have felt sorry for him, but these were not normal circumstances.

The second thing he remembered was that Suzanne went to great pains to emphasise that it wasn't *him* who was being made redundant, it was his *role in the company*. This struck Peter as faintly absurd. As if that made everything all right. He had been almost tempted to call her bluff and ask if it would be okay for him to take a different role in the company in that case. Perhaps he might be suited to a job in Personnel, for example, if it wasn't *him* that was surplus to requirements, being thrown on the scrapheap, put out to pasture, and all the other phrases that swirled around his mind as he sat there, mute, and listened to these two people end his life as he knew it.

'No hard feelings, mate,' Malcolm had said while Peter was packing up a cardboard box with all the detritus of the last twenty years of his nine-to-five existence. Peter had looked at him, perplexed. *Mate?* It took every ounce of restraint not to throw his Radio One *Steve Wright in the Afternoon* mug straight at the man's head. He and Malcolm had not spoken since.

Peter peeled himself out of the chair in his study, realising that at any moment one of his family might come looking for him there. He headed upstairs, passing a group of his neighbours coming in the front door. It was the tiny woman from down the road, dressed in a bright blue dress, followed by Rita, who he nodded at in recognition of their earlier exchange, and finally the almost comically tall son of the tiny woman, who everyone called Lurch. Peter smiled to himself, glad to be distracted for a moment, realising they reminded him of that class sketch with John Cleese. Prince trotted in after them, then immediately threw himself at Peter and followed him upstairs.

He had no idea why he gravitated towards Hanna's bedroom, except that maybe it was where Lydia was least likely to look for him. It had been a long time since he had been in his daughter's room. Gone were the days when she wouldn't settle down for sleep until he had sung her a song, her favourite being 'Fat Bottomed Girls' by Queen until Lydia overheard and disapproved, despite his insistence that she had no idea what the song was about.

He would often sing her to sleep, then leave with a kiss on her forehead as she lay curled in her bed, thumb in mouth, Tiny Tears tucked awkwardly under her arm.

Even though he knew Hanna would be downstairs, he knocked on her door first, having been trained to do so by the new, opinionated young person who had replaced his little girl. He could remember taking her to Woolworths to buy her first record with her pocket money. It was Showaddywaddy, and she had played 'Under the Moon of Love' over and over until Lydia limited her to once a day, much to everyone's relief.

THE BARBECUE AT NO. 9

Hanna had since rewritten the story of that first record to being Blondie, Showaddywaddy no longer fitting with the moody persona she now wore like a uniform. Peter missed the younger Hanna in a way that made his heart physically ache.

He was hit first by the smell of Impulse body spray – its musky scent another reminder of his daughter's adolescence – but he realised quickly that despite the room's teenaged aroma and decor, there were signs that the girl he remembered was still there. The walls may have been covered with posters of people he didn't recognise, wearing black, with gravity-defying hairstyles, but lying on her desk were exercise books covered in the colourful flowery doodles she had always drawn when her attention on reading and writing waned, which was frequently. And though the hard plastic Tiny Tears had been replaced too, in its place was the Cabbage Patch doll she had begged for only a few years before. Everyone had wanted one that Christmas and they had cost a fortune, but she had looked at him with those pleading eyes he found impossible to say no to, and given in and bought her one.

She very rarely looked at him now, pleading or otherwise, her eyes skittering away from him if he tried to catch hers in the hope of making her giggle. In fact, no one looked at him at all these days. Unlike Hanna, David was always focused on his schoolwork, his head in a book. He'd never seemed to need his dad in the way that Hanna had.

It would have been fine if he was still working. At least there he had always been the one everyone had looked to for advice or experience. But now that he spent his days driving around in the car, sometimes to the next town over, or sitting in the park, or, if it was cold, in the library, he could go whole days without having eye contact with anyone. The only person who occasionally seemed to notice him was Lydia, but when she did her expression was mostly one of scorn.

It hadn't always been that way. They had met in their late teens and their early days had been as carefree as they were careworn now. At first, he had worked hard because he wanted to give Lydia the best possible life, and his children the childhood he had never had. Peter was the only son of unhappy parents whose lives were haunted by the debt caused by his father's gambling habit. Peter's whole life had therefore been devoted to creating financial security. The problem was that no matter how hard he worked, or how much he earned, it was never enough.

At first, he had blamed Lydia for that. She always wanted more, and appearances became increasingly important to her as the years went on. Lately he had realised that he was just the same. He had been hoping that the house, the car, the hi-fi, the golf clubs, would finally fill whatever hole he had inside him, but he had failed. Not just at filling the hole, but at providing any stability for his family. He was just like his father. He had gambled the family's money on the housing market and Thatcher's promises to reward 'hard work, responsibility and success'. He felt consumed with shame.

The shame was why he hadn't been able to tell Lydia. He'd thought there was no point. He'd tell her once he'd got another job. It would be easy, right, a man of his experience and stature? His first few weeks of unemployment had been buoyed by optimism. He had enough money from his redundancy to see them through and in fact would probably end up using that to pay a chunk off their (very large) mortgage on no. 9 once he started his new job. He upgraded the car, seeing it as a necessary expense in support of his job search, imagining prospective employers seeing him arrive in his shiny new Volvo and thinking, There's a man that's going places. There was no need to ask Lydia to rein in her spending either, beyond a few vague mutterings about the cost of things that she always ignored anyway. He was never very good at saying no to her, or to Hanna, and why should he? He would get another job soon enough.

He began to worry when he was rejected after his fifteenth job application. He was still counting then. He had lowered his sights a little and applied for a job he was more than capable of doing. It paid less than the job he had left but had shorter hours, and he'd decided he would tell Lydia he'd chosen it deliberately so that he could spend more time with her and the family. But they'd declined to see him. Said he was 'too experienced'.

He had followed that up with a particularly humiliating interview conducted by a spotty young man in a shiny, ill-fitting suit called Darren who worked for a firm selling photocopiers. In a voice that sounded as though it had only just broken, he had explained to Peter that the company liked to 'see itself as at the vanguard of office efficiency' and had asked him about his familiarity with the new word processors and fax machine technology. Peter had to admit he'd never used them. His secretary had dealt with all his admin, painstakingly typing up his dictated memos and letters, then taking them to the post room. Nothing he did was of such urgency that it warranted sending a fax. On the rare occasions it was, he would simply pick up the phone and speak to the relevant person. Though he was at least savvy enough not to say it in the interview, he had always seen such tasks as beneath him.

Darren had smirked at his confusion at the question, staring knowingly at Peter, and Peter had suddenly felt as if he was emerging from a long coma to find that the world had changed. Things outside F W Savage & Company seemed to have moved on in the last twenty years and left Peter behind. He felt like a relic from another age.

Eventually he had signed on. He had braved the humiliation of the bleak, grey, damp-smelling waiting room at the Job Centre, full of defeated-looking men, and taken a number, like he was at a downmarket cheese counter. The shame of it was as sharp as a knifepoint. The judgements he had made about people who lived like this ricocheted around his head now that he had become one of them. He told himself that this would be temporary, that it was just to tide them over, that he would be a better man as a consequence of this hardship, but instead he had begun to take on the same defeated look as the grey, middle-aged men he found himself sitting among.

After a while he had become familiar with the people he saw each week and made up stories about them. He imagined their lives outside of the peeling walls and threadbare-carpeted place, giving them all pretty wives and healthy kids, just like his. Whenever he noticed that someone was missing, it gave him a momentary hope that they had found a job, just like he would. He never talked to anyone though, and he definitely didn't want to make friends there. If he did, it would mean he had become one of them.

His redundancy money had run out eventually, of course. Much quicker than he'd expected, thanks to the new washing machine Lydia had ordered, the bike for David, and Hanna's various musical requirements. Now his benefit money was the only thing they had coming in, and it simply didn't touch the sides.

He had stopped paying the bills a while ago. He remembered a trick he had learned from his father and would delay leaving home each morning until the postman arrived, intercepting him on his way out to keep the truth from Lydia a little longer. He felt shot through with shame that he was following in his father's footsteps, but then as his primary emotion was shame by that stage, what difference did more of it make? He'd kept on top of the bills to start with, using his time to write long letters and call people and negotiate payment plans from phone boxes with the sour tang of urine and other unnamed substances. Now, he just ripped up the brown envelopes with *DO NOT IGNORE. FINAL DEMAND* stamped on them in red letters and scattered the tiny pieces into separate bins.

Peter had no idea how long he'd been sitting there, on his daughter's bed, when he was roused by what felt like a roar from downstairs and what was unmistakably the opening chords to 'Bohemian Rhapsody'. Queen must be on. Something in him perked up, and he imagined Hanna groaning and her eyes rolling at what she now called 'dad music', but he knew she would want to watch. She loved them as much as he did. He would go down there and find her, and they would watch them together. Then he would work out what he was going to do.

'Come on, Prince,' he said, before realising that the dog was snuffling around in Hanna's school bag and had half-pulled it out from under the bed. She would be furious. Peter leaned over and shooed Prince away, pulling the bag all the way out and lifting it on to the bed to zip it back up again before he replaced it. He didn't intend to look inside. It seemed to him as though the thing just presented itself to him, hanging from the wad of tissue unravelled by Prince.

He knew what it was straight away, he and Lydia having tried for a third child a few years ago. His failure as a man had been underlined by plenty of these sticks. Now his failure as a father was being revealed by one. All the while he'd been worrying about not being seen by his family, he'd made everything about him, his life, his mistakes. In doing so, he had stopped seeing his daughter at all.

Rita – No. 15

Rita wondered what on earth had come over her. Something about the stillness of Steve and the way he listened had loosened the tight, coiled spring of tension inside her body. She'd felt herself relax for the first time in months, maybe years. She had been wholly herself for just a few minutes with this person she hardly knew. It was freeing. It was also intoxicating. She wanted more of it.

She was now back in the garden of no. 9, sitting with Steve and Tina on the uncomfortable wrought-iron chairs. She recalled being in Davina's garden earlier and smiled. At least these were matching, she supposed. The thought prompted her to look around for Davina and the girls, not having seen them for a while. She heard her before she saw her. Davina was standing with the O'Learys, laughing raucously, almost snorting. This woman seemed to have no vanity. There was no checking around her to gauge the reactions of the other guests. It made Rita feel awkward at first, as she looked around to see who might disapprove of Davina's exuberance, or the volume of her laugh. But the day had been a long one and most people seemed to be drunk, chatting away or lost in their own world. No one appeared to notice this woman laughing. Only Rita.

The thought suddenly struck Rita that if someone did notice, and didn't approve, why did that matter? What difference would it make to anything? It certainly didn't seem as though it would matter to Davina. Rita realised she had almost forgotten what it was like to be that unselfconscious in public. Yes, she had had her moment outside with Steve, but as soon as they had come back in, she had felt her body stiffen with what she thought was expected of her. She had almost felt herself shrinking as they stepped back into no. 9.

The change was accelerated by the fact that as they had stepped in the door, Rita had turned back, just briefly, and thought she caught a glimpse of the figure she had seen in the alleyway earlier, in the baseball cap. It was only a flash of something, but definitely a person standing at the corner of Delmont Close, still and staring, silhouetted against the early evening sun. Despite the heat, she had shivered. This time she was sure it was a man.

This second sighting had jarred her. Could this be someone looking for her after all? Had they been sent to find her? If so, why weren't they making themselves known? Were they just here to report back on her whereabouts? That didn't make sense. Whoever it was and whyever they were there, they had unsettled her. Back at the party, she had returned once more to the state of constant vigilance she had been in since the day she had given birth to Jacob.

Des had immediately been filled with contrition after the moment in the kitchen. He had scooped her up in his arms and got her to the hospital as quickly as their beaten-up old car – bought with contributions from the church congregation – could get them there. He talked at her non-stop the whole way, asking – no, begging – for her forgiveness and promising over and over that it would never happen again. 'I don't know how it happened,' he kept saying, as though it was nothing to do with him, it was just a thing that had occurred and he was as baffled as she was at what had caused it.

He had kept to his word, at least for a while. He'd fallen in love with Jacob as soon as he saw him, and it seemed that the birth of their son had given him a whole new perspective on her too. It was as if she had been transformed into someone more holy by becoming a mother, and she was so relieved that, to her present-day shame, she basked in the glow of the new reverence he seemed to have for her.

They were a family.

The following year was the happiest of her life. She was surprised by just how naturally and quickly she adjusted to motherhood as her primary role, the woman she had been before Jacob feeling like someone else entirely. Jacob was an easy baby, which Des put down to their skill as parents, but she suspected it was her son's nature. She had never articulated it out loud, but in her mind, something about the violence immediately preceding his birth had, like Newton's law, caused an equal and opposite reaction in her son. He was peaceful and calm from the moment he arrived in the world. She let her husband believe that it was down to them, knowing it would benefit her if he saw her as at least partially responsible for their son's gentle temperament.

The sheen of new motherhood wore off though. Once Jacob started walking, talking, and causing chaos in the home, as toddlers are wont to do, Des began to complain. At first, he would deliver his criticisms in benign-seeming comments. He would come home at the end of the day, survey the apocalypse-like scene caused by toys, food and various discarded items of clothing, and say things like, 'Hasn't my handsome boy made a mess.' She was wise to this though, she'd been through it before and knew where it ended, so she started to make sure that the house was neat and clean by the time he arrived home.

He began to comment on other women in his congregation too. 'Alice Henderson has snapped right back into shape, hasn't she? After two children as well. Terry is a lucky man,' he said one afternoon after church when she had just served his roast dinner, a tradition he insisted she keep, despite it being uncomfortable to prepare in the heat of an Australian summer.

She had only eaten half of what was on her plate that afternoon, and from then on stopped eating at all during the day, existing on salad in the evening, despite her almost constant light-headedness. She soon returned to her pre-Jacob weight. Anything to keep hold of the feeling of the first year of Jacob's life, a feeling she had craved forever, that of being safe.

She began to anticipate where Des's critical eye might land, and her life became a series of delicate manoeuvres in order to keep ahead of his disapproval. After a while she could hardly recognise herself at all. She stopped wearing make-up (for fear of being considered 'worldly'), she started wearing loose clothes to cover up her newly lean body (for fear of being 'enticing'), and she grew her hair long (in the hope of being more 'biblical'), and it worked.

Somehow, she navigated Jacob's childhood without any major wrongdoing in her husband's eyes. Yes, she sometimes needed instructions on how she should behave and appear, and she suffered at the hands of his silent anger when she didn't, but thanks mainly to his busyness with the church and his duties as pastor, much of her time was spent alone with Jacob, which suited her just fine. Rita began to feel as though she had cracked it, as if Des's moods were a code she just needed to decipher in order to make everything all right.

This ended abruptly on a trip to Sydney when Jacob was thirteen. Des positioned it as a reward for her 'making an effort'. It was really a chance for Des to meet with senior church leaders at their headquarters, where he was hoping for the chance of a new, bigger placement. 'It's time for me to spread my wings,' he had said. Jacob went to stay overnight with a friend, the son of one of the many women who clucked around both him and Des at church. Rita was jittery and anxious at the thought of being so far away from her son, but she had already learned to hide those feelings. Once, when she told Des that she was missing Jacob when they had gone out for a rare evening by themselves, Des remarked, 'You don't want to raise a mama's boy,' and she knew not to mention it again.

It was a long time since she had been in a city, and at first she was overwhelmed by Sydney's noise and bustle. She held tight on to Des's hand and stayed close to him, which he approved of, saying, 'I've got you' in a proprietorial tone, like she was a prized possession. When she thought about that now, she cringed at how that had made her feel at the time. She had mistaken it for love. She felt newly intoxicated by her handsome husband, like she had in their early days.

Eventually though, she remembered the buzz of being in London in the sixties, and who she had been then, though the green-and-cream buses in Sydney were very different from the red double-deckers of home. They passed the House of Merivale on Pitt Street and she felt a pang akin to heartache for the Biba boutique her younger self had spent almost every penny she earned in. She wanted to beg Des to allow her to go inside but knew he wouldn't and that the request risked irritating him. Outside the shop there was an ethereal-looking woman, leaning on the wall and smoking a cigarette, a scarf draped loosely around her neck. She was so cool, Rita felt her breath catch in wonder and something curiously like nostalgia. I could have been her, she thought.

The following morning, they decided to walk to Des's meeting at the church headquarters, Rita hoping to have time to return to the House of Merivale while he was in there. As they made their way through the busy morning throng, Rita almost missed someone calling her name until they tapped her on the shoulder.

'Rita, wow! Rita, is that you?'

It had been so long since anyone had called her by that name, she was confused at first. She had got so used to Rebecca, it felt like part of her. She was about to shake her head and explain to whoever it was that they had got the wrong person – in many ways they had – when she saw on turning around that it was Alistair. In the surprise of the moment, she forgot herself and instinctively stepped into his affectionate embrace – before recalling where she was, who she was and who she was with, and moving back to her husband's side.

Rita reached for Des's hand, but he resisted her attempt to touch him by putting his hand in his trouser pocket. Alistair looked from one of them to the other, seeming to sense the tension, then held his hand out to Des, an oddly formal gesture for the man she remembered but then, looking at him properly, she could see he had changed in other ways too, his hair shorter, his clothes smarter. Of course he had changed. So had she since those carefree days. He still had his dark, deep-set eyes though, and she felt like they were looking into her soul.

'Hi, I'm Alistair,' he said, then stared at Rita again, and she realised with a jolt that she should introduce him to her husband, despite every impulse telling her to run away from this situation as fast as possible.

'Alistair is an old school friend,' Rita said, willing him to go along with the lie.

She could hardly explain that Alistair was one of the loose gang of friends and acquaintances she had hung around with in London. That he was something of a drifter then, and an expert pickpocket who had once tried to teach her how to take people's wallets and purses without them ever noticing. How they had spent most of the day running away from people on Oxford Street after she had bungled it each time, then stopping in alleyways to double up in wheezy laughter. How he had been her best friend in the world before she had met Des.

Alistair was a wheeler-dealer. The kind of person who could get anything from anywhere, like the Artful Dodger. He was wily and funny, but actually her overwhelming memory was of his kindness. A moment of sadness hit her like a gut punch. How had she discarded her friendship with this man so easily? He was the only person who had never required her to be anyone or anything other than herself. She looked at him now and saw that kindness still reflected in his eyes.

'And this is Des, my husband,' she said, suddenly curious about what Alistair was doing there, while at the same time needing the situation to be over. The awkwardness of this meeting of the two, disparate parts of her life was suddenly so excruciating it felt like it might cleave her in two.

Des nodded at Alistair, his expression unchanging, though Rita could feel the rage coming off him in waves and he did not take the hand proffered to him. Thankfully, Alistair took the hint. There was no point in starting a conversation about how they came to be here and what had happened in the years since they had seen each other. Instead, he smiled and said, 'Well, it's lovely to bump into you,' at the same time as Des looked at his watch and began to say, 'We've got somewhere to be.'

Rita felt Alistair's eyes following her as they walked away.

The relief she felt was soon replaced by fear. How was Des going to react? What would he say? Or do? What should she say? Or do? Her mind scrambled for answers like reaching for footholds to avoid a sheer drop. She had nothing to cling to. She just had to wait. They walked down the street in silence, Des increasing his pace with each step until she was almost running, pushing her way past people, apologising as she bumped shoulders and arms with passers-by in her efforts to keep up with him.

When they reached the building that housed the church headquarters, Des simply said, 'Wait here,' before leaving her on the pavement outside. There was no chance of Rita going back to Pitt Street now. She did exactly as she was told, her eyes pinned on the office doors and the lopsided signage that said 'New Pentecostal Church of Australia', and waited for her husband.

The new placement didn't happen.

'The meeting didn't go well,' Des said when he came back an hour later, his face flushed and his voice ominously low, the words almost muffled by his clenched jaw. He didn't need to tell her it was her fault; his hardened expression made it clear that she was responsible. He waited until they had travelled home to hit her, but by the time he did, it came almost as a relief. The anticipation inside Rita had reached a level where it was unbearable; she flinched at every movement he made and cringed at every word. *Just get it over with*, she wanted to scream at him.

This time the violence was sustained. Eventually, he left her crumpled in a heap on the floor, telling her to 'clean yourself up before I get back'. Then he went to collect Jacob. The mention of her son's name hurt almost as much as the numerous kicks to her ribs, as she realised that, whatever happened, she must protect him, both from his father and from ever knowing what he had done. It was the thought of her boy that stopped her leaving that day and many others afterwards, along with the knowledge that she had nowhere to go.

Some weeks later, she discovered the piece of paper in the handbag she had taken on the trip to Sydney, unused since. *If you ever need anything, A.* was written on it, with an address and telephone number. She thought back to that frantic walk after they had met Alistair on the crowded street, and the bodies she had bumped into as she'd raced after Des. Had Alistair put this in her bag? How had he known?

She had folded the piece of paper up and tucked it between the photo and frame of a picture of her, Des and Jacob, a happy family, they had displayed on their mantelpiece. She didn't know when she would use it, but she knew she could, and it gave her comfort to know that she had it, like an 'in case of emergency, break glass'. She would often stare at the photo while he beat her, weighing up in her mind: Is it bad enough yet? The answer was always no. Until it wasn't.

Rita was brought back to the moment, and the barbecue at no. 9, by Davina smiling broadly and waving exuberantly at her, as though they were long-lost friends who had just spotted each other unexpectedly. Rita waved back, flooded with a sense of certainty she had not experienced for some time. She realised in that moment that the invisible bars on the prison her relationship with Des had kept her in were still as real to her now as they had been then, but they didn't have to be.

That is what I want, she thought, watching her neighbour as she walked towards her. I want to be like Davina. I want to feel safe enough to be myself.

Steve – No. 20

Steve surveyed the garden while they finished up what was left of the charcoal-like sausages and burgers from the barbecue. 'Let's get you something to eat,' his mum had said as they returned to the party. Steve knew she had rightly sensed that he needed something to focus on if he was going to stay.

'There's still plenty of food left,' she'd pointed out, then whispered, not very quietly, 'I don't think Lady Di and her friends eat anything other than lettuce leaves.' She had proceeded to pile her plate high with the most burnt-looking sausages she could find. *The more burnt the better* was her motto when it came to most food, but Steve never complained. How could he?

The party was beginning to thin out a little, with mainly the residents of Delmont Close left in attendance plus a few stragglers, including the small group of outcasts he considered he and his mum to be a part of, consisting of the O'Learys and Davina, along with a couple he didn't recognise.

He couldn't see Ryan though. He tried to tell himself that this would allow him to observe his other neighbours and look out for the watcher, but then he spotted Ryan's mum standing with Davina, and took a sharp breath. Maybe he was still here after all. The feeling was something like excitement.

Cheers from inside the house drew them all to see what was happening in the living room, and Steve trailed after his mum and Rita into the now packed space where every available seat was taken and it was standing room only. There were so many people in the room, Steve's breath became shallow and his eyes scanned the area for the exits. He was about to leave when his gaze landed on Ryan, who, on spotting them, signalled them over to stand with him.

Was it him who Ryan had seen, or the rest of them? Steve wondered. Did that mean Ryan wanted to stand next to him? Was he just being polite? Either way, his feet seemed to move of their own accord and he found himself standing next to Ryan before he had even thought it through. His whole body seemed to gravitate towards him. All other eyes in the room were glued to the television and it was only then that Steve realised the room was silent except for the music. He turned to the screen himself.

Freddie Mercury from Queen was at the piano singing 'Bohemian Rhapsody', accompanied by the entire Wembley audience. He felt the hairs on his arms rise and an inexplicable lump form in his throat. The opening of 'Radio Ga Ga' brought another cheer from the occupants of the Gordons' living room as well as those of Wembley Stadium. At the chorus, Hanna and her friends began clapping to the beat, and soon the whole room was clapping along in time with the audience, their arms above their heads in perfect synchronicity.

Steve remembered the strangely connecting feeling of being on parade, where every movement was timed to perfection. He felt a wave of emotion he could not explain, which was only heightened when Ryan turned towards him and smiled, his arms in the air too. Freddie stalked across the stage, and it was all Steve could do not to cry. He had almost forgotten the beauty of being entirely in the moment, not scanning his surroundings for danger. Freddie held all of Wembley and, it turned out, all of no. 9 Delmont Close in his thrall. It was magical.

The spell was eventually broken by Mike Wilson, who was standing next to Ryan. 'Wouldn't want to bump into him in the toilets backstage now, would you?' he said, flapping his hand in what Steve guessed was supposed to be an effeminate way.

'Mike, you are naughty,' one of the women next to him said, slapping his arm affectionately. She was giggling, while the men sniggered. Hanna, who was sitting on the edge of the sofa in front, turned around and stared at Mike, her expression unreadable.

'He's not one of them, is he?' said Gerald Chamberlain. 'I like Queen.'

THE BARBECUE AT NO. 9

'It doesn't stop you liking Queen, Gerald,' said his wife with a sigh. She seemed to have stopped crying now, Steve noted.

'I don't want to be mistaken for a poofter,' Gerald said, laughing, as Mike and the rest laughed along. Steve sensed rather than saw Ryan's reaction. Felt the body next to him go rigid. His instinct was to touch Ryan on the arm, to comfort or reassure him, he wasn't sure which, but he too just stood there, not moving a muscle. Mike cracked another joke that made the others laugh again, and Ryan turned away, leaving the room and heading back out to the garden. Steve was rooted to the spot.

The moment brought back all the mutterings about Cameron by the rest of the lads, the jibes at his friend that he didn't fully hear or was unsure about the meaning of, or simply blocked from his mind. At the time he had told himself it was because Cameron was bookish and less quick to join in the banter and jokes of everyone else. Now that felt naive of him. He knew exactly why Cameron had been a target. Though they had never spoken of it, he had known Cameron was just like him from the start, and he had long wished more than anything that he had told him that, instead of pulling away from him after they returned from the Falklands.

When Steve had left the army and come home, Cameron had gone to serve in Germany, and they had lost touch entirely. He had done nothing to support his friend, and he had not been honest with, or about, himself. He regretted that choice every single day, though at the time it had felt as though he hadn't had a choice, and now here he was. What should he do?

He was just about to go after Ryan when the door to the living room was flung open with a violence that made the whole room stop. Everyone turned away from the spectacle of Queen to that of a dishevelled Peter Gordon standing in the doorway, eyes bloodshot, face full of rage.

Hanna – No. 9

The contrast between the moment her dad appeared in the doorway of the living room, and the moment before, was almost too much for Hanna to process. Just before, she had felt, for a fleeting few minutes, truly happy. After what had happened with Rosie, the two of them had sat in the alleyway for a little while, listening to the music in the distance until they heard the opening to 'Bohemian Rhapsody'. All the memories of sitting on the rear seat of the car with David, with Dad driving, and them all singing along to the parts at full volume, including her mum, had come flooding back.

Rosie had smiled at her, as though the incident with Ned was all but forgotten, and Hanna had marvelled at her friend's ability to bounce back. 'Come on!' Rosie had said. 'Let's go and watch it,' and the two had headed, hand in hand, to the living room where the adults, in particular Lydia, were all so tipsy that they didn't particularly care about what Hanna and her friends were up to any more. She, Shane, David and Rosie all finally got to watch the concert together.

Shane had held her hand while they watched until

'Radio Ga Ga' came on and the whole room erupted. She had wanted to laugh out loud with the joy of it. Even her mum was singing with abandon, awkwardly clapping along, holding a shoe in each hand, clearly drunk and not so Krystle Carrington now. She had wanted to say to her mum, 'This is it. This is why music matters. This is why it's not silly and pointless.' She had felt swept away by it. She had wanted her dad.

Mike had almost spoiled it, but even that was a positive thing. In a few simple sentences any remainder of the crush she had once harboured was dismantled with his casual bigotry and interruption of what felt to her like a sacred moment. She had always been aware that her feelings for him weren't real, that it was an innocent crush, the kind teenagers were supposed to have and not act on. In her case it had always been a distraction from thinking about the very real issues she was struggling to face. She felt almost ashamed that she had ever thought he was nice, or cool, or any of the things she had thought about him. It was as though she was seeing him clearly for the first time. She wanted to laugh at the freedom of it. He was a creep, how had she not seen it before? If only her feelings for the baby's father were as uncomplicated.

She was so wrapped up inside her head, she almost didn't realise that the door had swung open, and it was only Shane's horrified face that made her turn around to see her dad standing there, his eyes unfocused and watery. In that moment, everything seemed to slow down. She heard her mum's voice saying, 'Peter? Pete?' while her dad's eyes roamed the room. He was searching for someone, and she wondered who it might be. She thought about the conversation she had overheard – was it Uncle Keith? Did he want to continue their argument? Lydia would go mad if he tried to do so in public. Her dad's eyes found hers and his expression changed. It looked like heartbreak. Then his gaze moved to Shane and his eyes became filled with white, hot rage.

Oh God, he knows, she thought. He knows.

Several things seemed to happen all at once, as if a giant pause button hovering over the room had been released. Her dad strode towards Shane, at the same time as Lydia moved towards her husband, her lips taut, face serious, all the drunk playfulness of only minutes ago gone. Hanna was about to move, to stand in front of Shane, to explain, to defend, to at least do something, when she felt Lurch take hold of her and pull her out of the way. She was going to shout at him when she realised that he was standing in front of Shane in her place, his pale, calm face looking down at her dad's red, spluttering one as he tried to get to Shane.

'Get out of my way,' her dad said through gritted teeth, pulling his arm back. The room took a collective breath in, and Hanna closed her eyes; she couldn't bear to watch her beloved father punch this sad, tall man. She opened them again almost immediately, realising it hadn't happened. Instead, Lurch had hold of her dad's arms, holding him back as though he was nothing.

'You don't want to do anything to that boy,' Lurch was saying, his voice quiet yet firm, his stance powerful, unyielding. 'Trust me. You don't.'

Prince seemed to appear from nowhere and stood between Lurch and her dad, his head to one side as though puzzled. The sight of him seemed to take all the potential violence out of the room. The fight left her dad's body at the same time as Hanna became aware of Shane's parents at the patio doors, alerted to the commotion somehow. Hanna finally looked at Shane, whose frightened eyes flickered between her and her dad, searching for something in their faces that might explain what was going on.

I'm so sorry, Hanna mouthed, hoping that he understood her, while knowing that once he knew what she had been keeping from him, he would never understand. He looked like the boy he was, not the man he was growing into, and Hanna was sideswiped by the guilt she felt for the situation she had placed him in.

'Peter,' Bob Mitchell said, moving at unusual speed until he was standing with Lurch and Prince. 'Is there a problem here?'

Hanna saw that, unlike earlier, her boyfriend's dad looked tall and solid, any sense of him not being confident, or not belonging in this house, completely gone. He was the strongest presence in the room other than Lurch.

THE BARBECUE AT NO. 9

'No,' Hanna found herself saying, her voice coming back to her slowly. 'No. It's just a misunderstanding. That's all it is. Just a misunderstanding. Right, Dad?'

She looked into her exhausted father's eyes, begging him to read the plea in hers to stop this. Bob led Shane away while Lydia seemed to snap into hostess mode and recognise that their social standing was teetering on the edge of a precipice. She clapped. Actually clapped. As though they were a roomful of primary-school children she needed the attention of, and any moment she might put her finger to her lips and instruct them to do the same. Hanna would have found it funny if the whole situation weren't so awful and if she couldn't hear the thinly disguised pain in her mother's voice.

'Please do carry on enjoying yourselves,' her mum said to the staring audience. 'Hanna here will get you any more drinks you need, and I will see to my husband, who may have had a few too many.' Then she tittered before leaving the room, as if this had been a minor indiscretion and not what everyone in Delmont Close would be discussing in the morning, like the latest episode of *EastEnders*.

Hour Ten: 7–8 p.m.

Queen, David Bowie

Hanna – No. 9

Hanna didn't know who to go to first, Shane or her mum and dad, then something inside her clicked into action, some sense of loyalty to her mum more than propriety, and she nodded at David. Without exchanging a word, the two of them began collecting glasses and cups and taking orders for drinks, and the room eventually turned back to the television, with low mutterings she knew would be expanded on later, when everyone got home. She could already imagine them discussing what had happened at the barbecue at no. 9 over their cornflakes and hangovers the following morning.

Hanna knew she would have to face her mum and dad at some point, but she would at least try to salvage a little of their reputation before then and give herself the breathing space to decide exactly what she was going to tell them, and how. Her hands shook as she picked up glasses and the paper plates that were strewn across the pine dresser, but she focused on the task as though there was nothing more important that she should be doing.

'Hanna . . . are you okay?'

She felt a gentle touch on her arm, and the woman

from no. 15, Rita, steered her through the living room and into the now empty kitchen. She removed everything from Hanna's hands and pulled out a chair from around the dining table for her to sit in, her eyes never leaving Hanna's, her face filled with gentle concern. 'Shall I make us a cup of tea?' she said, putting the kettle on. Hanna didn't drink tea, but saw it and accepted it for the act of kindness it was. She nodded, and while Rita made them both mugs of milky tea, she looked around the kitchen, in all its pineness.

As she did so, she realised something she had never noticed before: she couldn't see her family in it. Instead, there was only the impression that her mum wanted to give of the perfect family, only vaguely reminiscent of the real people who lived here. There was none of the music, laughter and mess that she knew they consisted of, or at least they once had. It was all beige wood and gadgets and carefully curated trophies of success and aspiration, with no room for people. Especially not people with problems who made mistakes like Hanna, and, as she had discovered today, her father.

Rita put two steaming mugs in front of them and sat down. 'Now, you don't have to tell me what's going on, it's none of my business. But at the same time, if you want to tell me and you think it might help, I'm here,' she said, then added with a smile, 'But most importantly, where does your mum keep the biscuits?'

'She keeps a packet of Jammie Dodgers hidden at

the back of that drawer,' Hanna said, pointing to the dresser. 'They don't go in the biscuit tin because Mum says they're common, and the biscuits in the tin are *just for show*, apparently.' For some reason Hanna wanted to be honest with this person, warts and all, feeling proud that she'd managed to make even a small confession. 'But I think it's really that Jammie Dodgers are her favourites, because I'm sure the packet is a different one every time I go in there.'

Rita smiled and pulled the red packet from the drawer. 'Well, let's make a dent in these ones, then. I'm a dunker, are you?'

Hanna nodded, and they dunked in unison and quietly munched their biscuits. Something about the ordinariness of the moment in the midst of this extraordinary day made her relax her grip on herself and it was as though a dam had broken. All the emotion she had swallowed down over the past few months spilled from her and she almost hiccupped with the force of each sob. Rita sat next to her and held her hand gently, letting her cry.

When the initial wave of emotion had passed, she finally spoke.

'I'm pregnant,' Hanna said eventually, aware it was the answer to a question that Rita hadn't asked. 'And I think my dad found out.'

Rita continued dunking and eating her biscuit, her expression not changing. There was no gasp, no shaking of her head, no clutching of pearls. The lack of shock gave Hanna the courage to continue. 'I haven't told the father,' she said. 'I wasn't actually planning to tell anyone.'

Rita nodded.

'I've been keeping it a secret, hiding it from everyone, including Shane, who I started going out with before I realised I was pregnant,' Hanna added, unable to stop talking now she had begun. 'I was planning to run away. But now this has happened. It's all just a mess.'

There was a long pause before Rita began to speak. 'I get it,' she said. 'I totally understand why you hid it. I do.' And Hanna believed her, feeling somehow absolved by this woman.

'It's funny, isn't it. When we hide the truth, it's usually for the best possible motives, but then the lie ends up hurting others or ourselves more than telling the truth in the first place would have. It doesn't seem fair.' Rita seemed to have gone somewhere else in her head, but Hanna nodded anyway. 'And maybe the only way through, once you realise that, is to be completely honest,' Rita said, 'because the thing is that no choice is consequence-free. You're either suffering the consequences of the truth or the consequences of the lie.'

Her look was so far away, Hanna wondered if they were even talking about her any more, but then Rita turned towards her again, her eyes soft with compassion. 'I know this feels like the end of the world,' she said, 'but I promise you it isn't. You will get through this. I can't tell you how, but I can tell you that you will. That's the thing about life. It keeps going, regardless. And I speak from experience on that,' she added with a small smile.

Hanna thought about this, about how she had got through the last few months somehow, and even though things had been hard, she was still standing, just. Maybe if she was strong enough to do that, she was strong enough to face her parents' responses to the truth. Maybe that was the right thing to do. She looked at the woman in front of her, who she barely knew but suddenly felt held all the answers. 'Do you think I should go and find Mum and Dad? Tell them the truth?' she said.

'I'm not someone you should really listen to, but if I was, I'd say that yes, maybe that would be a good idea,' Rita said, and Hanna knew she was right.

'You're very easy to talk to,' she said.

'Well, don't tell anyone,' Rita replied, lowering her voice and looking around her, even though there was no one else in the room, 'but I used to be a vicar's wife. It kind of goes with the territory.'

Hanna almost laughed, thinking of the dowdy, cross-faced woman who was married to the vicar of the church Lydia insisted they went to every Christmas, a man who could also be described as dowdy and cross-faced. 'You don't look like any vicar's wife I've ever seen.'

'Yes, well, I'm not one any more,' Rita said, 'but that's a story for another day.'

Hanna wanted nothing more than to hear that story now, to be distracted from going to find her parents, and Shane, and face whatever music was ahead of her, but it seemed as if Rita had disappeared back inside another room in her head and shut the door. When Rita eventually spoke again, Hanna somehow knew that the words she was saying were as much for herself as they were for Hanna.

'You know, I've come to the conclusion that so much of what the Church says is right or wrong is a load of rubbish and it's mostly just men trying to control everyone around them with arbitrary rules that no one can possibly keep to all the time,' Rita said.

Hanna wasn't used to hearing the adults in her life talk like this, and wasn't sure whether to be shocked or enthralled, but chose the latter.

'And then there are those moments when you read something from the Bible, and you can feel the truth of it, right in the very centre of yourself.' Rita's voice was low, her fingers pointing to her heart. Tears began to fall as she carried on.

'John, chapter eight, verse thirty-two. *The truth will set you free.*'

Peter – No. 9

Until recently, Peter hadn't found marriage that hard. He couldn't understand it when his friends, or at least the men he played golf with, his brother included, moaned about their wives and children, as though they were a noose around their necks. He'd certainly never considered having an affair or leaving them, as seemed to be fashionable in his circle as soon as a man got to a certain age. His family were his world, though he would never have said this out loud for fear of being laughed at. It wasn't a thing men admitted. If having affairs was fashionable, expressing emotion was most definitely not.

Peter knew Lydia had her foibles – she was far too focused on what the neighbours thought about them, and she spent too much money, though in fairness she didn't know they didn't have it – but he was also sure of her steadfastness and her love for both the children and him, even if he hadn't seen evidence of it for a while, hidden as it was under her scornful demeanour. They had been going through a difficult patch, sure, but he'd never considered that their marriage might be in real trouble. Until that moment. He felt as though he was waking up from a long sleep, to discover that everything had changed, even though it had all been happening around him; his daughter, his wife... He had never seen Lydia look like she did as she stood in front of him in his study.

She had bundled him in there after the scene in the living room. She closed the door carefully and quietly, though he knew her well enough to know that she had wanted to slam it with some ferocity. He supposed he should be thankful that she was still in sufficient control that thoughts of what their guests might think were still uppermost in her mind. Her expression, however, was clear. She was incandescent with rage.

They say that just before death, a person's life flashes in front of their eyes. Peter hoped it wasn't a sign of the demise of his marriage that he was now seeing moments from the twenty years they had spent together playing out in front of him as though on a cinema screen.

There was the moment they met in the pub, when he had decided to chat her up and, while attempting a confident swagger over to her and her friends, had fallen flat on his face in front of her. Lydia had laughed so hard she had snorted, which made him laugh in turn, and she had agreed to go out with him. He had been smitten from that moment on. More recently there had been the pain of the miscarriages and the grief of losing the babies they both wanted so desperately.

He knew that each one had affected Lydia deeply,

and that she had hardened her outer shell in order to hide her inner pain. She had become brittle, and her relationship with Hanna was the one to suffer. Peter knew that Lydia just wanted to protect their children and give them the best possible start in life, but Hanna was at an age where that was difficult for her to see. He, of course, could have stepped in. Should have stepped in. Instead, he had been almost entirely absent. Was it too late?

'Are you going to tell me what the hell is going on?' Lydia said, her fury just about contained, though he could sense it simmering and knew that what he said now would determine whether it boiled over. If he told her about Hanna, he realised, all Lydia's fury would be aimed in her direction. He could at least protect his daughter now. So, he made a different decision, saying words he hadn't planned to, shattering her world in a whole new way.

'I lost my job,' he said, 'last year.'

For once Lydia seemed stunned into silence. This wasn't what she'd been expecting, that much was clear. Her perfect forehead wrinkled as if he was speaking a language she vaguely recognised but couldn't fully translate. He decided to carry on. In for a penny, in for a pound, as Keith frequently said.

'I didn't tell you because I thought I'd get another one, but I haven't.'

She was still looking at him in confusion. 'But where have... where have you... what have you been doing all day?' she finally said, and Peter couldn't stop his rueful smile. It was so very Lydia to focus on that little detail, on the daily lie he had told in getting dressed for work and leaving in his car every weekday morning. Eventually she would get to the bigger implication, but for now, she needed to focus her attention there. He understood that. Admired it, even.

'Sometimes I've gone for interviews, sometimes I've sat in the park, sometimes I've gone to the library,' he said. 'But always, always I've been thinking about what to do, how to provide for us. I didn't want to worry you with it all. But now . . . well, now there's no avoiding it.'

Lydia's mouth tightened. 'What do you mean?'

Peter took a deep breath. There was no point in hiding how bad things were any more. He knew that saying it out loud would make it real, but the effort of pretending it wasn't happening was almost more exhausting than facing the truth, he realised.

'We've run out of money,' he said. 'Well, actually, we ran out a while ago. I kept thinking it would all sort itself out, that I would get another job, but it didn't happen and now the bills are all overdue and the mortgage hasn't been paid.'

'But . . . I mean . . . What have we been living off? Buying food with? You've been giving me housekeeping money and I've been spending it and . . .'

'I borrowed money,' Peter said, finding a curious relief

in finally saying the words. 'From people I shouldn't have. And the thing is that they want it back.'

There was a long silence while the words sank in.

'Okay, but Keith will help, surely. I mean, I'm the last person that wants to go to Beverley, cap in hand, I can only imagine the triumph on her face...' But Peter was shaking his head, wanting her to know he'd tried everything, that he would never have brought this to her door if he hadn't.

Lydia slumped down into a chair, her face pale, her expression no longer furious but shocked. Peter wanted to hold her, to tell her it was all going to be okay, but given that he was no longer sure it was, he instead sat down too, pulling his chair around to her so that he was close but not touching, not knowing whether his touch would be welcomed. Lydia sat up straight suddenly, as if a thought had occurred to her.

'The intruder in the garden earlier,' she said. 'Was that...?'

Peter shrugged. 'I don't know,' he said, 'but it could have been. They aren't the sort of people who ask politely.'

He watched his wife's face crumple as the tears finally began. Lydia hardly ever cried. Anger was her default emotion. There was energy and action in anger, and he knew she saw tears as a kind of surrender. The sight made his heart physically ache, and yet he had nothing. No solutions, no reassurance. All he had was his enduring love for the woman in front of him and their children. Could that be enough? In the face of their entire lives falling apart?

'I want to put it right,' he said. 'I want to make it all okay. But the truth is that I don't know how.' The admission felt to Peter like jumping off a cliff. His stomach rose with the velocity of it. He always knew what to do, that was his role in life, in this family. He'd never wanted to be seen as anything other than the provider, the strong one, so now Lydia knew the truth, who would he be in her eyes?

The silence between them stretched on, the only sound the faint twang of guitars. Peter could just make out the tune of 'Rebel Rebel' by David Bowie. Hanna loved this song, but Lydia thought Bowie a bad influence who would introduce their daughter to the 'wrong sort of ideas'. Oh, if only it was that easy to differentiate between the good and bad influences, and right and wrong ideas, Peter thought. He leaned his head forward to Lydia and she met him halfway, their foreheads touching.

'I'm so sorry,' he said eventually, realising that he hadn't said the most important thing of all, 'I'm so sorry.'

There was a gentle tap, and Hanna's face appeared around the study door. Lydia sat up straight immediately. The scene in the living room felt like a distant memory and Peter wanted to signal to Hanna not to speak, but her words came out before he could stop her.

'I know you will be really disappointed in me,' she

was saying to Lydia's evident bafflement, 'but the thing you always taught me was to take responsibility for my actions and that's what I'm doing now.'

Peter hadn't cried during any part of the conversation with Lydia, but he felt his throat close at the sight of his beautiful sixteen-year-old standing taller and stronger than he had managed to in the last six months. At that moment, Prince appeared at the door, snaking between Hanna's legs, then ran straight up to Lydia, launching himself into her lap and vigorously licking her face. It was the distraction Peter needed. He got up, went to his daughter and took her hand.

'Your mother doesn't know yet,' he said gently. 'I think we should all sit down.'

Steve – No. 20

In the aftermath of the scene in the living room of no. 9, Steve had been unable to move. He was only vaguely aware of the people around him as they went back to normal, watching the concert, drinking, chatting, the only change being the rustle of gossip about the Gordons and what had just unfolded. He could sense the glee in his neighbours' whispered tones, recognised their joy in someone else's misfortune. It reminded him of everything that had happened in Scotland and why they'd had to move.

He hazily registered his mum asking if he was okay and saying she was going to get him a drink. She had touched his hand, and he hadn't pulled back, had somehow recognised that it was her and not something to be afraid of. This was progress. There was a time when he wouldn't have been able to recognise anyone when he was in the middle of an episode and would have lashed out at her touch. Now, he knew that he had to wait. That this would pass. That he would feel his body once again and be able to move his limbs at will.

When that happened, he fully intended to get out of

this house and go home, to return to the one place where he knew he would be safe. He thought about what the woman from no. 15, Rita, had said to him: *I don't see you very much . . . Around the close, I mean.* This very situation was the reason why, he wanted to say to her now.

People were unpredictable, even people who seemed normal, like Peter Gordon. The only way to protect yourself was to have as little to do with them as possible, Steve had learned. He had also learned that sometimes he was the unpredictable one. That it was other people who needed protecting. Either way, he knew that life was safer without the complexity of relationships, even when those relationships involved family.

The day he had found out about Cameron's death had been a difficult one from the start. It was in the early days of returning home following his medical discharge from the army. He was living with his mum and Trevor in their old home, Trevor having moved in with Tina not long after he'd left, with Andy and his new wife only a few streets away. From the very start, Steve felt as though he was interrupting something, just by being there. His family had settled into new routines and ways of being with each other in his absence, and Steve knew his being home was a disruption.

The morning the letter arrived, Steve had had an episode. They were more frequent then, and more intense. This one had been set off by a team of removal men arriving to move their next-door neighbours. He had still been asleep and the crashes and clangs they made had inveigled themselves into his subconscious until he believed that they were something else entirely and he'd ended up in the corner of his bedroom, naked and cowering. Afterwards he was filled to the brim with the usual sense of shame at the tricks his mind played on him, and fury that he no longer felt in control of it.

Andy and his wife had come round for their usual Saturday morning cup of tea with his mum before going into town to do the big shop. They were sitting around the small kitchen table, where there were four matching chairs. Since he'd returned home, someone, and it was usually his mum, who insisted, had to sit on the spare stool they used to keep in the garage, the inconvenience underlining to Steve that he was an unwelcome addition, someone who didn't fit into this domestic tableau. He often made sure he was going out somewhere to avoid the awkwardness, but he was still feeling fragile that morning from both his hangover and the episode, and so didn't make it out in time.

The letter was from Cameron's sister. She'd enclosed a photograph with the note and Steve stared at that first, drinking in the details. It was of him and Cameron, taken in the first few months of them knowing each other, before the war that had changed them both. The two of them were in civvies, their white T-shirts contrasting with tanned skin from a rare hot British

THE BARBECUE AT NO. 9

summer. His arm was slung casually around Cameron's shoulder. He was grinning at the camera, while Cameron had his face in profile as he looked over at Steve. Just a glance at the expression on Cameron's face told Steve everything he needed to know. He had felt it too. Steve felt all the regret he had held at bay wash over him. He put the photograph down on the table and turned to the letter.

Dear Steven

I hope you don't mind me writing to you. My name is Irene, I am Cameron Hogan's sister. I found your details tucked in one of Cameron's precious books, along with this photograph. He told me about you after he came home from the Falklands, and I was so pleased that he had such a good friend with him, especially out there. For this reason, it felt important to write to you to let you know that sadly, after a short illness, Cameron passed away last month in Berlin. I can imagine your shock, as it was a shock to us all too. Cameron had always been so healthy, but it was a rare form of skin cancer that took him. The only blessing was that it was quick. He didn't tell anyone how sick he was and we only found out ourselves right at the end, but I know he would have wanted you to know. You were important to him.

Irene

'I said, do you want another brew?'

Andy's voice seemed to come out of nowhere, bringing him back to the room. Steve looked up from the letter to see his brother, and everyone else, staring at him, their faces expressing varying levels of concern. He shook his head absently, then read the letter again, breathing deeply to try and control the tremor in his hands.

'Y'all right?' Andy said, his voice quiet as he passed Steve to go and put the kettle on. Steve nodded again, walking slowly out of the kitchen and up to his bedroom, taking the utmost care with each step, having lost all feeling in his limbs, as though his body didn't belong to him any more.

He had no awareness of how many minutes he sat on his bed, looking at the words that no longer seemed to have any meaning, when he realised he had left the photograph downstairs. His body still not his own, he carefully and quietly made his way back to the kitchen where there was only Andy and Trevor left, the women presumably having gone to inspect the two new gnomes Tina had purchased for the garden, one with a fishing rod, the other a ukulele.

With a start, Steve realised that Trevor had the photo in his hands, and Andy was looking over his shoulder. They were both staring at it, their expressions not ones that Steve could read, though in that moment he wasn't sure he could have read anyone's. Everything seemed to

THE BARBECUE AT NO. 9

happen simultaneously. Trevor turned the photograph over and read whatever was written on the back. 'Seems a bit fucking gay to me?' he said, and Steve launched himself at him, punching indiscriminately. There was no room for thought or logic. There was only rage, a rage much bigger than the man in front of him and the words he'd said.

'What the . . .?' Andy said, pulling Steve away from Trevor, who was now cowering, arms over his head in an attempt to defend himself from Steve's bombardment, but Steve could barely hear him, was intent only on violence, and turned to his brother, swiping him across his face, catching his left eye with some force. Andy retaliated immediately, his fist curling around Steve's top, pulling him towards his snarling mouth, when the sound of their mum's voice in the doorway stopped them both in their tracks.

'Boys!'

Steve stared at his brother; one of Andy's eyes was almost closed, the other burning with Steve's own reflected anger.

'What the hell happened here?' she said, but Steve was in no mood for a post mortem of what had taken place. His anger was too big, and he needed to find a way to contain it. He picked the photograph up from where it was now lying – discarded on the floor by a terrified Trevor – and left the house, slamming the door as he went.

He had little to no recollection of what happened next. All he knew for sure, because he had been told, was that he was found some time later by a passer-by sitting in a street miles away, dirty and dishevelled. He had been weeping, hands gripped around the creased photograph. He'd apparently been unable to remember his name or where he lived, and had resisted any attempts to move him, so the police had been called and he'd been taken to a local hospital while they worked out who he was. They had eventually located his mum, who was by then frantic with worry. He'd had a long stay in that hospital. The first of many.

He had apologised to Andy when he came to visit, though it took a while for him to do so. The brothers had shaken hands, but something had shifted between them since that day. There was a guardedness, and it often felt as though they were circling around each other, one waiting for the other to strike. Trevor moved out shortly after. 'Your son is a nutter,' was his parting shot to Tina when he left. That had become the neighbourhood's view too: that he was a 'nutter'. When Steve had returned home, he started to notice curtains twitching when he walked down the street, and people crossing the road if it looked like they might bump into him. Never particularly comfortable around people he didn't know, Steve became painfully self-conscious in public, constantly scanning the horizon for anything that might upset his precarious balance.

THE BARBECUE AT NO. 9

His mum had been careful not to bring anyone new into their home since, managing their lives as if there was an exclusion zone around them, protecting her son, allowing him to feel safe, but the damage was done. The family was now tainted in the eyes of their neighbours, and she had eventually decided that the best thing to do would be to move them to a place where no one would remember 'the incident', as she referred to it. Steve would never forgive himself for the fact that she had effectively given up her whole life for him. He could never allow himself to think about the sacrifices she had made on his behalf, for fear that the guilt would fell him.

His mum appeared in front of him now, drinks in hand, and carefully led him out to the garden, handing him a large tumbler of what looked like whisky. 'Here, drink this,' she said, as though it was medicine. Steve did as he was told, closing his eyes as he swallowed.

He was somewhat surprised when he opened them again to find that everything was normal: the music was still playing and people were still standing around chatting, seemingly enjoying themselves, judging by the smiles on their faces. He often felt like the world stopped when he had an episode, reinforced by the fact that he usually ran away immediately, so he had never actually observed the aftermath. It was interesting to him to see that life went on regardless of the turmoil inside his head.

He was calm enough now to remember Ryan. Had he seen what had happened? Steve looked around the garden, unable to see him. He wondered if he had gone home and felt a curious mix of sadness and relief at the thought. What had he been thinking, coming here, talking to Ryan, allowing himself to hope that there might be a life outside his bedroom, that he might be able to function in the world? He wouldn't make that mistake again.

He turned to his mum, whose gaze had not left him.

'Do you want to go home, son?' she said, and he nodded, knowing that he had been right to avoid the messiness of life, that the barbecue at no. 9 had proved it to him. They left together, his mum not even stopping to say goodbye to everyone in her haste to return him to the safety of their own four walls.

Hour Eleven: 8–9 p.m.

The Who, Elton John

Hanna – No. 9

The conversation with her parents did not go at all as Hanna had envisioned. During the many sleepless nights she had suffered since finding out she was pregnant, she had played the scene over and over like a video recording in glorious Technicolor. In the soap opera version of the story that had kept Hanna awake, her mum had screamed and shouted at her, while her dad had looked on, a disappointed expression on his face, then turned away from her in disgust. This was the move which had broken Hanna's heart, and she had shed more tears at the thought of her dad's heartbreak than her mum's anger.

The reality was more muted.

The three of them had barely sat down before the words spilled out of Hanna. 'I'm pregnant,' she said, forcing herself to keep eye contact with her mum after she had spoken, despite the desire to look away. She expected to see fury or even disgust reflected back at her, but instead saw only sadness. She realised that her mum had been crying already and wondered whether she now knew about her dad too. She also realised that she probably had him to thank for Lydia's quiet, almost resigned response to her news.

'I was planning to leave,' Hanna said. 'I still can. If you want me to,' she added. Though she no longer wanted to go anywhere, she did want to give her mum a chance to opt out, to tell the neighbours that her daughter had 'got a job in London', to save what little of their reputation on the close was left.

Her mum listened in silence, then shook her head. Eventually she said, 'What does Shane think?', her voice without expression.

'He doesn't know yet,' Hanna replied, then took a deep breath before she added, 'because he's not the father.'

At this her own father stood up and began pacing around the room. Lydia's face was still so impassive Hanna wondered whether she had heard.

'I haven't told him yet – the father, I mean – but I'm going to,' Hanna said, 'and then I'll tell you about him. I just think he should know first.'

Hanna had decided this in that second. Realising it was unlikely that news of her pregnancy would stay in the family, that he was probably going to hear about it, she knew she had to tell him. The thought made her throat tighten with fear, but she was on this train now and there was no stopping it. She thought about the conversation she had had with Rita and had the strong sense that at least if she told the truth, there would be a freedom in that, whatever the outcome.

THE BARBECUE AT NO. 9

Her mum continued to sit, face and body inscrutable. It was unsettling. For a woman who usually had so much to say, her silence was unexpected and ominous. Her dad stopped pacing and was looking at his wife, his face also seeming to search for some sort of reaction. Lydia was always the barometer of the family's moods. This lack of response was disorienting for both of them. Hanna had been hoping that her mum might come up with a plan that would save them all, but still Lydia said nothing.

Then the doorbell rang, breaking the silence, making them all jump. It was followed by a loud, insistent knocking on the front door.

Rita – No. 15

After her conversation with Hanna, Rita knew she needed to leave the party. Emotions and memories were coming at her thick and fast, and she no longer had the defences to fight them off. The last thing she wanted to do was get a reputation for being the hysterical woman at no. 15 by bursting into tears in front of her new neighbours. There was being herself, then there was being *completely* herself. Rita wasn't sure that Delmont Close was ready for that; in fact, she wasn't sure that she was ready for that either.

She said goodbye to Davina before she left. She'd found her holding hands with Emmeline and Galina, the three of them dancing 'Ring o' Roses' style to 'Modern Love' by David Bowie in the now almost empty garden of no. 9. Davina wrapped her in a wine-fragranced hug and said, 'Please let's see each other soon?' and Rita nodded gratefully, unable to speak for fear of releasing a sob. Had she made a friend? she wondered.

By the time she had settled back down on the sofa and switched the television back on at no. 15, The Who had taken to the stage. Rita strained to hear the lyrics, as it was apparent that there was something wrong with the sound. The irony of Roger's voice having faded away against the twang of the guitars was not lost on Rita, and she found the performance almost unbearably sad, but she sat there, mesmerised, and wept for her own faded self.

She'd always believed that it was meeting and marrying Des that had led to her becoming a ghost of a person, but maybe it was just inevitable? Then she thought about Davina, and the spark of something she had felt earlier. Davina was vibrancy and colour, there was a richness to her age and experience, she held herself and the world around her lightly. Was that something Rita could aspire to, or was she too far gone? she wondered. Would she ever be able to get out from under the weight of everything that had happened?

As Jacob had grown taller, Rita felt as though she had got smaller and smaller, everything about her diminishing as her marriage went on. Even her voice had got quieter, so strong was her need to placate her husband and protect her son. Any hopes she had for the future were entirely centred around her gentle, sensitive boy. That sensitivity was becoming more apparent with each passing year, and more of a problem for Des, who began engaging him in activities designed to 'toughen him up'.

Disappointed that his son was no good at the rough and tumble of Aussie-rules football, Des decided that hunting and fishing would be the way to turn him into the kind of man he wanted him to be. Rita was horrified when he bought Jacob an air rifle for his fifteenth birthday, the two of them spending the day out in the bush.

There had always been guns in the house, but they were kept carefully under lock and key, and apart from Des having shown her how to use them 'for protection', Rita rarely went near them. It felt both strange and wrong to see her son holding one, a big smile on his face, when they returned. 'He wasn't half bad,' Des said, and ruffled Jacob's hair. The pink glow of pride on her son's face almost broke Rita's heart.

The beatings were a regular part of Rita's life now. She no longer had any sense of what might tip Des over the line, his criticisms of her indiscriminate and numerous. She only had to *smile* in the wrong way to incur his wrath, and she had got to the stage where she just accepted his violence as being part of her lot in life, as mundane as the endless laundry and washing-up that came with her role as wife and mother. Her only job was to make sure that she never cried out and that Jacob never heard or suspected what occurred between his mother and father under the cover of darkness.

The sun slowly set outside no. 15, until the house was in darkness except for the flickering television. Sitting on the sofa, Rita wept, noisily, messily and with abandon. She cried out every drop of sadness she had held in during those years. She was so overwhelmed with the decades of unshed tears she felt as though she was drowning. What had caused the release? Was it meeting Davina? Was it seeing the boy who looked like Jacob? Was it the conversation with Hanna, who reminded her so much of herself, with all her teenage rebellion masking a fear of being alone? Or was it the realisation she had while talking to the young girl that in order to be free, the truth had to be faced.

Eventually the tears ceased, and she turned her attention back to the television, where Elton John had taken to the stage. The rest of Wembley was now a sea of shadows, all eyes on the colourful spectacle of Elton at his piano. He opened with 'I'm Still Standing', and Rita sang along at the top of her voice. She *was* a survivor, that much was true, but was she really living? Or was she existing in the wake of her actions on that hot, sticky night? The night of Jacob's seventeenth birthday.

It had all seemed to go so well. They had hosted a small gathering at home with mainly church people in attendance. Des didn't like socialising with outsiders, a rule which stretched to his son, so the few friends Jacob had around were the sons of members of the congregation. The cake Rita made was baked to perfection and everyone complimented her on it. 'Rebecca, you're just the most wonderful hostess,' one of the women had said to her. Rita couldn't remember which one, they all blurred into a line of helmet-haired, modestly dressed women, like a paper-doll chain, each one indistinguishable from the other.

Despite the success of the evening, Rita knew she would be in trouble for something. Social situations caused her husband high stress, as he wasn't in full control of events. Rita often thought that church pastor was the perfect role for Des because it allowed him to be in charge, in an ordered, structured way. At social occasions there was less hierarchy, though of course even then most people deferred to Des and his opinions, he had that way about him, whether in God's house or his own. But the lack of order created by people doing and saying what they wanted, when they wanted, could unsettle Des for days afterwards and she knew she would have to be careful to tiptoe around him once everyone had left.

After Jacob had gone to bed, Rita cleaned the house quickly and quietly while Des sat at the kitchen table, brooding in silence. The mistake she made was in picking up what she thought was an empty can from the table. 'I was drinking that,' he said, his voice without intonation. Rita put it straight back in front of him, but the damage was done.

She didn't realise that Jacob had entered the room at first, as she was cowering on the floor, her arms over her head to deflect the blows.

THE BARBECUE AT NO. 9

'STOP IT!' he screamed at Des. 'STOP IT STOP IT STOP IT STOP IT!'

The room fell immediately silent. Even Des was completely still. Neither of them had ever heard Jacob raise his voice about anything. Eventually his father recovered enough to tell Jacob to go back to bed, that this was 'between your mother and me', but Jacob, now pale and quivering, shook his head. 'No,' he almost whispered, 'no.'

Des took a step forward, and for a moment Rita thought he was going to hit Jacob, but instead he walked out of the house and slammed the door so hard it felt as though the entire foundations shook under the impact. Jacob walked calmly to the door, picking up the keys from the rack, and locked it. 'He's not coming back in,' he said. Rita gathered herself.

'I'm so sorry you saw that,' she said, and was about to lie and say that it had never happened before. Then she looked at her son's face and realised he knew. He had always known.

'He can't keep doing this to you,' Jacob said. 'I'm a man now, let me protect you.'

'That's not your job,' Rita said. 'It's mine.'

She had no idea how long they stood there before the door handle rattled and the banging and shouting began. She could picture Des out there, fists hammering on the door, face bright red, incandescent with rage. It wouldn't take much for their flimsy door to give, and their neighbours were too far away to hear. What should she do to protect them?

The thuds on the door stopped for a few seconds, and she and Jacob looked at each other, eyes wide with desperation, wondering what he was doing. Then Des spoke. His voice was as calm and collected as when he was greeting parishioners at church.

'I am going to kill you,' he said.

Rita knew in her very soul that this was true.

She had been frightened for her life before: the feeling was nothing new. Her terror was that this time, he might do the same to Jacob. She knew she couldn't let that happen. The banging began again and she could almost feel the door buckling as Des threw his entire weight against it.

'Go get the gun,' she said to Jacob. 'I'll stay here in case he manages to get in.'

'It's loaded,' Jacob said when he returned, and handed Des's shotgun to her.

Rita closed her eyes briefly. How had they got here? How were they in the situation where her son had loaded a shotgun for her to defend them against his father? For a moment she faltered, considered putting the gun down and letting the situation play out, but then she looked at her boy and saw a dark stain growing down his trousers. He was so frightened he had wet himself.

Rita cocked the gun and aimed it at the door.

*

THE BARBECUE AT NO. 9

Rita stood up from the sofa. She could not replay the scene again. She saw it all the time in her dreams: the screaming, the gunshot, the blood. She had relived the panicked hours afterwards countless times, in the early hours of the morning when she woke up, covered in sweat, and wondered if she should have, or could have, made a different choice. The memories of the hours afterwards were more scattered. She could see fragments, not the whole, like a puzzle with pieces missing.

Her first thought had been to simply call the police and explain exactly what had happened. It was self-defence, after all. But then she pictured Des shaking the hand of the local police sergeant after the baptism of his youngest at church, the men smiling warmly at each other. Who would believe her? In the eyes of this place, they were the perfect couple, and Des was only one step down from Jesus himself. Jacob had been beside himself at the thought of her handing herself in too, crying frantically, 'You can't go to prison, Mum. You can't. I couldn't bear it. Please don't, Mummy, please.'

She got the number from the back of the photo frame instead and called Alistair, praying he still lived in the same place. She knew that Alistair would help her to think through what to do. It wasn't fair to put that on Jacob. A gruff-sounding man answered the phone, telling her, 'He's not here,' at which her heart sank, but he had called her back within an hour.

'You said if I ever needed you . . .' she said.

They'd made a hasty plan for her to run, using her old identity, the one no one in this small town knew. There was nothing in her name here, Des had never allowed it, it was as if she didn't exist. Once she got to the UK, she could access the small inheritance left to her by her mother, and Alistair had connections, ever the Artful Dodger, to help her disappear again.

'As soon as you turn eighteen, I'll find a way to get you to me,' she told Jacob as she kissed his face over and over, inhaling the scent of him, before she drove off in the early hours of the morning, leaving her son in his bedroom with instructions to call the police and his grandparents once she'd got a head start.

The thought of leaving him there, with Des lying dead in the kitchen, filled her with a horror she would never get over, but what could she do? It was prison or run, and she couldn't take Jacob with her. She knew his grandparents would look after him. They adored him, after all. And Jacob knew she loved him, didn't he? She was doing all this for her son.

At the time she had felt that would be enough, but she wasn't sure any more. She may have managed to run from the scene, but she hadn't run from its consequences, and the pain of the separation from Jacob was more than she could bear. Her entire life had become a lie, and she was tired of all of it.

Rita picked up the phone in the hallway at no. 15 and made the call she thought she would never make.

Then, while she waited, she went upstairs to get the photographs tucked into the lining of her suitcase, the ones she had resisted looking at since the day she'd arrived, the ones of her and Jacob, the ones filled with love. She had no idea how long it was she sat looking at them before someone began ringing the doorbell repeatedly.

Steve – No. 20

Steve was itching to go straight to his bedroom as soon as they stepped into the house, but something stopped him. Maybe it was his mum's uncharacteristic silence. She opened the front door and went immediately to the kitchen, slumping down into a chair, her tired face contrasting sharply with the shimmering bright blue of her dress. Something tugged deep inside Steve. I've done this to her, he thought.

'Shall I make us a cuppa?' he said, and she nodded without looking at him, occupying herself by lighting a cigarette, though he noticed her hand trembling.

While he bustled around the kitchen, making the tea, he glanced surreptitiously at his mum. He never saw her as anything less than sparkling. She was always so full of life, and energy, and confidence. She had made it okay for him to need her. Had never once expressed a need for anything from him. He would never be able to repay her for that. He could see the toll it had taken on her though. All her hopes of a fun afternoon at the neighbours' house ended by him. He thought about Trevor, and Andy, and how her defence of him had led to her relationships with both of them changing. He thought about how sociable she was, yet she could never have anyone around because of him.

He placed a mug of tea in front of her and sat down opposite with his. 'I am so sorry, Mum,' he said, his voice breaking. 'I'll be better . . . I mean, I'll try to be better.'

She shook her head at him vigorously. 'You don't need to be anything other than who you are,' she said. 'There's no need for you to be sorry. I'm just tired.'

'But there is, Mum. There is.' He took a deep, shaky breath. 'Maybe it's time I got some help.'

Tina was quiet for a few moments. Steve could imagine the conversation inside her head. The insistence that he didn't need help, that everything would be all right. More than anything, his mum wanted everything to be all right. But it wasn't all right.

'Maybe,' Tina said, her voice almost a whisper.

Steve knew what that admission would have taken from her, but he could see the features on her face relaxing and felt his body respond similarly. He thought briefly of the watcher, but he couldn't seem to summon up the energy to care any more about whether anyone had been spying on them. A Russian agent? The IRA? It just didn't matter.

They sat for a while, the only sound the out-of-sync ticking of the many clocks that his mum had collected, before she spoke again. 'You know, you stood in front of that boy this evening, and you stopped Peter

Gordon from hitting him,' she said, as though they were just filling each other in on the events of the day. 'And I thought, that's my beautiful, brave son.'

She blew on her tea before taking a sip. 'Mind you, did you see Lady Di's face when it all kicked off?' Steve smiled, and they drank their mugs of tea in comfortable silence, until the doorbell began to ring.

Hour Twelve: 9–10 p.m.

Elton John, Freddie Mercury & Brian May, Paul McCartney, Band Aid

Steve – No. 20

Steve immediately jumped up at the sound of the doorbell and was about to go to his bedroom without a word when he realised what he was doing. Once again, he was leaving his mum to deal with things, letting her take care of everything when he couldn't.

'It's okay, you go on up. I'll answer the door,' she said, as though reading his thoughts.

Steve disappeared up the stairs and into his sanctuary, expecting to feel a sense of immediate relief, but instead all he noticed was the stale smell of cigarettes and unaired sheets. It was as if the realisations of the day, along with the conversation downstairs, had turned the volume up on his senses. It wasn't a sanctuary; it was a prison. He went straight to the window in his alcove and opened it and was about to turn away when he saw a police car driving slowly into Delmont Close.

Steve instinctively went to grab his notebook when he heard his mum's voice from downstairs, calling him. He'd momentarily forgotten there was somebody at the door. He felt caught between the two versions of himself: the one who wanted to sit down and observe the progress of the police car and record every last detail, and the one who wanted to be engaged in the act of living.

The sound of his mum's voice calling him again decided things for him. He turned away from the window and headed downstairs once more. His mum was standing at the bottom, all the exhaustion in her expression erased, her eyes bright and almost saucer-like as she watched his descent. *Ryan's here*, she mouthed theatrically at him, while pointing in the direction of the ironically little-used living room which she kept for best.

Steve stopped still. Ryan was here. In their house. He swallowed so loudly he almost wondered if Ryan would be able to hear it. Tina began flapping her hands at him, as though the action would somehow propel him down faster. It worked, however, and he found himself gently guided into the living room at Tina's insistence, where she promptly turned on her heels and left him.

Ryan was looking at the curiosity-packed sideboard. Every single ornament and souvenir was lovingly dusted weekly by his mum and repositioned back into a precise order that Steve had never fully realised was there, until he once moved one of them – an angel carrying a gilded harp – by accident and she noticed immediately. To him it looked like a car-boot sale, and judging by Ryan's bemused expression as he too stared at them, he thought the same.

Ryan was holding a china cup, which Steve knew

were kept at the back of the cupboard and only used for company. There hadn't been much of that for years. Ryan looked at Steve, a loose curl settling in front of his glasses, and Steve found himself unable to speak. Ryan's eyes flickered downwards to his tea as though suddenly shy under Steve's silent gaze.

'I'm sorry to call in like this,' Ryan said. 'It's just . . . well, it's just, I realised you'd gone, and I didn't say goodbye, and I heard what happened with Peter Gordon, and I wanted to see if you were all right, and there was the thing that bloke said . . . and I should really shut up speaking now.'

Steve could see that Ryan's cheeks had flushed pink. He cleared his throat. 'I'm glad you came,' he said, light-headed with the effort of speech.

Ryan looked up again, a smile spreading across his face. He moved the curl out of the way of his eyes. They were a pale blue, Steve realised. He found himself smiling back and the two men beamed at each other, no longer needing to say a word.

Peter – No. 9

Lydia shook her head at the insistent sound of the doorbell ringing. 'You'll have to answer that,' she said. 'Look at the state of me.'

Peter looked at her ashen yet always beautiful-to-him face, and wanted to tell her that to him she was perfect, but he knew it wasn't the moment. Would it ever be the moment again? He decided he would do as she said, and maybe give mother and daughter a moment alone together. They had barely exchanged a word following Hanna's revelation.

Peter didn't recognise the young woman at the door at first. 'Can I help you?' he said, automatically casting around for his wife, despite knowing she was still in the study – *fixing her face*, as she called it. He was surprised when Lydia appeared at his side, as if conjured up by his thoughts of her, looking as immaculately put together as ever. He could almost believe his family hadn't completely fallen apart during the last hour. He found himself wanting to laugh. Even now, his wife's sense of social decorum hadn't failed her.

THE BARBECUE AT NO. 9

'Oh... Mrs Allan – sorry, I mean, Natasha, isn't it?' said Lydia. 'Did you leave something behind?'

Peter had just realised he had seen the woman earlier, at the barbecue, when she crumbled in front of them, her face dissolving into tears and her body seeming to fold in on itself. He caught her just before she fell. 'Come in, come in,' he said, and looked at Lydia. With one glance they shared an unspoken understanding about what they should do with the weeping Natasha, using the kind of shorthand that comes with a relationship the length of theirs. Peter felt momentarily comforted by it. He hoped that Lydia might have noticed it too.

Together, they helped Natasha into the study and the chairs they had just left. Hanna stood as the three of them entered the room, and Peter saw that Natasha's distraught expression was mirrored by his daughter's. Peter worried for a moment that Hanna might pass out, and gently sat her down again. He would normally have let Lydia take charge in this kind of situation, but Peter decided that the least he could do in the light of everything was to handle this, if he handled nothing else.

While Lydia sat and held Natasha's hand as she cried, Peter went to the bottom drawer of his filing cabinet, taking out the bottle of whisky he stored in there and pouring the woman a generous measure. 'Do you want to tell us what's happened?' he said, handing it to her.

Natasha took a large gulp, then almost wailed, doubling over in what looked like physical as much as emotional pain. Lydia finally spoke. 'Whatever it is, I'm sure it won't be as bad as you think,' she said, and the woman looked at her with pleading eyes, as if begging her to make everything okay. Peter recognised that expression and was reminded of a time when Hanna had arrived home from school choir practice in floods of tears – almost inconsolable because she hadn't been chosen as a soloist – and Lydia somehow managed to combine empathy with a reassurance that everything was all right really – with just her presence. His wife was a magician, he thought.

He glanced over at Hanna, who remained frozen, staring at Natasha, and Peter debated whether she should even be there, while at the same time not wanting to let his daughter out of his sight until they'd had a chance to discuss everything properly.

'It's Laurence,' the woman eventually said, and Lydia nodded, knowingly, while Peter wondered who Laurence was. He guessed it must be her husband or boyfriend, but he had no idea how this couple fitted into the complex web of people that formed his wife's network. She knew everyone on the close, and indeed sometimes he suspected she knew everyone in a twenty-mile radius.

Lydia must have spotted his confusion and stepped in. 'Laurence is Hanna's music teacher,' she said, 'Mr Allan. This is Natasha, his wife,' and though Peter was none the wiser about what she was doing in their house, he felt an overwhelming sense of relief that Lydia was there. Though he knew the thought made him a bad person, he hoped that seeing another couple in crisis might make their own predicament less shocking, if not more palatable.

'He's been behaving oddly for weeks,' Natasha was saying. 'But today has been the worst. He kept coming and going from the house' – she stopped and blew her nose noisily on the tissue that Lydia had just handed her – '"disappearing off for "walks",' she said, making air quotes with her fingers, her expression showing the disdain for this excuse. 'He kept saying he needed time to think. Then he'd get home all hot and bothered, but of course he was hot and bothered! He was wearing dark clothes and a hat, like it was some sort of bloody disguise! On a day like today as well. No wonder he was boiling. Then he'd take it off, but within an hour he'd put it back on and off he'd go again. I kept asking him what was going on, but he wouldn't tell me.'

At the mention of the clothes and hat, Hanna audibly gasped, and Lydia raised her eyes to Peter, widening them meaningfully, to his confusion. What was his wife trying to tell him? He was a little lost and felt as though he was one step behind in understanding what was going on, not for the first time. He nodded at Lydia though, letting her think he had understood, wanting to do anything to demonstrate their togetherness, despite his confusion.

'Then he decided that we'd come here. To the party,' Natasha said, and took a deep, shuddering breath. 'He was suddenly all excited, and back to normal, and I wondered if it was him going mad or me. But then when we left here, he wouldn't speak to me until we got home. As soon as we got in the house, he said . . . he said that things weren't working. That he needed to go out again. Then he left.'

She delivered all of this at such speed, Peter was struggling to keep up, and judging from Lydia's expression, she was now too. What did any of this have to do with them? Only Hanna seemed to be comprehending what the woman was saying, though the expression of anguish on her face worried him greatly, and something began to prickle at the edge of his awareness.

Natasha took another deep breath and seemed to calm herself a little. 'So, I looked through his things,' she said, 'and I found this.'

She handed Lydia a piece of paper, but her eyes didn't move from Hanna, her expression now unreadable. His daughter's face was white with shock, which turned quickly to despondent resignation as she seemed to comprehend what was on it. His wife stared at the page too, then up at him. Peter moved to her side, gratified that Lydia had looked to him first. That gratification was immediately wiped away by what he saw on the piece of paper she was holding. He recognised what was written on it instantly. It was the song that Hanna had written, the one that won the competition. The one that was about the kind of love that teenagers dream of, that adults know isn't real.

But it wasn't the song that caught his eye. It was the message at the bottom of it, in his beautiful daughter's handwriting, surrounded by love hearts.

I Am Yours Forever, it said, in her bubbly, childish hand.

Hanna – No. 9

Eventually Mrs Allan spoke again. 'He left. He's gone missing,' she said. 'I thought he might have been here . . . that he might have come for you.'

Hanna could only shake her head.

'I think he must have been the person in the garden earlier,' her mum said, and Hanna was so relieved to hear her mum's voice, she barely took the words in, while her dad looked at her, aghast. 'I can't be sure, I couldn't see him that clearly, but from what Natasha says, he was wearing the same clothes as the man I saw. Can you think of any reason he might do that now?' She turned to Hanna as she said this, her voice sounding calm and controlled, but Hanna knew her mum well enough to know that underneath it lay the fury she would no doubt unleash later. Hanna could almost hear the cogs whirring in her mum's mind as she worked out what had happened.

Hanna remembered the last conversation she'd had with Laurence. She had ended things months earlier, around the time she had started going out with Shane, and before she found out she was pregnant. Though Laurence had not been happy about things ending, he didn't have a leg to stand on as far as Hanna was concerned.

When they had last spoken, just before school had broken up, Laurence had asked her to stay behind after a lesson and had been pushing to meet her during the summer holidays, telling her he missed her and couldn't bear the thought of not seeing her for months. By that time, however, she had already made her plan to leave. She still found it hard to lie to him, so instead avoided references to the future beyond that weekend and swerved around the fact she wouldn't be here any more, hoping he wouldn't pick up on it. Maybe he had? She had always thought he could read her so clearly; it was one of the things she had thought was special about him.

'I don't know,' she said. 'Maybe he thought . . . he could have thought . . . guessed that I was going to run away.' Had he wanted to stop her? Come with her?

'So, it's true, then,' Natasha said, flatly. 'You were . . . together? You were in a relationship?'

Hanna nodded her head slowly and waited for her mum to explode. She felt something strangely akin to relief settle over her. They knew it all now. Everything she had tried so hard to avoid, had made a mess of avoiding. The relief was followed immediately by an overwhelming sadness. This was the moment when her parents saw her as she truly was and rejected her. Hanna felt the tears begin again and made no attempt to stop them.

When her mum spoke, her voice was icy and controlled, the words crisp.

'That's not how I would describe it,' she said. 'Not how I would describe it at all. There's something very wrong with a grown man, a teacher at that, pursuing a child.' She stopped for a moment and took a shaky breath in. 'My. Precious. Child.'

The tears that Hanna could feel flowing freely down her face matched her mum's as she turned to look at her daughter.

'It's all right,' Lydia said. 'None of this is your fault. None of it.'

Hanna almost fell into her mum's embrace, then felt her dad's arms surround them both, cocooning them. 'It's all going to be okay,' Lydia said.

And just for that moment, Hanna believed there was a chance it might be.

Rita – No. 15

The policeman at her door was so young and fresh-faced, Rita almost laughed. He looked nervously down at his notebook then back up at her, before saying, 'We've had a call from this address about wanting to confess to a murder in Australia?' His expression was one of scepticism, as though she might be playing a trick on him.

Another, older policeman was standing alongside him, smiling benevolently at Rita. She suspected he was letting the younger, clearly less experienced one speak because they all believed she was a crank. The woman she had spoken to on the phone had sounded almost bored when she told her that she wanted to confess to killing her husband. She had at least expected an intake of breath, but instead had been asked to spell out her name and address repeatedly, with as much enthusiasm and urgency as if she was calling to report a car stuck up a tree.

'You'd better come in,' Rita said, and the two men followed her into the living room.

They perched on her sofa, the younger man looking ill at ease, the older one faintly amused. Rita took a deep breath and told them everything. About leaving the UK for Australia, about Des, about her name change, about Jacob, about the violence, about that hot, fateful night. She left out the part about Alistair. She didn't want to get him involved any more than he already was.

Rita watched as the expressions on the policemen's faces changed throughout her account. When she had finished, the young one was about to speak when the other one – she was sure they must have told her their names, but this whole evening was starting to take on the quality of a dream and she couldn't remember if they had or not – stopped him with a touch on his arm.

'Maybe we should have a chat down the station, love. Get all of this on record,' he said, and his colleague nodded vigorously.

Rita calmly gathered her things and let herself be led down the drive, knowing from the movement of curtains up and down Delmont Close that she had been spotted and would be the talk of her neighbours the next day. It didn't matter though. She knew she wouldn't be coming back.

From the rear seat of the police car, as it drove slowly out of Delmont Close, Rita could hear the distant strains of the Band Aid song 'Do They Know It's Christmas?' playing through the open windows of the houses as Live Aid came to an end. The sound echoed into the hot summer night.

PART THREE
One Year Later

Saturday, 12 July 1986

Steve – No. 20

Steve took a deep breath before entering the Happy Shopper with a long list in his mum's flouncy writing clutched in his hand. It was a Saturday and would likely be busy, but needs must if he was to get everything they needed for Debbie's christening the next day. He was still uncomfortable when he was with a large group of people, but Hanna had promised him the gathering would be small and that he would know everyone anyway.

'Big day tomorrow,' Madge said with a nod of the head at his full basket when he got to the till. His eyes must have given away his nervousness, so she followed it up with 'But you'll make a wonderful godparent!' as she rang everything through, fingers moving across the numbers at the speed of light. 'And Ryan will be with you, won't he?' she said. 'He'll make sure you're all right.'

Steve winced before looking around the shop, making sure no one else was in earshot. He adored Madge, but she was less than discreet in acknowledging his and Ryan's relationship, and unexpectedly more tolerant on the subject than most people around Delmont Close. He didn't want the rest of the neighbourhood knowing.

It had been difficult enough telling his brother, but his mum had encouraged him to be open. 'It's time to build bridges,' she had said, and as ever she had been right. The conversation had seemed to solve a mystery for Andy, and though his reaction had been awkward at first, that of a polite stranger as opposed to a brother, over the months their fortnightly phone calls had become easier.

Fiona Chamberlain wandered into the shop, her expression downcast, nodding at them both before making her way down the aisles. 'Microwave dinner for one, no doubt,' Madge shout-whispered while Steve cringed again at the volume of her pronouncements. 'Antoinette's with her father and his lady-friend this weekend,' she said, sniffing her disapproval. Gay relationships were no problem at all for Madge, but divorce was beyond the pale.

'Has the father reappeared yet?' Madge said.

Steve didn't need to ask her who she was talking about. The whereabouts of Laurence Allan had been the subject of endless hours of discussion and speculation. There were rumours he had disappeared off to France, and might even be teaching again, but the police had shown little to no interest in following that up, and his wife had left the area shortly afterwards.

'No, and I don't think he will anytime soon. He's vanished from the face of the earth,' Steve said. Madge sniffed again.

'Mind you, he wouldn't last long if he did show up around here. Peter Gordon would make mincemeat of him,' she said.

Steve was just about to leave when Madge pointed at the newspapers on the racks by the door. *Base Invaders*, one of the headlines read, and beneath it was a photograph of a group of women attempting to scale a tall fence. 'Recognise anyone?' she said. Steve picked the newspaper up and looked closely at it, smiling at the familiar face of one of the women triumphantly waving a fist in the air. It was Davina, from no. 16, who seemed to be trying to break into Greenham Common airbase.

'Good on her,' Steve said, while Madge shook her head in sorrow.

Outwardly, Steve's life had changed very little. He still kept to his routines, he didn't much like crowds or loud noises, and he had the occasional episode. But his inner landscape had changed almost entirely. Ryan loved him completely and without judgement. As a consequence, he had begun to see himself differently. Instead of viewing himself as a broken man who needed fixing, he could accept that he was no more or less imperfect than the next person. He, and everyone else for that matter, were like his mum's shelves of mismatched souvenirs and ornaments. They were full of quirks and imbued with memories and meaning for those closest to them, but not to everyone's taste. That was good enough for him right now. This realisation had somehow loosened his hold on the world.

The next morning, before the ceremony, he smiled at Ryan's attempts to control his unruly hair. He had it slicked back with gel, which, combined with his youthful features, made him look like a cast member of *Bugsy Malone*. His mum was in the kitchen, hair in curlers, making sandwiches to take to the Gordons, for afterwards. Steve was starting to feel that the day had too much significance, and with that thought his breathing began to get faster and his palms clammy.

He remembered something that Rita had said to him in a recent letter. *I've realised that the fear of doing something usually feels worse than doing the thing itself,* she wrote of her decision to tell the truth about her husband's death. *And the only way out is through*. The truth of that had struck him at the time, and he was becoming more able to see it in the moment, including this one.

The news that Rita had been arrested for the murder of her husband had rocked Delmont Close to its foundations. It had relegated Hanna's pregnancy to that of distinctly second-tier gossip, which Hanna had been grateful for, a fact that she had shared with Steve when she came round to thank him for stepping in between her father and Shane during the barbecue.

The two of them had tentatively become friends, bonded in their outsider status. Apart from Rosie, many of Hanna's schoolfriends had drifted away, encouraged by their parents to distance themselves. But Steve and Hanna had forged a quiet friendship which withstood the Gordons' house repossession and subsequent move to the Blackthorn Estate. They were now fully established in each other's lives.

They had both been as shocked as the next person to discover Rita's history; neither had dreamed for a moment that the woman they'd met had been capable of murder. 'It's the kind of thing I think I should've spotted,' Steve once said to Hanna, though he had never told her quite how much he had observed the neighbourhood's comings and goings, including those of her family.

Steve used the considerable energy he'd once channelled into researching and unearthing conspiracy into finding out more about what had happened to Rita, including where she was being held, and had written to her, his hands itching to do something now he no longer recorded everything in his notebooks. Over the course of their letter-writing, Rita had told her own story, a story which had opened Steve's mind further to the possibility that the distinction between good and bad wasn't always as clear-cut as he had thought.

Maybe the enemy was rigidity.

He loosened his tie and got a glass of water, which he sipped while helping his mum butter thick slices of white bread and cut the finished sandwiches into triangles.

Hanna – No. 75 Blackthorn Avenue

Hanna's instinctive movement on waking was to reach for her daughter. She sat up immediately on realising that the small cot next to her bed was empty, her brain wildly searching for context to make sense of where she was, when it was, and where her daughter might be. The green digits on the clock on her bedside table told her it was early. How long had it been since Debbie's last feed? Time had stopped having any meaning after the birth of her daughter.

She breathed out again at the sound of her dad singing 'Fat Bottomed Girls' to her daughter somewhere in the house, his voice travelling through the paper-thin walls, her eyes beginning to smart at the memories from her own childhood. She got up and went downstairs. 'Oh good, you're up,' her mum said as Hanna wandered into their tiny kitchen, the size of the downstairs loo in Delmont Close, where she was standing over the oven.

'We've got a lot to do to get everything ready for after church. We can't have people thinking we're *that family*

THE BARBECUE AT NO. 9

who don't put on a decent spread. It's my granddaughter's christening, for goodness' sake.'

Hanna attempted to stifle the laughter bubbling up inside her. It was of course at her mum's insistence that the christening was happening at all, which Hanna had agreed to as a way of saying thank you for the last year. 'Shall we tell the vicar that she's named after Debbie Harry?' Hanna had said, slyly. 'No need,' her mum had said. They had compromised on the godparents, Lydia agreeing that Hanna could choose Steve and Rosie, alongside David.

Given their very public fall from grace, Hanna found it amusing that the correct etiquette – according to her mum, anyway – continued to matter so much. 'Mum, we are definitely *that family*,' she said, 'but whatever you're making, it smells good.'

'Delia's quiche Lorraine,' said Lydia.

Hanna nodded, knowing that the fact this was Delia's recipe was as important for her mum as the food itself. Lydia's way of making peace with now having to cook everything from scratch, given they could no longer afford the ready-made versions of things, was to insist on following Delia Smith's recipes to the letter. They were, after all, the *only* option in Lydia's opinion, the TV chef having recently overtaken Princess Diana as her role model of choice. 'She's a successful working woman,' she would say, 'just like me.'

Lydia's job on the beauty counter at the department

store in the shopping centre had been her saving grace. She loved it. She called all her customers 'my ladies', and they were as devoted to her as she was to the free samples of make-up and skincare that the job afforded her. It had given Lydia a new lease of life. 'I'll not be one of those old-fashioned grannies,' she insisted, even if it meant she was constantly going on at Hanna to make more of herself and attempting to persuade her to 'have her colours done', whatever that meant.

'Go and chivvy your brother up,' Lydia said. 'We need to be ready to go in thirty minutes and counting.'

Forty-five minutes later the Gordons – except Prince, who had rarely left Hanna and Debbie alone since the birth, much to the annoyance of Lydia, who had taken to carrying chicken treats in her pockets in order to tempt him back to her side – arrived at the church. The little dog had been left at home and watched them all from the window as they trooped off down the drive, a melancholy expression in his eyes.

They walked over from the Blackthorn Estate, Lydia insisting that the fresh air would do them all good. Hanna and David exchanged amused glances at this pronouncement, knowing the real reason was that their mum didn't want the family arriving in the second-hand, somewhat clapped-out orange Cortina that had replaced Peter's Volvo.

Though their dad had a new job, it would be a while before their debts were paid off, and though he didn't seem to mind what he drove any more, Hanna knew that her mum felt the loss of status. It was with exactly the same tone that she called their house on the Blackthorn Estate 'cosy' and declared that she was 'no longer into the more ostentatious style of Delmont Close', as if this was all a choice, as if they hadn't had to move when the house had been repossessed, and everything of value sold by the bailiffs.

Overall, though, Lydia had surprised them all with how she had dealt with everything. Once she had accepted that this was their lot, her planning and organisational skills had been brought to the fore, and she had managed everything with the precision she had previously brought to leading the summer fete committee. Hanna had realised that while small, seemingly inconsequential things might set her off, when it came to the big stuff, her mum was unflappable.

When they arrived home after church, Prince flung himself at them all as though they had been gone for a week, not a couple of hours. The Gordons' social circle was smaller these days, not all of the Neighbourhood Watch had stuck around, but everyone who had was now cramming themselves into Blackthorn Avenue.

They no longer had a dining room, but the living room was at least freshly painted, Hanna's mum having rolled her sleeves up and managed it herself. Hanna's dad put his tape of Queen's *Greatest Hits* on the small cassette recorder to play quietly in the background, the state-of-the-art stereo stacking system having been a casualty of the repossession, and the family stood at the centre of the gathering, with Steve and Rosie.

Steve was holding Debbie like a comfort blanket, having taken her from Hanna as soon as they got into the house, while Rosie chattered in his ear. After a while Tina tottered over to him, arms outstretched, hands in a grabbing motion, and snuggled Debbie into her arms. Tina adored Debbie. She and Hanna's mum nodded frostily at each other.

'Christina,' Hanna's mum said.

'Lydia,' Tina replied. 'I saw your Beverley in town the other day,' she carried on and Hanna took a sharp intake of breath as her mum paled. 'But I don't think she can have seen me, she walked right past without saying a word.'

'She was probably a bit preoccupied,' Hanna's dad said, in his dry monotone voice. 'Keith's being investigated by the tax office for fraud,' he added, and Hanna thought she could detect the smallest hint of a smile on his face which he attempted to wrestle into a more appropriately solemn straight line and her mum changed the subject.

'Right,' said Tina, nonplussed for once.

No one mentioned Laurence, and Hanna was grateful for that. She hadn't yet reconciled her own complicated mix of emotions about him and had very little capacity to deal with anyone else's opinion. Her time and energy were all focused on Debbie. Her feelings about Laurence could wait.

The room settled into silence as her dad began clinking a spoon against the stem of his wine glass. Her mum put her hand on his arm. 'Don't break it,' she hissed, while smiling widely at the assorted guests.

'Thank you, everyone, for coming,' Peter said. 'And for sticking by this family over the last year.'

Lydia's smile was something of a grimace now: her husband clearly hadn't run the content of his speech past her.

'Things haven't necessarily been easy,' he said, and Hanna could imagine the telling-off he would get for *airing their dirty laundry in public* later.

'But in some ways, it's been the making of us all. I am so proud of my daughter, not just for bringing her own daughter into the world, but for doing so with such strength and grace. I've watched David become an uncle, and his love and care for his niece makes me proud of him.'

At this her dad's voice broke and Hanna glanced at David. She put her tongue out, pulling a face at him. He pulled one back, but Hanna could see his eyes were glistening.

'But the person I am most in awe of is my wife, Lydia. She still insists that she is too young to be called Grandma . . .' He paused, and everyone laughed. 'But every day I marvel at the courage she has shown throughout this time, and I thank my lucky stars that she took "for richer, for poorer" quite literally.'

He turned to Lydia's horrified face and kissed her, dipping her like a ballroom dancer, so that the horror turned quickly to blushes and giggles. David rolled his eyes at Hanna. They had both had to get used to their parents' embarrassingly teenage displays of affection over the last few months. Hanna took Debbie back from Tina's arms and held her close, breathing in the smell of her.

'This is your family,' she whispered to her daughter. 'This is love.'

Epilogue

Rita – Long Bay Correctional Centre, Sydney

The unexpected visit from her lawyer, Eloise, was a welcome break from the monotony of Rita's days. She liked Eloise very much. She was a poised, professional woman who Rita could never have afforded to pay without assistance from Davina, who not only donated towards Eloise's fees but also galvanised other activist women to do the same. Rita had no idea how she would ever repay her. Especially if she was found guilty, which she supposed was inevitable, despite her plea of self-defence.

The two women met in a small, airless room, and Rita was surprised to see Eloise almost, but not quite, smiling. She had never seen her lawyer with anything other than an expression of stiff seriousness, entirely in keeping with her tightly ponytailed hair and buttoned-up suits, whatever the weather.

'I have news,' she said, in her customary clipped tones. 'Someone has come forward. Someone else who was abused by Desmond. And they have evidence.'

It took Rita a while to process what Eloise was saying, but it seemed that the woman who had been Des's girlfriend before Rita's arrival had paid Eloise a visit. This woman had told a story so similar to Rita's own experience at the hands of her husband that Rita started to weep at Eloise's retelling. Their relationship, which Des had told her had ended because 'the woman is insane', had in fact fallen apart after Des had attempted to strangle her one night when he was drinking heavily. The woman had tried to report him to the police at the time but, just as Rita had feared for herself, she had been brushed aside and dismissed by the local force.

'But there are medical reports of her injuries,' Eloise said. 'And photographs.'

'Right,' said Rita, almost breathless. It wasn't just her. It had never been just her. 'What does that mean for my case?'

'It speaks to a pattern of behaviour that we can now prove,' Eloise said. 'And this woman is willing to testify, and credible,' she said. 'He had a type,' she added, her eyes softening.

After Eloise left, Rita sat in her cell and cried, imagining telling Alistair when he next came to visit, and wondering whether to tell Jacob when he came to see her later. As soon as he had turned eighteen, with Alistair's assistance, Jacob had moved to Sydney, both to start university the next year and to be closer to her. He visited as often as he could, and though she had resisted that at first – wanting him to live his life – he insisted, and she treasured every moment she spent with him. She was so proud of the man he was becoming. A man who knew his own mind. Was it right to share this news with him at this stage? He had accepted that she was in prison, mainly because she had told him that it was better than running and living in the constant fear of being caught. That it was better than living a half-life. And that was true. She had found a strange peace in recent months.

She had written to Steve about how the acceptance she had come to in prison – about the unfolding of her life and the choices she had made – meant she felt freer than she had living in Delmont Close. If she had tried to outrun those things forever, she would always have been looking over her shoulder, waiting for them to catch up. She had tried to explain this to Jacob too, the sense of freedom she now felt, and the fact that she had realised it wasn't contingent on her circumstances, but she suspected he thought she was just trying to make him feel better.

This news from Eloise risked threatening that peace with the tantalising promise of a different kind of freedom. Could she dare to hope that maybe she might not spend the rest of her life in prison? Had the risk she had taken paid off? The risk of telling the truth, but not the whole truth.

The version of events she had told had always felt like the best choice from the selection of terrible choices she had in front of her at the time, and she had certainly got close to the truth. Wasn't that what people said about lies? That the closer to the truth they were, the more plausible they seemed? And after all, Des was indeed a violent man. He had threatened to murder them that night. He was killed in self-defence. He had died of a gunshot wound.

But the part she had kept to herself, had held inside her ever since that night, was the part where her son had grabbed the shotgun back from her in the seconds before Des battered down the door of their house.

'I'm a better shot,' he had said.

It was Jacob who had got his father in his sights and pulled the trigger.

Sure, the truth would set her free, but she would never, ever tell it. Her love for her son and her need to protect him outweighed anything else.

Acknowledgements

How to thank all the people who have changed my life over the last couple of years, by publishing *The List of Suspicious Things* and now *The Barbecue at No. 9*?

Nelle, agent of dreams and woman of integrity, plus the whole team at RML, who have my back, and I feel it in every way, thank you.

Venetia, thank you for holding on while I freaked out before I wrote this book. Your belief in me means everything.

I love working with the team at Hutchinson Heinemann and feel lucky to have met you all.

Ailah, Charlotte ('get down, Shep'), Isabelle, Rebecca, Alice, Aspen, Georgie, Ceara (whose covers are a thing of beauty) and the whole team. I am so grateful for your support and friendship. Getting to do this with you again is a joy. (We miss you, Claire!) Thank you to Joanna and Caroline for your copy-editing care and attention too.

Then there are the many friends I've made through writing, and who have been by my side while I've written this novel, especially Samuel Burr, whose daily voice

ACKNOWLEDGEMENTS

notes have kept me going and made me laugh so hard. Thank you for metaphorically holding my hand while I wrote this book. Your friendship means the world to me.

Sophie Hannah, who was my first reader and also gifted me Lydia's obsession with being thought of as 'that family' (Ben Shift, thank you for letting me use it!) as well as for the Dream Author programme, and in particular the Marlborough Manor retreats. Can't wait for the next one with a Johanna Spiers road trip thrown in.

My WhatsApp group of debut authors (Amy Twigg, Ania Card, Emily Howes, Jessica Bull, Sarah Marsh, Sarah Brooks, Flora Carr and Laura Shepherd) and the semi-colons (Jodie Robins, Asha North and Sarah Lupton) have been a constant source of advice, cheerleading and laughter. For someone who didn't do WhatsApp groups, you have all converted me.

Cathy Rentzenbrink, who has been a voice of calm wisdom at the other end of a phone (and sometimes in person), and whose Sunday Sessions have been the source of many of the scenes in this novel, thank you so much.

David Headley, I will never be able to thank you enough for the support you and Goldsboro Books have given me. You are so generous, and your friendship has become so important to me, despite your proclamations of being a working-class Yorkshire person, just like me ☺

Chloe Timms, whose friendship and endless Zoom

ACKNOWLEDGEMENTS

calls I treasure. I feel lucky that writing and Book Twitter brought us into each other's orbit.

Rachel Joyce and Marian Keyes, for being the early readers of this novel, THANK YOU. Your generosity to me means the world, as do your brilliant books.

Huge thanks are also owed to my Substack readers who helped to 'unfreeze' my writing after the publication of *The List of Suspicious Things*, which meant that this novel got written.

Thank you to Peter Kay – reading your book about television reminded me of the term 'video nasties', which is in this book, so thank you for that and for all the laughs (there is a further nod to you in this novel), and also to John Robins, who when you dressed up as Freddie Mercury on *Taskmaster* (unbeknownst to you) gave me the sign that I should write this book.

Bloggers, including and especially Jules, Bex, Tilly, Colin, Michaela, Rich and Tash – all of whom have become such an important part of my bookish life, along with all the incredible booksellers at Taunton Waterstones (especially DAVE of course!), Alex and the team at Berts, Emma + Hannah and everyone at Bookish, the team at The Grove, Criminally Good Books and the team at Truman's. But honestly? Every single blogger and reviewer and bookseller and library worker has my unending gratitude.

To Michael Neill, who answered my emergency email just before *The List of Suspicious Things* was published,

ACKNOWLEDGEMENTS

and sparked a whole new phase of my spiritual life, thank you!

Of course, I need to thank The Barkers – the best people I know – for the blue plaque on my house, and the 'practical love' I constantly receive from you.

And my oldest friend, Sam Wintle, for the millions of Live Aid reels you sent to me that I never looked at. Our friendship of 40+ years is a shining light in my life. Thank you for always having a bed for me.

This one's about family, and I couldn't have written it without mine, adopted and otherwise.